C000008212

Strand of Faith

Choices and Consequences: Book 1

By Rachel J Bonner

When the choice is between love and life, how can anyone decide?

This is a work of fiction. Names, characters, organisations, places, events and incidents are all used fictitiously. Any resemblance to actual persons, places or events is purely coincidental.

ISBN: 978-1-912890-03-3 (paperback)

Text copyright © Rachel J Bonner 2018

The right of Rachel J Bonner to be identified as the author of this work has been asserted by her in accordance with the Copyright, Designs and Patents Act 1988.

All rights reserved. No part of this publication may be reproduced, or stored in a retrieval system, distributed, or transmitted in any form or by any means including electronic, mechanical, photocopying, recording or otherwise, without prior express written permission of the publisher except in the case of brief quotations for review purposes.

Published by Isbin Books, Lancashire

Cover artwork and design by Oliver Pengilley
Cover artwork © 2018 by Rachel J Bonner

Editing by Sarah Smeaton

This book is sold subject to the condition that it shall not, by way of trade or otherwise, be lent, resold, hired out, or otherwise circulated without the publisher's prior consent in any form of binding or cover other than that in which it is published and without a similar condition including this condition being imposed on the subsequent purchaser.

Dedication

To my husband, David, without whose love and
support this would never have happened.

And in loving memory of my Dad

1934-2013

Description

A girl and a monk have compelling reasons not to fall in love. But those they expect support from are manipulating them both because their choices will have consequences for the rest of the world.

After a stormy youth, Brother Prospero has found comfort and fulfilment in the monastery. That is, until he discovers something that forces him to reconsider his whole vocation. To follow his heart, he'll have to face his demons again, outside the security of the monastery. Is it worth the risk? Can he beat them this time? Or will they finally destroy him?

Orphaned and mistreated, Leonie has found sanctuary and safety at the Abbey. All she wants is to learn how to manage her unusual abilities so that she is not a danger to those around her. When she comes into contact with Prospero everything threatens to spiral out of her control. Whether she leaves or whether she stays, how can she possibly avoid destroying – yet again – those she has come to care about?

Abbot Gabriel is faced with an impossible choice. He can do nothing and watch the world descend into war. Or he can manipulate events and ensure peace – at the cost of two lives that he is responsible for. He knows what he has to do but is he strong enough to sacrifice those he loves?

Table of Contents

Prologue

The young lord slowed his horse and dropped behind the rest of the hunt, sickened by his discovery of what their quarry was. His companions glanced at him with little curiosity, no doubt assumed he was feeling the after-effects of last night's drinking, then went on without him. He took a circuitous route away from the hunt, in no hurry to return to their starting point. He stopped at a convenient stream to water his horse and then sat on the bank lost in his own thoughts.

Gradually he became aware he was being watched. It took him a few minutes to spot the source. There was a child lying along a branch low over the water all but hidden in the leaves, one hand dangling in the stream. All he could make out were her eyes, large and dark in a dirty face.

"You're not safe there," he said. "Come back to the bank."

The child laughed, surprising him. "Your kind hunts mine," she said. "This is as safe as anywhere."

His guilt intensified, cutting him to the core with her apparent easy acceptance of her role as prey.

"Not me," he said. "I left the hunt." He tried another approach. "Are you hungry? I have food in my saddlebag."

She hesitated, clearly thinking it might be a trick. He stood up, fetched the food and placed it on the ground between them before returning to his seat. With little sound, the child disappeared from her perch and materialised on the bank. Seen out in the open she was about eight or nine years old, dressed in rags and so filthy he couldn't be sure of either her skin or hair colour.

She studied him for a moment then dashed forward and grabbed the food before retreating a pace or two to squat and eat, still watching him, her body poised for flight. He held still, trying to appear unthreatening. Slowly she sank into a sitting position, legs crossed, licking her fingers and ensuring she got every last crumb.

"You're the one the Lady expects to marry," she said between mouthfuls.

That was true enough. As probable heir to one of the other ruling Great Houses, his alliance with the daughter of this Great House would be welcomed on both sides. The details were still being hammered out between their High Lords but he was supposed to formally ask for her hand on this visit.

"No," he said impulsively, "I won't be aligned with those who think you should be used as prey."

The child grinned at him, mischief now dancing in her dark grey eyes. "She's planning to run off with the stableman anyway, soon as she can. Her father thinks marrying her off will stop her."

He stared at her, trying to take it in. *This brat knows more than I do?* That was the underlying reason for what he was being asked to do? He – and his House – were about to be tricked? As most of his mind processed this, some part noticed that the brat was shivering. He shrugged out of his coat and tossed it towards her.

"You're cold," he said. "Take this. Put it on."

She paused, uncertain, then slipped it on and wrapped it round herself although it dwarfed her. He was aware of her eyes following him as he paced up and down by the water's edge thinking about his next action.

"I'm not putting up with this," he said more to himself than to her, "I'm leaving. Now." He turned to the child who was sitting watching him, the food now gone. "Come with me, I'll take you somewhere safe. You'll be safe at Taylor House."

She shook her head and scrambled to her feet to back away from him.

"If you stay they'll hunt you, too," he told her but she shook her head again.

"They won't catch me," she said as she backed further away and then disappeared into the trees.

He went after her but he couldn't see her. He closed his eyes and reached out with his mind, looking for the spot of light in his head that indicated the presence of another human. The spot flickered – he still hadn't fully mastered this skill – and when he opened his eyes there was nobody there.

"Taylor House," he shouted into the empty space around him, in the hope that she would hear. "Remember Taylor House."

He didn't continue to search for long knowing that carrying a reluctant, struggling wild child wouldn't be practical with what he needed to do next. He didn't understand why she mattered so much to him, why he felt so hurt that she'd rejected his offer. Telling himself that he was being silly, that saving one child would make no difference at all, he returned to the House he was visiting, told the High Lord of his decision, packed his belongings and left.

To himself, he swore that he would be back to find and rescue this child.

The child watched him from a perch high in one of the trees. Like many of her pursuers, he hadn't thought to look up. As soon as he was out of sight, she scampered down the tree and hurried back to her nest, a makeshift shelter deep in the forest. The other children clustered round her; despite her age, her skills at finding food and building shelter made her the natural leader.

"I met an angel," she told them, eager to distract them from the fact that this time she'd returned without food. "He gave me this coat."

The other children pestered her. "What's an angel? Tell us!"

They snuggled into a pile with her at the centre, sharing body warmth, one or two of the smallest huddling into the coat beside her.

"He was tall," she said, "a bit like a grown-up, only much nicer. Angels look after people. They're never mean. They give you food and warm things."

"Did he give you food? Did you bring us any?"

"Yes, he gave me food." She felt a flare of guilt that she hadn't saved any for her nestmates. "He watched me eat it. When angels give you food, it's just for you, you have to eat it then. But we can all share the coat."

"What was his name? Where did he go?" The other children were insistent.

What was his name? she thought. What was that name he'd called after her? Taylor, that was it.

"He was called the Angel Taylor," she told them. "He said I could go with him, but he left before I could come and get you all. I couldn't go without you. I don't know where angels go. I'm sure it's somewhere warm with plenty of food and other kind angels to look after us and be our family."

The littlest child burrowed more deeply into the coat. "Will he come back?" he asked.

She smiled down at him. "I hope so. We'll all have to hope so and look out for any angels. There might be others around. But we'll have to be careful they aren't grown-ups trying to trick us."

She made up new stories about the angel every night to help the children sleep. Angel Taylor became the nestlings shared symbol of hope. Gradually the stories took over in her mind and merged with the real experience until even she could not distinguish between them.

Chapter 1

October

Prospero

Late again, Prospero would have no chance of making it to the Abbey on time if he followed the conventional routes at a conventional speed. But there were alternatives he'd discovered through many years of similar situations. He surveyed the corridor with his mind to ensure it was clear, ran along it, pushed open the window at the end and jumped, unconcerned that the ground was two floors below. Using his telekinetic ability on himself meant he could land gently and, this time at least, he remembered to use it to close the window behind him.

The Abbey itself was central to the campus and the other buildings had grown organically in courtyards around it. Having been built at different times, the courtyards did not fit exactly together and the consequence was a number of small, forgotten spaces like the one Prospero was now in. At the upper levels, it provided light into various corridors. At this lowest level he was faced with a door. Despite its imposing appearance it wasn't locked and it gave him access to the extensive cellar storage that spread under the campus, which meant he could run directly across rather than having to zig zag round the courtyards.

Part way through, he pulled up suddenly, sensing the presence of another person nearby, someone he didn't recognise. He hesitated for a moment, torn between curiosity and his urge to reach the Abbey. But, whether or not they were supposed to be here, he certainly wasn't. If he stopped to investigate, not only would he be late, but there could also be some very inconvenient questions about why he was in the cellar in the first place. His compulsion to be with his Brothers won out and he set off again, trying to push thoughts of the stranger to the back of his mind. At the far end of the cellar he ran up a flight of stairs, slid carefully round a corner then merged into the line of Brothers as they filed into the Abbey.

The stranger refused to stay at the back of his mind. At the slightest lapse of his concentration during the service in the Abbey they danced back to the forefront of Prospero's thoughts, the remembered sensation of spotting them tickling at his mind, an itch he couldn't relieve. Andrew nudged him as they were leaving the Abbey.

"You were almost late, and you haven't been paying attention," he whispered.

Prospero just grinned, glanced around to make sure no one was looking and pulled Andrew into a cupboard under a flight of stairs.

"Come on," he said. "There's something I want to check out."

He reached for the back of the cupboard, where another long-forgotten door gave access once more to the cellar storage. In the middle of the cellar, they met Pedro, head chef, checking on his supplies. He raised his eyebrows at them.

"What are you two doing here?" he asked.

Andrew just shrugged but Prospero was happy to explain, "I was in here earlier and I'm sure there was someone else here, near the back, the older part."

"That's hardly surprising, there are often people in here. And what were you doing here then? Were you late again?"

"Maybe." Prospero grinned. "But if it was anyone who was supposed to be here I'd have recognised them. And I didn't, so I want to find them."

"Well, they won't still be here, not now, not with the noise you're making," Pedro told him.

Prospero acknowledged that, "I know they're not still here, or I'd be able to sense them. But there may be some sign that they were here, and of who they were."

Prospero was quite certain about where he'd sensed whoever it was, but there was no sign that anyone had been there and nothing seemed to be missing or to have been disturbed. Puzzled, but unrepentant and still convinced of what he'd sensed, Prospero headed back to his duties, taking Andrew with him.

***

Late one evening, Andrew and Prospero walked across the courtyards to the monks' residence after fulfilling their medical duties at the hospital. The cold season was well underway and both men shivered slightly, pulling up the hoods of their outer tunics and covering their hands with their sleeves. The night Shields were on, protecting the campus, but limiting the range Prospero could mind search.

As a skilled adept, Prospero had an extended awareness of the presence of others over a range of several miles. He could even identify and locate specific individuals, seeing them as glowing spots in his mind, each as individual as a face, superimposed on a mental image of their location. Each time he used this skill and saw only those he recognised he was reminded of his failure to find the stranger.

"It's not any of our Brothers, nor the Sisters," he told Andrew. "In fact, it's not anyone from the Great House at all. I know everyone here, and it wasn't someone I know."

"You're looking for that intruder again, aren't you?" Andrew asked. "Honestly, there are plenty of people you don't know. Especially in the college, and some in the hospital."

"Not that many," Prospero said shortly, his frustration building. "And anyway, if they were on the staff anywhere, I'd have spotted them by now even if I didn't know them personally. And no one else should be in the cellar."

"You know you're being ridiculous about this, don't you? Just forget about it." Although his face was hidden in the dark, Andrew's feelings showed in his short, sharp tone.

"I can't. It's nagging at me. All the time." Prospero was insistent.

"Have you thought, maybe you just made a mistake?"

"I didn't. I'm sure of that."

"Well, then, someone who shouldn't have been in the cellar. A student, or a random stranger."

Given that neither a mistake, nor a random stranger could provide a satisfactory solution in Prospero's mind, he continued to scan the college part of the campus for students. Once or twice he thought he caught a mental glimpse of his intruder but they always disappeared before he could track them. He thought about staking out the cellar in case they returned, but duties and events conspired to stop him. He'd still look, every time he used that route as a short cut – even when he didn't need it.

Pedro

As soon as he was sure that Andrew and Prospero had left the cellar, Brother Pedro returned to where Prospero thought he had sensed someone. He circled the shelfing once or twice, studying its contents while thinking hard. Then he reached for a large box on an upper shelf and was unsurprised to find it light and empty. Behind the box he saw a concealed space, big enough for a person to curl up in. He spotted a couple of old blankets, a book, a water bottle and a small food tin. Putting the large box on the floor, he opened the tin, and smiled to see that it contained a couple of his signature chocolate chip cookies. *So that's where they've been disappearing to,* he thought.

He put everything back as it was and decided to keep his findings to himself. If Prospero's intruder was what Pedro now thought they were, Pedro would keep their secret as long as necessary and provide all the help he could. Prospero might mean well, but this particular intruder would be easily scared off and that wouldn't help anyone.

Instead, every night before he left the kitchens, Pedro put extra food, old items of clothing, and anything he supposed might be useful, in places where they might be thought of as having been discarded. He wasn't surprised when they disappeared promptly. He thought about trying to communicate with this secretive creature but he knew his presence would scare them off and he very much doubted that they could read, so for now he did nothing more.

Gabriel

Lord Gabriel started dreaming again. The first dream was simple; a jewel, a glowing red ruby, fell into his hands. He knew that he had to do something vital with the jewel but not what that was. He awoke in fear of what the dream meant – not in itself but the consequences of it happening at all.

"Not again," he prayed. "Please not again. Please take this burden from me."

He dreamt again the next night. This time he was holding an emerald when the ruby fell into his hands. He tried to keep them apart but they were drawn to each other and began to merge together. He woke suddenly, unsure whether they had merged to form a new jewel or disintegrated to dust in his hands.

He prayed again, "Show me what this means. Give me the strength to do your will."

Chapter 2

November

The stranger

I opened the door to the Old Chapel just far enough to be able to look in and make sure it was empty. It was, so I slipped inside and hurried to my hiding place, underneath the altar table. This was one of my favourite places to hide out, where I could relax and sleep without fear. It was on the edge of the campus, near the river and clearly one of the first buildings on the site, built not that long after the Time of Devastation. It wasn't used now, but it was dry and looked as though it was still cared for even though I never saw anyone else visit it.

I suspected that it was cared for out of respect for the memorials inside. There were three memorials along one wall commemorating the events of the Time of Devastation, but it was the fourth one, on the opposite wall, that drew me most. As the world had repopulated after the Devastation, some of those in their late teens had started to discover they had additional skills, things they could do with their minds. Some could communicate with each other, or sense where people were without being able to see them. Others could move things, or start fires, or predict the future. Those who didn't have these skills had been scared of such magic, and the first generations were persecuted and often killed. This was a memorial to those early adepts and to those who had died assisting them.

As more people developed the abilities, having such skills became more acceptable, though there were still many who feared them. Engineers had developed a shield which could be used to prevent anyone under it using their gifts, and shields were used anywhere people thought they might be unduly influenced, such as in shops or any building used for religious purposes.

The Old Chapel still had a working Shield, triggered whenever someone entered. That was one of the reasons I thought it was still well maintained, and also one of the reasons I liked being there. Being a telepath I could always hear a background chatter of other people's thoughts. I'd learnt how to ignore it, but under a Shield everything became quiet, peaceful, which was such a relief. Also, I'd found that I didn't have nightmares or sleepwalk if I slept somewhere that was Shielded. My mind always felt slow and sluggish the next morning though, so I didn't do it too often.

Once I was safely curled up in my hiding place, I started to think about my current situation. I was almost happy living in this community, despite the inherent dangers and risk in what I was doing. The whole place felt peaceful, safe and non-threatening. Of course, I had to be on my guard and I did my best not to be noticed but that was the case anywhere. Now I was afraid I had been spotted.

A couple of weeks ago I'd been hiding out in the cellars under the Abbey buildings. Someone had come rushing through and I had felt a current of power around them, the sort that indicated someone was using their gifts. I'd been hiding my presence physically rather than mentally, and I was pretty certain they'd spotted me where I shouldn't be. I had got out of there as soon as the coast was clear. I'd been back once or twice, making sure I hid my presence properly, but I hadn't risked sleeping there since because I couldn't hide my presence mentally when I was asleep.

Nothing more had happened, so I'd thought I'd got away with it. But today, I'd had classes at the college, and, as I'd been where I was supposed to be – at least as far as anyone here knew – I hadn't been hiding my presence mentally. Doing that took a fair bit of energy so I didn't do it when it wasn't necessary. As I'd walked across the courtyard after class I'd felt that current of power again, whispering past my mind. I'd been surrounded by other students, but this whisper had come from a distance and I was afraid I'd been recognised. I'd shielded myself immediately, but I was very concerned that someone might have been looking specifically for me, and that they'd know me when they found me.

As I thought about it, I figured I had two options. One, I could leave, find somewhere else to live, but I had nowhere else to go. And I was finding the classes in how to use and control my gifts useful, which was a bonus as it was something I very much needed to learn to avoid disaster. Or, I could stay, but I'd have to be much more careful and much more watchful. I didn't like to think about what might happen if I did get caught.

I'd have to be more rigorous with hiding myself mentally, of course, which took energy. Using my abilities always left me hungry but I could scavenge food from the kitchen, as I had today. The real danger was sleeping, as it always had been. If I started sleepwalking they'd find me, without a doubt, and I couldn't spend every night in the Old Chapel. I figured I'd just have to sleep out in the woods more, even though the cold season was here now. I could have a fire if I was careful – it wouldn't be too much of a hardship.

More settled in my mind, I left the Chapel and set off to take some of this food I'd scavenged to those who needed it even more than I did.

Chapter 3

Mid December

The stranger

I was running, fighting, trying to escape Them as I had so many times before. They were dark, nebulous, never clearly defined, bodies shrouded in black cloaks, faces hidden. They shadowed me, following, looming, certain to grab me if I let them get close enough. I fought where I had to, ran when I could. I knew exactly what would happen next; I would find a hiding place, deep, dark, secure and as I entered it, I would wake. Usually, I would wake to find I was some distance from where I had gone to sleep, with a trail of destruction behind me where I had tried to fight Them off. I tried – so hard – to find ways to sleep without risking the devastation of my nightmares.

As I filled my normal role in this dream world, part of me was already thinking about what I would lose this time. I'd had such hopes, been doing so well, this time. I knew here, this college, this Great House, was where I needed to be, and I'd survived months without anyone noticing me. Now I would be discovered and I would have to start all over again – if I survived the consequences of being caught.

Then the dream changed, subtly at first; there were more of Them. Still undefined, they were solider than usual, more direct, starting to approach me. I grabbed for a weapon and found my hands around a large, loaded catapult. I fired it at the nearest one and it ducked out of the way. Another approached from the side and I swung round to kick it in the stomach, meaning to bring the catapult down on the back of its head as it bent over. As I did so, the catapult turned into a sword, and the Them faded away like a ghost, leaving me off balance as my foot failed to connect. I dived, somersaulted and came back up and now there were two more advancing. My sword turned into a pillow – that's the problem with dream weapons, they are totally unreliable – so I threw it at them, and again they ducked away, but they didn't retreat. I gathered the power and launched that at them, but again they didn't falter. Now there were four of them, closing in on me, blocking my escape routes.

I felt another behind me, turned to attack and found myself immobilised, its hands on my upper arms. As it pulled me closer, I looked up, partly terrified, partly curious for more definition, more information about Them. I felt something like an electric current run through my body, not painful, but exhilarating, followed by the certain knowledge that I had found whatever I had been looking for…and I woke up.

Struggling for comprehension, I realised I was still being held, still immobilised.

I stared into the wide open, dark blue eyes of one of the monks. Several thoughts competed for my attention; this time I was not going to be able to deny, hide or rectify my trail of destruction. And this man had now discovered one of my secrets. In dismay at what I'd forfeited, I closed my eyes again and sagged, my forehead falling against his chest. I felt him lift me up into his arms, and he spoke to me. I understood the words, they just didn't make sense in context.

"It's you! I've found you!"

Of course I am me, who else could I be? And he most certainly had found me out.

"It's okay."

No, nothing is okay, how could it be?

"It's over now."

Well that bit makes sense, life here is definitely over.

"You're quite safe, nothing will harm you."

I knew that had to be nonsense—I'd never been safe. Except that, for a moment as I woke, his mind had been open to me, just as mine had to have been to him. There'd been no malice, just consuming curiosity and a desire to help. I gave up trying to understand and succumbed to the exhaustion that always followed the nightmares.

Prospero

Brother Prospero hadn't been surprised, when the night-watch team had called him to assist with a sleepwalking student. Each group of students included a few of those rare youngsters with two or more strong Gifts, and they inevitably suffered the devastating nightmares brought about by the development of these Gifts. As he had responded to the call, he had run through likely candidates in his head. To find that the troublemaker running riot through the central courtyard was Leon had surprised him; the boy was unassuming and easily overlooked, his abilities barely sufficient to qualify him for this group. Nonetheless, it never paid to underestimate a dreaming student especially one who was frightened, and more strongly Gifted than anyone had thought.

Despite being asleep, Leon had used telekinesis to move benches and plant pots to block his pursuers, and pyrokinesis to set small fires and smokescreens to add to the confusion. The team had slipped into a well-practiced routine, two members in front of the boy, attacking and distracting, forcing him to concentrate on them. Two others had focussed on protecting their teammates, and the environment, dousing fires and restraining moveable objects. Prospero had slipped round behind Leon, shielding his own presence and radiating feelings of reassurance and calm. Carefully, he had crept closer until he could reach out and had then pulled the boy close, immobilising him as he had placed a mental shield over the pair of them. Within the shield he had touched Leon's mind, intending both to soothe and wake him. What he had found there had shaken Prospero so deeply he had almost let the shield drop.

Breaking the mind contact, he swept the – dreamer was probably the best word he thought – into his arms, and looked around for Andrew, who was duty doctor.

"I've found them!" he whispered exultantly to Andrew. "This is our intruder!"

Andrew just shook his head. "Intruder or not, what's important is dealing with whatever they need now," he said. "Bring him back to his room and I'll take care of him."

Once he had consigned the dreamer to Andrew's care – and made sure that Andrew knew exactly what he was dealing with – Prospero headed for Lord Gabriel's office at the centre of the complex. He knocked on the open door, and walked in without waiting for an answer. Despite the lateness of the hour, Lord Gabriel was still seated behind his large oak desk. As the High Lord of the Great House St Peter, demands on his time were never ending, but he considered his most important role to be that of Abbot, spiritual leader to the Brothers and Sisters, and his door was always open to them. He looked up at the sound of someone entering and smiled when he saw Prospero.

"I hear you successfully halted another student nightmare again tonight."

Prospero nodded. "Actually, it was that I wanted to talk to you about. It's not what it seems."

Lord Gabriel rose from his desk and gestured to a comfortable seating area. He raised an eyebrow in query as they both sat down. "So? You have some issue concerning the boy involved?"

"That's just it, Father – he's a girl!"

"Interesting." Gabriel leaned forward in his chair. "You are sure?"

"I'm sure," confirmed Prospero. "At the moment – she – woke up we connected, just for an instant."

"What have you done with her now?"

"She's back in her room, asleep, sedated. Andrew is with her. I said I'd go back."

Gabriel thought for a moment. "This all suggests that Leon is both more Gifted and more skilled than we thought. What do you think?"

"She used pyrokinesis and telekinesis whilst asleep; both were skilfully placed to deter rather than to hurt, which also suggests a very high awareness of the location of others. Clearly she's telepathic, whether she has precognition or teleportation skills I couldn't tell. When we connected, I had the impression of very high strength."

"And she's managed to hide all that from us for weeks, which certainly makes her very highly Gifted," Gabriel agreed. "I wonder why she chose to hide both her ability and the fact that she's a girl?" He looked over at Prospero. "Was there anything else to report?"

Prospero felt uncomfortable, realising that he would have to confess. He sighed. "A few weeks ago I sensed someone I didn't know in the cellars. I've been looking for them since – this is her." He hesitated. "There's something about her that disturbs me."

"Can you tell what?"

"No, I can't really describe it. Now, I can see her with my mind even without trying, but I've spent the last few weeks looking for her and I've been unable to find her."

"I expect it will become clearer in due course," Gabriel reassured him. "For now, you'd better return as you promised."

Chapter 4

The next morning

The stranger

When I woke, I didn't open my eyes immediately. Instead I used my mind to scan the area and assess the situation so as not to arouse the suspicions of anyone who might be around. It was morning, I was in my own room, but he was still there, sitting in the chair, giving out an aura of calm relaxation. There didn't seem to be anyone else around, either in the room or in the area outside.

He spoke, "You might as well open your eyes—I know you are awake." His voice sounded amused.

I sat up and looked at him. "Have you been there all night?" I asked.

He shook his head. "Someone has. Not always me."

"Ah, guards," I deduced with a snarl.

"No, doctors," he claimed. "To make sure you are unharmed after last night's escapade. You aren't a prisoner. You are free to walk out that door and go wherever you want, if you wish." He smiled. "But if you are going to do that I suggest you get dressed and have some breakfast first."

He indicated a tray on the table piled with food. I was hungry and the smell was overwhelming but I wasn't going to give him the satisfaction that easily.

"I need the bathroom."

"Fine. I'm sure you know the way."

He didn't try to stop me, and once safely in the bathroom, with the door locked, I took the time to think about my options. I could escape now, out of the window, but I'd be hungry, inadequately dressed, and, if I was a prisoner, there'd be a guard out there or not far away. I wasn't too worried about the guard, but if it was that easy to escape now it would be easy later, too, and I'd be fed and dressed. If it wasn't that easy now, I'd just make my situation worse by trying. On the other hand, if he was right, and I was free to go, I might as well take the meal and the clothes first. Possibly my logic was affected by hunger, or perhaps curiosity, a characteristic which had got me into trouble many times. Still, I'd got out of all that trouble too, and no doubt I'd find a way to get out of whatever mess I might get into this time.

I returned to the room. He was still there, a fact which I knew already, being far more aware of his presence than that of anyone I had known before. I was certain that he was connected with the feeling I'd had last night that I'd found whatever I'd been searching for, though I didn't know what that was or how it involved him. I wasn't even sure that I knew that I'd been searching for something.

He smiled at me and indicated the table and the tray of food.

"Perhaps introductions are in order," he said. "I'm Brother Prospero, and you"—he paused—"are very definitely not Leon."

I dropped the spoon I'd just picked up, all thoughts of hunger gone, and stared at him in horror. Of course, he knew I wasn't Leon, I'd realised that last night, but I'd put it to the back of my mind in hope that it had been forgotten when he didn't bring it up immediately. I started to back towards the door, very conscious of how little I was wearing; now I understood what he would want from me, why there was no one else around. He didn't move, and to be fair, I felt no hint of threat or menace from him.

"Don't run," he said calmly. "I told you, you are quite safe here."

My fears must have shown in my face; he sounded exasperated as he added, "Honestly, whoever you are, this is predominantly a monastery. You're probably safer here than you have been anywhere else in your life."

I doubted that—I'd known a fair number of religious types whose private morals rather differed from their public vows. On the other hand, I'd been here for a while, and I'd seen no evidence to contradict the claim that these monks kept their public vows even in private. He must have noticed my hesitation as he went on.

"At least sit and eat, I won't move from here while you do, and you can stay closer to the door. We have a proposal for you, but it is entirely your choice as to whether you take it up."

Then he was silent. *Fine*, I thought, *play on my curiosity*, but the food was tempting me again and I sat and started to eat.

"I still don't know your name," he said mildly. "You don't have to tell me, but I'd like to know what to call you."

I studied him carefully. He looked relaxed and comfortable, confident that he was both in the right and doing the right thing. Even sitting down he looked as though he was tall, and broad shouldered. His eyes drew me for a moment; I could get lost in them. They were such a deep blue they were almost navy. He stared back and I could feel my skin starting to heat. I turned back to my food to hide my blushes.

"My name's Leonie," I admitted between mouthfuls.

"Ah, very sensible. That's close enough to your assumed name to make your deception that much easier, isn't it?" He didn't wait for an answer before continuing, "Do you have another name, a family name, a House name, or is it just Leonie?"

I shook my head. "Just Leonie. I don't have any other

name."

"Well, Just Leonie, once you have eaten we would appreciate it if you would dress – as Leon for the time being – and then the Lord Gabriel requests the pleasure of your company."

I started to eat faster. Whatever the circumstances, prisoner or free, you did not keep any High Lord waiting, particularly not if you wanted them to look on you at all favourably. Prospero looked amused.

"Take your time," he ordered. "Gabriel can wait, he's in no hurry, he's got plenty else to do."

I rapidly reassessed Prospero. To speak so casually of the High Lord, he had to be very senior in the House himself, and yet he looked too young. Several years older than me, certainly, but surely too young to be on first name terms with a High Lord?

I hadn't paid much attention to the hierarchy here; I'd been concentrating on learning what I could in class, keeping my head down and making sure that I kept out of sight and out of mind. I continued to eat fast. Prospero leaned forward in his chair, making me jump.

"Slow down," he insisted. "You'll get indigestion or make yourself sick. I told you, there's no hurry."

I looked at him in disbelief, but slowed down a little, which seemed to satisfy him as he leaned back again.

"A proposal?" I queried, curiosity coming forward now some of my hunger was satisfied.

"I'm afraid you'll have to wait until we see Lord Gabriel," he replied, "but it's a good one. It should be better for you than what you've been trying to do here."

He gestured broadly at the student room. Clearly I was

going to have to wait so I returned to eating and ignored him, which seemed to amuse him. He noticed as soon as I finished and spoke again.

"I'm going to move now," he said, "and go and wait outside while you dress. Come and find me as soon as you are ready, okay?"

I nodded, and watched while he got up and left the room. As quickly as I could, I pulled my clothes on and dragged a comb through my hair. I leaned against the inside of the door for a moment before opening it, trying to get my feelings in order. I was confident I could get out of this mess, nervous about what the price might be, what I might lose. I was reluctant to go and see Lord Gabriel, but eager to be with Brother Prospero again. *Eager to be with Brother Prospero? Where did that come from?*

I couldn't put it off any longer so I opened the door to find him waiting outside, leaning against the wall looking quite at ease. I tried not to look nervous as we set off, but he must have been able to tell because he spoke.

"It will be alright, you know," he said gently. "I know you don't trust me, but could you perhaps trust my vocation?"

Funnily enough, I realised I did trust him; it was the situation I was wary of. I wondered why I trusted him. Was that to do with how we'd connected last night when he'd woken me? I looked him straight in the face as I answered him. "I'd rather trust a person than a role."

He didn't have an opportunity to respond as we had reached our destination. He led the way through the open door without knocking. I was right, he must be very senior. No ordinary member of a House would just walk into a High Lord's office like that. Lord Gabriel looked up at Prospero then came towards us and indicated that we should sit down.

"Hello, Leonie," he said, and sat down opposite me.

I couldn't think why a senior member of the House would take any time over me, let alone the High Lord. My deceptions, my crime, my punishment were surely minor enough to be dealt with at a much lower level. Had I totally misjudged the situation? Did they consider what I'd done far more serious than I'd thought? Did they know what I'd been before? Had they somehow found out what I'd done in the past?

I'd never come across anyone like Lord Gabriel; he had a glow, an aura of such goodness, and when he looked at me I thought he could read me through to my very soul. I immediately decided that this was one person to whom I would always tell the truth. Possibly not the whole truth, but never a lie.

Chapter 5

Prospero

Leonie looked very composed as she sat down opposite Gabriel and responded to his greeting.

Gabriel continued, "You've caused us quite a challenge you know. The thing that interests me most is why you have disguised yourself as a boy and come here?"

Leonie looked at him with some surprise. "But you don't have girl students, not amongst those with extra skills."

Prospero had difficulty stifling his laughter and turned it into a cough, which earned him a look from Gabriel.

Gabriel smiled at Leonie. "Well, we do, but they live at our sister house on the other side of the campus, and tend to need different classes, for their different Gifts. But you could also simply have come to the college as a student."

"I thought that the college students couldn't access the same classes as the adepts," Leonie explained. "And anyway, I just knew that this was where I had to be."

"Sister Elizabeth would not have had the facilities to manage all your abilities anyway," Gabriel reassured her. "But you said you 'just knew' this was where you should be? How did you know?"

Leonie took some time to reply, picking her words slowly and carefully. "I used to feel a pressure to move on, keep going, but when we got here, to the town, it stopped, just disappeared. The person I was with then, she knew of my gifts, and she told me about here. She said that usually the gifts appear in teenagers and they either fade away by the time you are eighteen or grow much stronger, and that very few have more than one gift. She told me that you pick out those with more and take them as a special group – the adepts – but only boys and you only find a few each time."

Leonie paused to gauge how her revelations were being taken, but Gabriel motioned for her to continue.

"Before she died she told me I should find a way to be one of those few. And the others in the group didn't think I should stay with them once she'd died, so when they moved on, I stayed here and worked out how to come to the college." She looked up again and continued more quietly. "I have to learn how to control the things I can do, before I hurt anyone. I didn't mean last night to happen."

"Don't worry about that, it's in the past. You've covered the why, so how?" queried Gabriel.

"Forged papers are pretty easy to find, if you know where to look, and have something to trade," Leonie confessed. "That got me everything I needed for an application. When I came for an interview the interviewer wasn't expecting to see a girl, so he didn't. I shielded my thoughts so he only saw what I wanted, distracted him when I thought he was getting too close, tried to do the tests only just well enough to get in…"Her voice drifted off but picked up again, "And then when I got here, I just tried to stay out of sight of everyone, not get noticed, just be average – I've had a lot of practice at not being noticed. It seemed to work, until last night."

Gabriel agreed, "It certainly did work—you're very good at it, but we are going to have to be rather more rigorous with our recruitment in future!" He thought a moment, and studied the girl with interest.

"Leonie," he asked, "were you with a caravan of Traders?"

Leonie nodded as he continued, "Katya's caravan? She died while they were here, some time ago."

Leonie could only nod again but she met Gabriel's eyes, even though her own were full of sadness.

"I had a lot of time for Katya," Gabriel said. "If she felt you should be here, then I am certain she was right." He paused. "You do want to stay here with us, don't you, Leonie?"

For a moment Leonie's eyes and face were full of hope, before clouding over with caution. "You mean as a girl, but here still, to learn how to use what I can do?"

Gabriel smiled. "Yes, as a girl, to study what is appropriate to your levels of skill and ability."

Briefly, Leonie was speechless, and then she whispered, "But how?"

"You will be my ward," Gabriel told her. "It will appear that Leon leaves for the Christmas break tomorrow and does not return, while Leonie will arrive tomorrow afternoon. Your rooms will be in the main House, rather than with the students, but within the main Shield. I think that is important for all our sakes. Brother Edward will sort out clothing and equipment, and we'll find you a duty assignment in the kitchens with Brother Pedro. All clear so far?"

Gabriel looked at Leonie who was watching him in wonderment. She nodded, still speechless.

Gabriel continued, "After the Christmas period we will assess your skills and strength properly and plan a suitable curriculum for you. Now, in terms of other details, I assume that as your application papers were forged, all the information in them is also incorrect?"

"Mostly," Leonie agreed.

"Do you know your real date of birth?" Gabriel asked.

"The twenty-ninth of February," Leonie responded, her voice little more than a whisper.

Gabriel looked up sharply, and Prospero sat up, suddenly more interested.

"That's Leap Day," Prospero said. "Last year was leap year, and that means you're seventeen." He turned to Gabriel. "We don't need her consent."

"I'm not a child," Leonie muttered, but mostly under her breath.

"It's irrelevant," Gabriel told Prospero. "I want Leonie to be happy with what we decide."

He turned back to Leonie. "We take new students in every quarter. Why did you choose to come now, and not next April, after your birthday?"

Leonie looked down at the floor and scuffed her foot, sheepishly. "I didn't expect it to work, not the first time, I was trying to find out where the problems were, what else I would need to do to get in. But it did work so I didn't want to pass it up."

It was Gabriel's turn to laugh. "You've had us completely fooled, haven't you? Still, at least you are safe with us now. Do you know anything about your parents?"

"I was told my father died before I was born, and my mother died giving birth to me. I lived with my aunt until she died, then after a while I joined Katya's caravan."

Gabriel stood up, dismissing them but still smiling. "We'll leave it at that. Brother Prospero will take you to meet with

Brother Edward."

Chapter 6

Leonie

I followed Brother Prospero through doors, down stairs and along corridors into a large space that resembled a cavern filled with treasure. He led me across to a room on the edge of the cavern, lined with racks of fabrics in all the colours of the rainbow, and well-lit by a wall of windows. Another monk was seated there at a long work table. My head was spinning with all the new things I had to think about. The sheer size of the storerooms didn't help and by the time we entered the inner room, the spinning felt real, not just figurative. Brother Prospero introduced me to Brother Edward and I know Brother Edward spoke to me but it didn't seem to make sense, and then he seemed to be swaying from side to side. I heard someone call Prospero's name urgently as if from a great distance, and then I was sitting down with a hand gently but firmly holding my head down by my knees.

"Don't move, breath slowly," I was told – Prospero again – and for once I felt inclined to do what I was told.

After a moment he moved his hand from my head and let me sit up, though I realised he was still holding my wrist. He was squatting down in front of me, so that his dark eyes were level with mine.

"Better?" he asked.

I nodded and regretted it as my head started to spin again.

"You don't eat properly, you don't sleep properly and your life is far too stressful. It's no wonder you nearly passed out," he accused me.

I growled back, "And you know this how?"

"The pup has spirit," Edward laughed from somewhere

behind Prospero.

I would have snarled at him, too, but couldn't find the energy.

Prospero ignored him to respond to me. "You're nothing but skin and bone, you've got dark circles under your eyes, and you've been living a life of deception for the last three months at least, if not longer."

Edward passed him a mug and he paused to press it in to my free hand. "Drink!" he commanded.

I did. It was hot and sweet, and sipping gave me time to compose myself. Truth be told, it was Prospero himself who was having a major effect on my senses. The man acted like he was always right, was far too sure of himself, and yet I trusted him instinctively. His touch made my skin feel like an electric charge was crawling across it – how could he not feel it? I wanted to bait him, annoy him, disrupt that calm exterior and make him feel as disorientated as he was making me feel. I was sure he was connected with whatever I had been seeking, and that made me feel insatiably curious, because I didn't know what I had been seeking, and I was without any way of finding out – and that irritated me too.

I reached out with my mind – something I should have done much sooner if I'd had my wits about me – to touch his mind and see what I could find out. No telepath could read or hear more than the surface thoughts of any non-telepath's mind – even with another telepath it was like talking without using your voice – but I thought it might give me a clue to his actions. I found a blank, a telepathic shield, and backed off. I hadn't expected him to be a telepath – in my experience men rarely were. Then I realised that Lord Gabriel had known my name before Prospero had had time to tell him out loud; they had to both be telepathic.

Amongst the Traders, it was the women who were telepaths, like Headwomen Katya. I still missed Katya deeply. She had taken me in as her apprentice, provided me with food, a place to sleep and training. Maybe I was an Outsider, but she'd always treated me well. I could have done with her wisdom to talk over all the things that were happening now. I pulled myself away from these past memories, aware that Prospero was still watching me. I realised that I'd finished the drink, so I passed the mug back to him, and he took it and put it on the table.

"You'll do for now," he said, "though I wish I'd taken the opportunity to take you into the hospital last night when I had the chance."

I shuddered, I did not like hospitals, but before Prospero could comment, Edward spoke.

"She'll be fine here with me. You get off to wherever you are supposed to be right now."

Prospero turned to him. "Make sure she gets a decent lunch," he said and then looked back to me. "If you don't eat properly, I'll know."

I hoped that was an empty threat but as he headed towards the door, I felt an unexpected fear flare up in me. Despite the fact that he unsettled me beyond measure, Prospero had been the one steady focal point in all that had happened in the last few hours, and now he was disappearing and leaving me in an unknown and potentially dangerous situation. I wasn't aware that I'd said anything but he turned back and squatted down again so our eyes were on a level.

"Don't worry; you'll be safe with Edward," he said quietly. "I'll be back for you in a couple of hours."

Then I was on my own. I don't think Edward heard that

last reassurance for he smiled at me and said, "He's a very good doctor, and monk for that matter, even if he can be a bit bossy!"

"Bit bossy!" I responded with a cautious smile myself.

Edward laughed and, as I looked up at him, I thought maybe I was going to have to reconsider my views about these monks. Although the college was run by the monastery, I hadn't had much to do with the monks or the nuns up to now. The Great House was arranged in courtyards around the Abbey and the monks occupied a separate courtyard from the student adepts. There was a shared dining hall and some classes were taught by monks or nuns. My policy had been to keep out of the way and keep my head down because I hadn't felt it was safe to get to know anyone, whether they were monk, nun or student.

Right now, I realised that Edward was also studying me so I dragged my thoughts back again to the current situation. Despite this, his first question took me totally by surprise.

Edward

Now in his mid-fifties, Edward had been a monk for more than thirty years. Although he didn't possess the abilities that Prospero and many of the others did, he had found the monastery a haven from the harsh world outside. In another place, another time, he might have succumbed to an unhappy conventional life as a reluctant husband. Here, celibacy was a relief to him and he revelled in being able to use his creative abilities to design and make glorious vestments, altar cloths and wall hangings. He was also responsible for clothing requirements across the monastery, the convent and the lay House, but, whilst there were a number of females in the lay House, being asked to provide a full wardrobe for a teenage girl was unusual, particularly one with such a high status as ward of the High Lord. He was looking forward to the challenge and regarded the girl carefully.

Despite the fact that she was dressed as a boy, he could see she had a delicate bone structure. Far too thin, he thought, but beautiful; dressing her well would be a reward in itself. Something struck him as odd so he looked more closely, trying to analyse it – clear skin the colour of honey, deep grey eyes with just a hint of green, short dark brown hair – ah, that was it, those colours didn't work together.

"What's your natural hair colour?" he asked.

Leonie looked up in surprise. "Red," she admitted. "It's rather noticeable, so I tried to hide it. It's curly too so I've tried to straighten it," she added.

Edward nodded. "That makes sense," he agreed. "We'll take that into account when we're choosing colours. No boring browns for you." He looked down at his own clothing – brown trousers, white undershirt and hooded brown over tunic. "Not that brown is boring, of course, far from it, but it won't do for you," he added. "Now, I've got a list here of what you will need."

He glanced down his list, then back at the now speechless Leonie. "What's up?" he asked, seeing her face.

Leonie just shook her head. Edward waited patiently. He was one of those people that others talked to, often saying more than they ought or than they had planned to. In the early years, he had struggled with gossip, eager to pass on what he had heard, but with maturity had come the ability to distinguish between what should be confidential and what needed to be passed on to an appropriate person. People still talked to him more than they should, and this put him in a unique position to identify synergies and apparent coincidences that no one else spotted – a trait Lord Gabriel valued very much. Right now, though, he was quiet, waiting for Leonie to be able to express her concerns.

"I don't need much," she said. "I never...I never had new

clothes before."

"No?" queried Edward, unsurprised, given the basic nature of what she was wearing. "Well, there's a first time for everything." His voice held a trace of amusement. "You have a role to take on as a ward of the House, and you need to dress appropriately for it so as not to let Lord Gabriel down. It'll just be what is necessary, no more."

Phrased like that, Leonie seemed to find the idea more manageable, so Edward carried on. "Are you up to walking round the stores with me now?"

Leonie nodded, words clearly still difficult, and they set off through the caverns of supplies.

Leonie

Edward was patient and kind, and I warmed to him as we started to find the various supplies he seemed to think necessary. I felt it seemed excessive given how little so many people had, but I succumbed to the pleasure of new clothes, just for me. Whatever the catch was in what Lord Gabriel was offering me, I found myself unwilling to let him down; I would keep up my end of the deal.

Edward didn't ask questions that weren't related to what we were doing and he chatted on with snippets of information about the monastery, the House, and the monks, which I stored away for future reference as I followed him round. He kept pulling things off shelves and piling them into my arms.

"Gorgeous grey, for everyday wear for you, I think," he said. "That'll bring out the colour in your eyes."

But he chose loads of other colours, too.

"Not red," I said impulsively, as he reached for something. "I can't stand wearing red."

He looked at me, but didn't say anything, and left whatever it was on the shelf. In the past I'd been made to wear red, just so that others – lords and ladies – could laugh at me and mock me. And anyway, I thought it looked dreadful with my hair. We took everything he'd chosen back to the long work table where Edward sorted it out and picked out a selection.

"Go and try these on," he said, handing them to me and indicating a changing cubicle to one side. "And then come back out. I need to check the fit."

I went, obediently. What he had handed me was a basic everyday outfit – trousers, undershirt and tunic. The monks and nuns always wore brown trousers and a loose fitting tunic – no wonder Edward had said brown was boring – with a white undershirt, but they seemed to vary sleeve length on both shirt and tunic. My outfit had trousers in a soft grey cotton weave, and a matching short-sleeved tunic that fastened down the front. The long-sleeved undershirt was emerald green, a silky fabric that clung to my skin. I did the tunic up and found it was shaped to my body, accentuating the few curves I had. I might have twirled in front of the mirror, admiring it. I wasn't anything to look at but these clothes were lovely.

Edward nodded his approval, pinned a few minor adjustments to the trousers and tunic then gave me some more to try on. Soon we had three piles on the table – those things he approved of, which he then consigned to a trunk, those he'd rejected and those that need alterations. In the late morning we heard the Abbey bells ring; they did that four times a day to call people – monks and nuns anyway – to the services. I was surprised that Edward made no move to go.

"Aren't you going . . ?" I asked, the words just slipping out and then drifting off as I realised it wasn't my place to question him.

"It's not compulsory, you know," he replied gently. "However much we might want to attend, sometimes we have other responsibilities. Can you imagine a surgeon stopping in the middle of an operation?"

Well, no, I couldn't, but neither did I think what we were doing was as important as all that.

"Lord Gabriel has told me that you are that important, if not more so," Edward insisted. "Now we've sorted out everyday wear we need to make you some items for special occasions."

He pulled some pattern books towards us, starting to show me examples and finding samples of fabrics, buttons and other trimmings. My mind was still on how services in the Abbey and work duties all fitted together for these people, so, feeling brave, I started to pester Edward with questions.

"Well, the monastery came first," he said. "Both monks and nuns, living separately but worshipping and working together. Our priority is the worship of God." He must have realised that contradicted what he'd said earlier because he went on, "We also serve God through our work, which is about taking care of others. That started with the hospital, treating the sick, which led to the college to train healers, which then expanded to train people in other areas, to enable them to improve their lives and the lives of others."

"But there are people who live here who aren't monks or nuns, aren't there?" I asked.

He nodded. "Yes, the lay House is for those who are affiliated to the college or hospital who aren't or can't or don't want to be monks or nuns. And the House sometimes takes on wards, like you, adopted children. It acts in the role of parent to them."

Well, I didn't remember my parents at all, so I guessed a House could do the job as far as I was concerned.

"What about those with gifts? How do they fit in?"

Edward took his time replying. "I'm not blessed that way myself, though I can see that the Gifts are a wonderful blessing, properly used. But they are a burden too, and can be difficult to control and use responsibly. Many of the adepts who come here find that putting their Gifts at God's service gives them a framework in which to control them and use them well. Often, that is within the monastery, but there are those within the House, too. The student adepts get the opportunity to learn to use and control their Gifts and explore that framework for themselves in a safe environment without making a commitment before they are ready."

"Is that why Brother Prospero came here?"

"Prospero?" Edward responded. "I think he always wanted to be a doctor—I'm pretty sure he had no intention of being a monk. He was pretty wild as a student to start with, and the nightmares he had..." Edward's voice drifted off in memory.

I looked up suddenly. "Nightmares?"

"Yes, like I hear you had last night," he answered, in a very matter-of-fact tone.

Honestly, does everyone know?

Edward continued, "His were some of the worst we've ever seen. It's a good thing he never got the hang of fire-starting, or he'd have burnt the place down long before he graduated!"

That was more information for me to store away, so I

returned my concentration to our work while I digested it.

I was aware of Prospero as soon as he returned, his presence like a current in the air around me. He stood at the door for a while, calmly surveying us as though he was checking up on what we were doing, then walked in like he owned the place. I was afraid my time here – to my surprise I'd been enjoying it – was over.

Prospero

By the time Prospero returned to find Leonie, she appeared to be on excellent terms with Edward. As he entered the workroom he saw them at a table partly turned away from him, conferring over patterns and fabrics. He was hit by a sudden flash of jealousy, which irritated him; she was just a student, of no special importance to him after all. To regain control of his feelings he took a moment to look around the workroom. A slightly battered trunk was on the floor against the desk, perhaps three quarters full, mainly with clothing but he also saw books, stationery, toiletries and other student paraphernalia in there. The work table nearest the door was covered with bolts of fabric; idly he thought the sapphire blue would suit Leonie very well, and then had to drag his mind away from such thoughts. On the desk was the detritus of a working lunch. As he glanced over at Leonie, it was clear her improved colour and energy suggested she had eaten a proper meal again. That reminded him of his medical duties. He moved towards Leonie at the same time as she looked up towards him.

"How are you feeling now?" he asked her by way of greeting but without waiting for an answer he also reached for her wrist to check her pulse.

Edward answered first, "We've been fine here, thanks, and I think we're doing well, aren't we, Leonie?" He turned towards her for confirmation and she nodded in agreement.

Prospero continued with his questioning. "You had a decent lunch?"

Leonie nodded again, and Prospero glanced almost imperceptibly towards Edward who also nodded from behind her. Prospero let go of Leonie's wrist and checked her forehead with the back of his hand.

"No shivers or shakes, dizziness, feeling sick, anything like that?"

Leonie shook her head this time.

"Well then, you seem to have recovered from last night and this morning." He smiled at her, sure that if anyone had been feeling his pulse they'd be able to tell the effect she had on him. "I'm happy to escort you back to your room when you are ready."

"Do I have to go now?" Leonie asked.

"No," replied both Prospero and Edward together and then looked at each other in amused surprise.

Prospero continued, "You're not a prisoner of any sort; you're free to go wherever and whenever you wish, but I think you've got a bit to finish here." He looked towards Edward who confirmed this with a nod. "Besides," Prospero added, "out there it's heaving with students and their families coming and going as everyone packs up and leaves for Christmas. It's much nicer in the peace and quiet here!"

"Does that mean you're hoping to hang around here until Leonie is ready?" asked Edward with a grin.

"Oh, I think I could," answered Prospero slowly, as he acknowledged with a grin that his ruse had been discovered. "I don't suppose anyone will miss me for an hour or two."

"Fair enough," confirmed Edward, "but I'm not having idle hands round here. You can start by finding some coffee."

"Sure," replied Prospero. "What about you, Leonie? Tea, coffee, hot chocolate perhaps?"

Leonie nodded at the last option, and Prospero ambled off, collecting the lunch plates on his way to return them to the kitchen.

Chapter 7

Leonie

Prospero meekly going off to get drinks and clear our lunch plates didn't fit in with the picture I had of him at all. I felt his presence again as soon as he returned to the room. It was like a current in the air, making all the fine hairs on my skin stand on end. I struggled to stop my hands from shaking as he passed me a hot drink and our fingers brushed. I hid it by nursing the mug in both hands and taking a sip. He gave the other mug to Edward, and spoke to me.

"So, what do you think of your new outfits then?"

I looked over the rim of the mug and said the first thing that came into my head. "I didn't know one person needed so many clothes."

Prospero laughed, "I'm sure Edward's only found you what is necessary."

"That's true enough," confirmed Edward, "and beautiful you'll look in them too."

Prospero smiled and agreed, "I'm sure that's true."

I looked from one to the other, blushing and confused at the idea that anyone would think I was beautiful under any circumstances. Edward saved the situation by turning to Prospero. "Anyway, I think I told you I wasn't having idle hands round here? You can start clearing up that work table."

He pointed to the other work table where we had spread out all kinds of buttons, ribbons and other accessories, and, again much to my surprise, Prospero dutifully set to work. I'd regained my composure a few minutes later, head down over our worktable, when Edward spoke again.

"Now that's just showing off."

I looked up, not sure what he meant, and found it had been directed at Prospero. Far from using his hands to sort the buttons, he was using telekinesis and a stream of blue buttons was leaping off the table and into their box.

"I need to keep in practice," Prospero responded.

The temptation was definitely too much for me, and I reached out with my mind and shifted the box so that the next button missed. Prospero looked round, startled, but there was a definite gleam in his eyes when they met mine. There was a clear challenge as I felt him take hold of the box so it wouldn't move. He had control of the loose buttons but he'd forgotten the buttons already in the box. I felt for them and brought them up in a long arc over his head then added the buttons from another box; he hadn't thought to guard them either.

Prospero grinned. "Like that is it?"

For the next few minutes we competed for the control and movement of the buttons. He set patterns in the air and I followed them and elaborated, setting more complex ones. Soon the space over his head was a swirling rainbow pattern of buttons and ribbons. I revelled in the opportunity just to play openly with my telekinetic skills like this; up to now I'd used them surreptitiously and only where necessary to provide the essential needs for myself and…others. Here I could just enjoy them and I tested and stretched myself with the number of items I controlled, the range and delicacy of movement. I could tell from Prospero's face he was enjoying it too, and his actions were encouraging me to try more and more.

"This is all very entertaining and pretty," Edward said, "but it's not getting the things put away."

I thought Prospero looked slightly chastened at that, which made me giggle quietly, and I hid my face so he wouldn't notice. Together we directed all the buttons, ribbons and other bits and pieces towards the right boxes and drawers. That was nearly as much fun as playing with them, and I made my streams of buttons and ribbons circle round Prospero a few times before they landed in the boxes. I was pretty certain that Edward was also amused by it all but he just acknowledged a job completed and then set Prospero to putting away the bolts of fabric that we'd finished with. I was given Edward's list and told to go and check off what we had already put in the trunk and pack it neatly.

Just as I was about to make one of the bolts of material move, Prospero reached for it and he spoke to me – telepathically.

I jumped although his greeting was friendly enough.

"Yes, I was sure you were a telepath, too."

Unable to formulate any words I just looked up at him, no longer comfortable, and scared of the consequences of being discovered.

I'd never thought telepathy to be that much use really, often more of a nuisance. Everybody, telepath or not, had superficial thoughts and feelings floating at the surface of their mind. A strong telepath heard those without trying; a weaker one had to choose to read them. Either way, they were usually very boring – 'did I remember to do this', 'did I forget to do that', 'I like his new outfit', 'that colour doesn't suit her', that sort of thing. I wasn't above checking these thoughts to see if there was information that I could use to help me, to protect those I was responsible for, but I didn't do it as habit because I thought it was intrusive, boring and I very rarely found anything useful. I'd learnt to ignore the background hum of all this in my mind, but that was one of the reasons I liked churches and shopping markets – they were Shielded so no adept could use any of their gifts in there, and that made them quiet and restful, at least for me.

Telepaths usually shielded their thoughts so no one else could read them. Two telepaths could talk to one another, in their heads, without speaking out loud, but that was nothing like as useful as it seemed, not least because you had to find another telepath first. Katya had said she knew of telepaths who could communicate over one hundred miles or more, but she'd refused to tell me any more about them. For most, their limit was perhaps one hundred feet, often less. Katya and I had managed a couple of miles once, but that was the furthest I'd had the opportunity to try. Then, it was just a voice, purely verbal, so you lost out on all the other elements of communication like tone, expression, body language – it was actually easier to misunderstand a telepathic conversation than a normal one. I'd never used a telephone, but I'd seen them and I knew what they were; I'd decided that telepathy had to be something like a telephone conversation but without the equipment. The only real use we had ever found for telepathy was to consult about someone Katya was healing when we had thought it better they didn't hear what we were saying.

As Leon, I'd been very careful not to be identified as a telepath in the early tests, and I was pretty sure I'd got away with it then. After that, no one had checked again, until now. I should have expected it but I still wasn't thinking and planning carefully enough.

"You must have been very controlled to fool our assessors," Prospero continued, *"because they noted Leon as having no telepathic powers at all."*

Then he stopped, sat down on the floor beside me and the trunk and spoke out loud. "What's the matter? What's worrying you?"

I still couldn't find the words to explain my feelings so I shrugged, and he went on, "Are you concerned that you're in trouble for deceiving us?"

That was closer, so I nodded.

"You're not in any kind of trouble," he reassured me. "I'm just astounded and impressed at the range of abilities you have. I didn't misunderstand? You did enjoy what we were doing with the buttons and things, didn't you?" He looked very concerned.

I nodded as much to reassure him as to answer the question.

He carried on, "Have you not had much experience with telepathy?"

I shook my head and ventured a few words, "Just Katya to talk to properly...and all the thoughts around, when I can't ignore them."

"You can hear people's thoughts, without making the effort to read them?"

"Sometimes, some people, not everyone clearly, and it's mostly just a background hum where I can't make out specific words and voices."

He raised his eyebrows but then smiled at me. "That's impressive, too. Being able to hear others without trying is a sign of a very strong telepath."

Edward interrupted at that moment, calling across to find out if we'd finished our tasks. We both had, near enough, so he suggested that we'd done all we could for today. Prospero rose to his feet and offered me his hand to get up. I took it and felt again the electric current crawl across my skin as we connected. His expression didn't change – how could he not feel it, or react to it?

"Right," he said. "Perhaps you'd allow me to escort you back to your room?"

It didn't seem like the sort of question to which I could answer no, but I was concerned about what happened after that.

"Do I have to stay there now?"

He raised his eyebrows and those deep blue eyes opened wider. "No, of course not. I keep telling you, you're not a prisoner. You've successfully fooled us all and had the run of the place as Leon, you can carry on being Leon and go wherever Leon can go until you become Leonie tomorrow. I don't suppose anyone else will know any better."

I was somewhat reassured by that. Anyway, I'd bet my ability to escape against anyone's ability to hold me, it just always helped to know the terms under which I was held. Edward passed me a parcel containing clothes for becoming Leonie tomorrow and confirmed that everything else would be delivered to my new room. Then Prospero did indeed escort me back to my old room. He left me at the door with a funny little bow.

"Until tomorrow, then," he said.

I waited until I was sure he was well away and that no one else was around and then I left too, for one of my favourite hiding places, to contemplate all that had happened over the past hours and what I was going to do about it.

Chapter 8

The next day

Prospero

Lord Gabriel had assigned Brothers Andrew and Prospero the task of collecting Leonie from her old room and escorting her to her new ones. Prospero was not at all sure that this was a good idea despite acknowledging the fact that he didn't want to entrust the task to anyone else. It had been little more than eighteen hours since he had escorted Leonie back to her room from Edward's workroom. During that time he had participated in worship, worked a shift at the hospital and slept and yet he had not been able to get her out of his mind. He had managed some mental discipline to drive her from his thoughts in the chapel and while concentrating on working but the consequence had been that she had run wild through his dreams and he had awoken feeling less than rested. He told himself that there was no reason he should have anything to do with her once she had been safely delivered into the care of Lady Eleanor. Eleanor ran the secular part of the House and would act as Leonie's guardian for all practical purposes. His path would not need to cross with Leonie's, other than in the dining hall where he could easily keep his distance.

If he was honest he could, and probably should, have walked away from the situation already; there was no way he should consider himself responsible for Leonie. He could have had someone else sit with her that first night, or have taken her to meet Gabriel or to Edward, but he'd been fascinated by her from the first moment he'd realised she was the person he'd been seeking. Far from walking away from the situation, he'd taken every opportunity to become more deeply embroiled in it. He'd manipulated events to be able to re-join her in Edward's workroom. Testing her abilities had been far beyond his remit but she'd been one of the few people he'd met whose Gifts had the potential to rival or even exceed his own. Her telekinetic abilities had certainly challenged his, and telekinesis was his strongest ability. Difficult as he found it to admit, despite being all but untrained, she had outclassed him, managing and manoeuvring multiple items more accurately than he could. He didn't think she'd realised this and it just made her all the more fascinating to him.

"You've been on edge all day," Andrew accused him as they headed towards the student rooms.

"It's nothing." Prospero shrugged. "I didn't sleep well."

Andrew gave him a disbelieving look, and Prospero confessed, "Truly, I didn't sleep well. But it's this girl. Something about her unsettles me. And it shouldn't. She's just a student, Gabriel's ward, a minor."

"She's not a minor, though, is she?" Andrew said astutely, "Not where I come from, nor you. It's this House that says she needs a guardian. We were considered adult by sixteen."

"Not by my mother," Prospero said darkly, surprising himself by the rare mention of his family.

Andrew didn't have time to respond because they'd reached Leonie's room. He knocked at the door and Prospero took a deep breath to help compose himself. It didn't help much. The sight that greeted his eyes when the door opened didn't help at all.

The best word to describe Leon had been nondescript – small, slight, with dull brown hair and shapeless clothing in muted colours. That description could not be applied to the Leonie now standing in the doorway. Leonie had copper red hair, clustered in unruly curls about her head. The outfit that Edward had found her might have been simple but it was well cut and showed off her shape admirably – too thin he thought, but very definitely feminine. The eyes were the same, though, huge and dark and distracting. Yesterday morning they'd been guarded, unreadable, but in the afternoon, when he and she had been playing with the buttons and ribbons, her eyes had lit up with mischief. Something flashed across them now – fear, anger perhaps, he wasn't sure – and he dragged himself back to the present.

Andrew had greeted her, "My Lady Leonie, we've . . ." but Leonie was objecting to the title for some reason and had backed away. He stepped forward to intervene and she turned accusing eyes towards him.

"You didn't tell me..." she started.

But he didn't let her finish. "As the ward of the High Lord, you do, of course, have the courtesy title Lady," Prospero said smoothly, "but we're very informal with titles here. People may greet you the first time with your title, but if you'd rather just be known as Leonie, all you have to do is invite them to do so. Some of the Brothers here are also entitled to be addressed as Lord outside these walls, but most prefer the title Brother, and within the complex we tend just to use given names."

That appeared to mollify Leonie, and she turned towards Andrew. "Please, just call me Leonie," she said.

"I'm Brother Andrew," he responded, "and this is Brother Prospero."

Leonie looked towards Prospero and this time there was challenge in her eyes. "Yes, Brother Prospero and I have already met."

He acknowledged the challenge with an inclination of his head towards her. "My Lady Leonie." He indicated a holdall and a box sitting on the bed. "Are these your things?"

Leonie nodded, and Prospero scooped up the box, whilst Andrew took the holdall and gestured for Leonie to lead the way from the room. Prospero could not fail to notice that she chose to walk beside Andrew, leaving him to bring up the rear, nor could he fail to notice that she had emphasised his title without taking the opportunity to invite him to ignore hers. He was much amused; life with Leonie around was clearly going to be fun.

He watched her as she walked ahead of him, and thought again that she was too thin. Given the powers and Gifts she had, she probably burnt off energy using them almost faster than she could eat. He should have a word with Pedro to make sure she always had access to food and snacks; three good meals a day was fine for most students but the really Gifted ones burnt off so much energy using and taming their abilities, it just wasn't enough. The student supervisor was supposed to watch out for such things, but as Leonie had been trying to avoid being noticed, he couldn't have had a chance. Her duties would be in the kitchens, which would make things that much easier; Pedro could be persuaded to make sure she had free access to what she needed. And he could watch her himself at meal times to ensure she ate properly then. Andrew would help when he wasn't around, so would some of the others. They had reached Leonie's new rooms before Prospero remembered that he had planned to keep well away from Leonie and the temptations she offered.

Gabriel

Gabriel paced backwards and forwards across his office, guiltily ignoring the work piled on his desk. His legs and knees ached from a sleepless night spent in prayer and meditation. Although he was now certain of what he should do, he had no confidence at all in his ability to do it. He sank to his knees once more, again wrestling with his problems before God.

Introducing a female ward into what was primarily a monastery had to be asking for trouble somewhere. Anyone with any sense would put her firmly under the care of Sister Elizabeth on the other side of the campus. However, it was not without precedent despite being many years since the monastery had last had a female ward, under a previous Abbot. That had worked out well for all parties despite being both painful and disruptive. Everyone had thought that Abbot mad, even suggested he'd been going senile, and no doubt they would be saying the same about Gabriel soon. He thought what he was doing was totally at odds with what was reasonable, so that reaction seemed perfectly fair to him.

He'd had another dream about the jewel the night before they'd discovered Leonie. This time, he'd had to hunt for the ruby, knowing he had to find it and keep it safe, knowing the jewel would be the focus of something that would affect not only his Great House, but all the others. It wasn't clear whether he had to use the emerald to keep the ruby safe, or keep the ruby away from the emerald to keep it safe. He had been surprised to find a girl masquerading as one of their students, but he had been certain she was the ruby of his dream, whatever that might mean.

Far more troubling had been the explicit waking vision of the future he'd had since then. He had these moments of precognition, dreams and visions that he considered messages from God, and he had learnt over many years not to ignore them, much as he disliked them. It was not good to know about the future.

As he knelt now in his office, the visions started again, consuming all his senses as if he were physically in them. He knew this was normal; the visions would repeat time after time with changes as he made decisions and took actions.

He was sitting at his desk, aware that several years had

passed. Leonie had left, no longer his responsibility. Brothers Andrew and Prospero were still part of the monastery, and everything seemed normal. But as he looked at the papers and reports spread across his desk, he realised things were far from normal. The simmering tensions between the two largest Great Houses had boiled over into all-out war. The other Houses had each aligned with one or other of these two, and there was no part of the world unaffected, no part that wasn't suffering loss, death and destruction. This report was about food shortages, another showed his hospital was struggling to cope with the levels of injury and disease. He could see no prospect of an end to the suffering.

The vision wavered and merged into a different future.

Again he was sitting at his desk, again several years had passed, but now he was aware of an overwhelming feeling of sorrow. He looked at the reports in front of him. They indicated prosperity and peace; this one showed that the long-established feud between the two largest Great Houses had been diffused and they were now working together as allies, if not friends, with other Houses following their example.

He rose from his desk and walked down to the river, stopping at the edge of a small clearing leading down to the bank. Brother Andrew was there, kneeling on the ground, his back to Gabriel, his hands moving back and forth as he tended a grave. Without even seeing the headstone, Gabriel knew it was the final resting place of Prospero and Leonie and the source of his sorrow. The reason for the shared grave wasn't clear to him but their connection and death had somehow precipitated the peace that enveloped the world.

As the vision cleared Gabriel felt a sense of urgency; he would have to act soon.

He rose from his knees and started pacing once more as he

thought again about his options. If he stuck strictly and obediently to the traditions, rules and principles of his House and Order, he should keep Prospero and Leonie separated. And if he did that, his vision suggested there would be worldwide war. *Is that what God wants of me? Absolute obedience to the rules even in the face of things I don't understand and that don't seem fair? Can war be good for the world, in the sense that a forest fire can clear the way for new growth?* He pondered this for some time, until it became clear to him that he considered this the easy option. He wouldn't have to do anything unusual or uncomfortable, he wouldn't have to stick his neck out, he wouldn't appear responsible and no one would know of his involvement.

He needed to work for the peaceful option. In this case, obedience to God was going to involve going against the flow and changing things that had been considered normal for many years. With a sigh, knowing that this was going to challenge him to the very limit of his abilities and probably beyond, he moved on to thinking about what he was now being asked to do.

He decided that the way to deal with a teenage girl in a monastery was not separation as seemed logical, but a counter intuitive approach of integration. The vast majority of his monks had to deal with females every day, not just the nuns but also those in the lay House, or colleagues and patients at the hospital or students and teachers at the college and they did so without any major problems. If Leonie had all but free run of the place – except the restricted areas, of course – perhaps the younger ones would consider her in the light of a sister and the older ones as a daughter. Gabriel thought this an approach worth trying though he suspected it would add fuel to the view that he was going mad.

But to precipitate peace he also had to encourage a close relationship to develop between Leonie and Prospero. That seemed a far more dangerous proposition and he had no idea how to do it safely, let alone in such a way that he could attempt to justify to his colleagues. Whilst making Leonie part of the family, so to speak, was one thing, it could hardly be reasonable, let alone good, for any one of his monks to be placed in frequent and close proximity to such a temptation, and Prospero's past history suggested great potential for trouble.

There had been girl children within the lay House before without trouble and, of course there had been Melanie. Although it was probably best to keep any thoughts of Melanie out of this situation. She certainly wasn't an argument in favour of what he proposed.

He planned to spend some time over the next few days discussing the interpretation of his visions and what action should be taken with one of his closest advisors. Not Prospero, it would be necessary to keep him entirely in the dark. But it would be essential to involve Andrew to some extent which would be both painful and blatantly unfair.

Gabriel stopped pacing and sat down, thinking now about the relationship between Andrew and Prospero. They'd been all but inseparable since they'd met on their first day as students, and he needed Andrew's influence on Prospero if he was going to pull this off.

Aware of the dangers of close and potentially exclusive friendships forming among his monks, Gabriel had, as a matter of course, separated Prospero and Andrew when they'd entered the Order. Prospero had seemed a particularly unlikely candidate, and Gabriel had been concerned that he had been following Andrew's lead rather than God's calling at the time. Matters had soon proved otherwise, but he had kept them separated as far as possible on principle, difficult as it was with them both undergoing medical training. Sometime later, Gabriel had realised that Prospero and Andrew, acting and working together as a unit, was much greater and more effective than the sum of them separated and had relaxed about the issue. He'd never had cause to regret this.

Clearly, the advent of Leonie was going to impact on this dynamic and despite his concerns Gabriel was more than curious as to how this would work out. Most people thought of Prospero as the leader and Andrew more of a follower; Gabriel's view was that the relationship was far more complicated than that – he was counting on that for Andrew's influence. They worked as a team, and Leonie was bound to disrupt this. He was also aware that Prospero had been restless for some months, and was ready for a new challenge, even though Prospero himself had not realised this. Andrew, on the other hand, was entirely settled.

Gabriel stood up again, and paced over to the window. Looking out, he saw Prospero and Leonie sitting on a bench in the courtyard, talking intently. Perhaps it wasn't going to take much at all to precipitate this relationship. That was a worry in itself.

Chapter 9

Leonie

Brothers Andrew and Prospero had shown me to my new rooms and introduced me to Lady Eleanor, who seemed to be in charge. I'd nearly got off on the wrong foot with Brother Andrew, but Prospero had smoothed things over. I knew I should be grateful, but he was always so confident, so sure he was right, and this time at least he was right, and that just made me mad, and I knew I had been off hand with him. I thought I'd got on alright with Andrew after that, but I'd felt the heat of Prospero's eyes on my back. Now I'd been left to settle in for a while, but Prospero would be back soon to take me to meet Pedro, who I'd be working for in the kitchens.

When Prospero did return to collect me, I was ready and had resolved to be both polite and friendly towards him. We walked together across the courtyard, and I summoned up my courage to ask him about what was troubling me.

"Can I ask you something about all this?"

"Of course." He indicated a bench. "Shall we sit?"

I nodded and we did so. He sat silently, waiting for me to speak but I couldn't think how to start so I just came out with it. "What do you want from me?"

He stared back, his eyes wide. "Nothing. I don't want anything from you."

I shook my head in frustration. "No, not you. The college, the House? When I was a student I understood – I paid, you taught – that was the deal. Now, I don't pay, but you provide still, so what do you want from me in return?"

I really didn't understand the deal here. As a student I had to pay for my room, food and tuition, as well as provide my own books, clothes and similar. As a ward, I had better rooms, and Lord Gabriel would cover my tuition and provide my food, clothes, accommodation and anything else I might need. In return all I had to do was a few hours duty each week in the kitchen; such generosity just didn't make sense to me.

I felt there had to be something else they wanted from me, although I couldn't work out what. I could not see where Lord Gabriel or his House would benefit from this deal with me, and that made me both nervous and curious.

Prospero seemed to understand. "Firstly," he said, "you have to appreciate that, apart from worship, our purpose as a House is to care for those who do or should need care. Not just the sick, although the hospital is a large part of it, but also the elderly, those without families, orphans. Whether you like it or not, and however independent you are, here it's our responsibility to take care of you."

He must have seen the rebellious look in my eyes, for he paused.

I struggled with my resolution to be polite. "I can look after myself."

"Yes," he replied, "you can. You've more than proved that. But wouldn't it be nice not to have to? Not to have to worry about how to keep warm or where your next meal is coming from? Not to have to hide who you really are or what you can do? To concentrate on learning to manage your skills instead of having to fight to survive?"

He knew the buttons to press.

I took a deep breath and tried a different tack. "There are loads of orphans out there. You don't provide them all with a home here and all that you've given me."

"No, we don't," he agreed. "But we do provide those we know of with homes, care, food, clothing and an appropriate education depending on their needs. What we've done here is what Lord Gabriel feels is appropriate for you, especially given your abilities."

I noted his careful wording with interest. "Lord Gabriel? Don't you agree?"

"Actually I do." He looked me straight in the eyes. "I think you will cause chaos wherever you are. I don't know anywhere else that has the facilities or the ability to deal with that. But there will be plenty who think Lord Gabriel is wrong."

Funnily enough, the thought that these people could disagree about the right thing to do made me feel better. If they were uncertain, then it was okay for me to be confused. "But I still don't understand what you want from me, what the terms are? What do I have to do? How long does this last? What do I owe if I leave? Can I even leave?" The questions burst out of me, their very speed expressing my frustration.

"How many times do I have to tell you? You're not a prisoner. You can leave at any time you want and owe nothing, I promise you that. Until you are eighteen, if you leave without telling us, we'll come looking for you because we've chosen to be responsible for you. But if you do decide you want to leave, please come and tell us first because we might be able to sort out whatever the problem is."

Two months that meant, just over two months. I might want to be here, but I didn't want to be trapped here. I hated to feel trapped. But I could survive two months and then I'd be free to do what I chose – even if I chose to stay.

He carried on, "We'll continue to provide for you until you are twenty-one, or have finished your studies at the college, whichever comes later, and at the end of that you will still be free to leave, and will still owe nothing. But if you want to stay, then we'll welcome you as a member of the House in whatever role is appropriate. In the meantime, what we expect of you is that you make the most of the opportunities here, do your best at your studies and work assignments, and don't do anything that might reflect badly on the House."

I shook my head. "Nobody does anything for someone for nothing in return."

"Don't you think so?" he queried with a smile. "We do. I don't know any catch. So, what do you say, will you stay? Not try and run away?"

I thought about it. "Once I'm eighteen, if I think the price is too high, I can just leave and no one will chase me?"

He sighed. I was exasperating him which I took an undue pleasure in.

"There is no price, but yes, you can leave."

He was wrong about that, there was always a price, it just might not be money, nor obvious. Clearly at least part of the price for the next couple of months was my freedom, but after that it could be anything. I still didn't understand why they were doing this or what they wanted from me but I made a decision.

"Okay then, I'll stay. And I won't try and run away, or leave without telling you."

Like I was actually going to leave without finding out how he was connected to my nightmares and my unknown search—but he didn't need to know that.

He smiled. "Good. Now, shall we continue to the kitchens and meet Pedro?"

I liked kitchens, despite everything. They were always warm, there was always food to scrounge and usually any amount of nooks and crannies and hiding places. And I knew my way round them and how to make myself useful. I made good bread and I wasn't so bad on a whole range of other items.

Brother Pedro was nearly as wide as he was tall, and clearly very busy. He smiled a welcome at Prospero as we walked in and then glanced across to me. For a moment a strange look appeared in his eyes, and I thought he'd worked out what I was and what I'd been doing. But the look disappeared so fast I must have imagined it, and he smiled at me too.

"Welcome to the kitchens, Leonie," he said.

Prospero left us to it. Pedro put his hand gently on my back and guided me round the kitchen as he discussed my duties with me, questioned me as to what my abilities and skills were, and went through the rotas with me so I knew what I was supposed to be doing when. Although he appeared to concentrate on me, his voice calm and his questions unhurried, his eyes still constantly surveyed the room. As we passed each station, each worker, he murmured a quiet instruction or gave a word of advice about the meal preparations which took place around us. Shortly before the meal was due he took me out into the dining hall and delivered me to Lord Gabriel's table. This was going to be the scariest thing I would face today. Individual conversations with Prospero and Pedro were one thing. Eating at the high table with all those very senior members of the House and monastery was quite another. The me of the past had been turned away from the kitchen doors of even the lowest Houses, had had to fight with the dogs for the scraps, and now I was expected to sit at the high table in a Great House, one of the Greatest? It still didn't make sense or seem real.

Lord Gabriel stood up as I approached, took my hand and showed me to a seat. His table was at one end of the hall and anyone seated there needed to arrive on time and was served their meal. For everyone else it was self-service from the counter and you could arrive any time within about half an hour of the official meal time.

I looked around the table. It seated perhaps sixteen to twenty and was pretty full, although the dining room was more empty than normal as so many had left for the Christmas break. Generally, those sitting at this high table were Lord Gabriel, various monks and nuns, senior members of the House and anyone Lord Gabriel chose to invite. As Lord Gabriel's ward, I was entitled to sit there too, whenever I wanted, although I didn't have to. That was something of a shock; with this and my courtesy title, I wondered what other things Brother Prospero hadn't thought it necessary to tell me.

For this meal, I was seated next to Lord Gabriel himself, and on my other side was Brother Benjamin. He was about the same age as Lord Gabriel, and he smiled at me.

"Would it help if I told you who people were?" Brother Benjamin asked quietly.

I nodded.

"Lord Gabriel has several deputies," he said. "I run the hospital and Brother Richard over there deals with anything in the monastery." He nodded his head towards three ladies, seated together at one end of the table. "Sister Elizabeth – she's the one with white hair – is Richard's equivalent in the convent. I think you've met Lady Eleanor. She's the Seneschal, and next to her is Lady Sarah who runs the college."

"What's a seneschal?" I asked.

He grinned. "Power behind the throne, if you ask me. Only don't tell anyone I said that. She's Lord Gabriel's second in command, responsible for running the whole administrative and domestic side of the House, leaving him freer for spiritual and strategic matters."

He went on naming people sat round the table. Some I knew already, like Brother Edward. Others I didn't know, although I'd seen them about the campus. It appeared that senior roles could be filled by monks, or nuns, or lay people of either gender.

Prospero was also seated at the table, some way from me, with Brother Andrew.

"They're two of my best doctors," Brother Benjamin said. "They're very good individually, but even better when they work as a team. They both work with the Gifted, but Andrew concentrates on the development of Gifts, whilst Prospero's area is more dealing with the consequences when things go wrong."

He turned to look directly at me. "I understand that you are Gifted yourself? That burns off a lot of energy and you might find it difficult to eat enough to compensate. If you find you feel hungry between meals, go down to the kitchen and see Pedro, he'll help."

Hungry just between meals? I was always hungry. But there were also those I felt responsible for who had even less than I did. At mealtimes here I'd load my tray with things I could wrap and pocket, and later I'd sneak out to share them. I figured that the less I ate, the more there would be I could share. That was a welcome addition to what I'd found in the kitchens, in the waste pile. I didn't think either of those activities were stealing, at least not when I was a paying student. I'd have to think about whether I could justify taking extra now the House was providing all my needs. Today, there would be no opportunity to pocket anything so I took full advantage for me, and ate all I was offered.

The meal was nothing like as overwhelming as I had been expecting. These all seemed to be genuinely nice people, polite and friendly without being intrusive. I felt welcomed without anyone being too demanding, nor was I left out of the conversation. These were certainly very strange experiences for me and it was going to take me some time to work out what was happening here.

At the end of the meal, Lord Gabriel beckoned to a couple of people, including Brother Prospero, to come over to where we were sitting. He introduced me to Lady Sarah who was to assess my academic ability and learning, and plan a study programme for me, although not until after the Christmas break, as she was about to leave for a few days. She asked what level of schooling I'd had already; Lord Gabriel answered which was a good thing, because I had no idea what I should say.

"Circumstances have prevented Leonie being formally educated. Instead, she has learnt what has been necessary for her lifestyle," he said. I thought that was getting a bit close to the mark, but he continued, "I think we'll find that in some areas she could probably educate us, whilst in others she might have no experience. That's why I want you to assess her and plan a tailored programme."

Lady Sarah agreed and said that she'd see me when she returned. The others he'd called over were Prospero and Brother Andrew. Lord Gabriel asked these two to assess my gifts, and again to plan out a suitable training programme, liaising with Lady Sarah to develop a timetable. Clearly I was going to be kept quite busy. They agreed readily enough and then Prospero turned to me.

"We're heading your way," he said. "I'm going over to check the control centre because I'm on duty later tonight. Would you like to come and see it?"

Of course I would; I tried never to miss an opportunity to learn about something new, you never knew when it might turn out to be useful. Besides, the more time I spent with Brother Prospero, the more chance I had to find out how he was connected to whatever I was searching for and to my nightmares.

Chapter 10

Andrew

Andrew followed Prospero and Leonie to the control centre, where he leaned against the cool stone wall and watched Prospero explain the various monitors and pieces of equipment to Leonie. Really, he thought, Prospero could be a very good teacher as long as his students were enthusiastic and attentive. Leonie was certainly that; she appeared to be absorbing information like a sponge.

"There are three types of shield," Prospero said. "First, there's the Dampener, which stops anyone under it using their Gifts at all. Then there's the Defender, which prevents anyone outside the shield affecting anyone inside it with their Gifts. And, third, there's the Container, which is like the Defender only the other way round. If you're inside a Container shield you can't use your Gifts on anyone or anything outside it."

Leonie nodded, and pointed to one of the screens fastened to the wall, which showed a map of the whole campus. "What does that do?"

Prospero walked over to it, gesticulating at it. "It shows what shield is being used where. The campus is divided into zones, so we don't have to have the same type of shield over all of it at the same time. Any zone can be covered by any shield, either just one type or any combination. The Abbey itself is covered by all three types all the time, but other than that we mostly just use Container shields at night because of the nightmares." He paused for a moment. "Oh, and some rooms have individual shields and controls for teaching purposes."

Andrew studied Leonie, as he had done throughout the meal. He was curious as to why Lord Gabriel was treating her in this way, and particularly why she had made Prospero feel so unsettled earlier. He saw a beautiful young woman, perhaps a head shorter than Prospero. Her curly red hair and honey-coloured skin were a stunning combination. During the meal she'd seemed shy, uncertain of herself, keeping her eyes on her plate, perhaps overwhelmed by the company. Certainly she'd been quiet, answering when spoken to, but not initiating any conversation or volunteering any comments. Still, he'd have been the same himself, under the same circumstances.

Right now, she didn't look shy and nor did Prospero look unsettled. They were both smiling, talking freely, and gesticulating to make a point. Leonie was looking up at Prospero, her eyes – *what colour were they? Dark grey? Green? Some combination of the two?* – alight as she questioned him. Her attention had moved to the next screen.

"That one?" she asked. "What about that one?"

"That's the night scanners," Prospero answered. "They look for the energy pattern of a nightmare, so the watch team can go and help."

Andrew knew all about the scanners, of course, and so his thoughts drifted off, back to the interesting, if somewhat uncomfortable, half hour he'd had with Gabriel earlier. Of course, Prospero had told Andrew on that first evening that Leon – Leonie – was a girl masquerading as a boy, but he'd have expected a girl to have been transferred to the nuns' area of this campus. Gabriel's explanation for keeping her was that she was very talented in areas that weren't normally within the remit of the nuns. That might be true enough – he'd been a witness to her use of telekinesis and pyrokinesis himself just a couple of nights ago – but he was quite sure that Sister Elizabeth was more than capable of dealing with her.

Gabriel's reason for involving Prospero in Leonie's assessment and training was that if two such talented adepts managed to work together they might achieve something significant. That was another viable reason, but again something hadn't rung quite true for Andrew. He was very concerned about expecting Prospero to work so closely with a Gifted female, feeling that it was putting unnecessary temptation far too close.

Is Leonie Prospero's type? As far as Andrew could remember – it was a long time ago and a lot of alcohol had been involved – Prospero's preference was simply female and willing. *Or has she been planted here to snare Prospero?* Given who he was, at least outside the monastery, there were some High Lords who might seek an alliance by stealth. It wouldn't need marriage, either. One careless lapse, one unfortunate chance, and he'd be easy to control through any child he fathered. Aware that his thoughts were running away with him, Andrew shook his head slightly to dispel them.

He hadn't hesitated to voice his concerns to Lord Gabriel and he supposed that Gabriel had at least acknowledged them. Andrew's role was to lead on Leonie's assessment and training and to act as a chaperone. He was also to encourage a friendship between Leonie and Prospero. That worried him and he'd continued to express his concerns. Gabriel had told him firmly to think very carefully about his vow of obedience.

"We discussed this before you joined the Order," Gabriel had said. "Do we need to cover it again?"

No, he didn't. He really didn't. That was a time he didn't care to remember.

Instead, he had spent part of the day in the Monk's Chapel within the Abbey in prayer and meditation. His conclusion had been that, given Lord Gabriel had decided on this course of action, he needed to support it. If he was so concerned, then his actions should be what Gabriel was asking anyway, acting as chaperone and protecting Prospero as necessary.

His final role was to keep the peace between Prospero and Leonie; now that was an interesting requirement. There didn't look to be any need at the moment, but then Prospero could be quite arrogant, and, however shy she'd seemed earlier, the Leonie he was watching now looked like she'd probably stand up for herself. If she was very talented, Prospero wasn't used to being challenged in any of his Gifts, and if by any chance she was better than him at anything that could certainly spark trouble. Andrew was beginning to think he might have been assigned a very tough task indeed.

Chapter 11

Christmas

Leonie

Pedro took advantage of my bread-making ability and I grew to enjoy our early sessions in the kitchen together. He was a great source of information.

"What do you know about Christmas?" he asked me one morning as we were shaping bread rolls.

I shrugged. "Not a lot." That wasn't quite true. When I'd lived with the Traders, Christmas had been another rest day, a day to cook special food, to take time with family, to sing and to dance. Amongst the Traders it was any excuse for a rest day – anniversaries, weddings, births, deaths, festivals, or just because there hadn't been one for a week. "But I've read the story, in a Bible," I confessed. "And I know it's a big festival, here."

I'd often used old churches as a safe place to hide out and there were almost always Bibles around. With nothing else to do, I'd read them, not all the way through, but quite a bit of them. I'd be the first to say I didn't understand that much of the Bible, but I'd always liked some of the stories.

"It's not the big festival here, though," Pedro said. "That's Easter. Christmas is a lot quieter, because Lord Gabriel sends almost everyone home to their families, whatever part of the House they belong to. He keeps just enough people here to make sure everything works, that's all."

The word family always made me feel a little jealous, and a little lonely. I kept my eyes on my work as I spoke. "Will you be leaving?"

"No, not me," he said. "I've got no family left outside.

There's a few others who'll stay, too. Lord Gabriel and Lady Eleanor, of course, Benjamin, Edward – he's got family but they disowned him when he came here. Andrew, because he was orphaned as a child and then his grandfather brought him up, but he's died too. Prospero has family, but he always volunteers to stay—I don't know why. I think he doesn't like to leave Andrew."

That seemed pretty odd to me. It might be thoughtful of Prospero to let others go whilst he stayed to provide cover, but if I had family I'd want to be with them whenever I could. Taking turns seemed fairer on everyone, and it wasn't as if Andrew would be alone either. Pedro carried on with other names, but I didn't know them.

"Just wait until Easter, though," he finished, his eyes lighting up. "Everyone comes here then, we're packed to the rafters—that's the best time of all."

After that I hadn't expected much from Christmas and was quite taken aback when Edward brought a package for me to the evening meal on Christmas Eve. He seemed amused by my surprise.

"You knew we were making you some other outfits," he said. "I've got this finished in time for you to wear it tomorrow."

I managed to stammer out some words of thanks, but I didn't open it until I got back to my room.

He'd said he would make me an outfit for special occasions and I remembered the fabric and the pattern we'd chosen, but this was far lovelier than I'd expected. The tunic was long sleeved and came to mid-thigh length over close-fitting dark trousers. In deep blue velvet, it had embroidered cuffs, neckline and hem and subtle embroidery continued across it. There was a matching cloak, fleece lined, with fur trim, and soft blue leather ankle boots, also fur lined. I couldn't resist, I had to try them on. I think Edward must have woven some magic into the whole outfit. I didn't normally bother much with mirrors; I knew I was nothing special to look at, and as Leon I'd used the mirror just to make sure I wasn't noticeable. In this room I had a full-length mirror and the girl who looked back at me was beautiful. Clearly well-made clothes could work miracles. I hung it up very carefully and went to find another favourite hiding place to think about things.

The floor-plan of the Abbey was in the shape of a cross, with different parts allocated for different purposes. But the building was tall, and there was a narrow gallery about halfway up the wall. There were recesses in it at the corners where the arms crossed the upright and I'd found that I could curl up there quite comfortably, unseen and undisturbed, when I had something I needed to think through. Sometimes I went there to sleep too because I seemed to be safe from nightmares in the Abbey, but it always left me feeling sluggish the next morning.

This time I must have dozed off without meaning to because I woke to the sound of people coming into the Abbey. I'd forgotten there was to be an extra, late-night celebration across midnight to mark the start of Christmas Day. Still, I was safe enough where I was and nobody would spot me if I didn't move so I stayed put to enjoy the service. It wasn't a long one, no sermon, just readings, singing and prayers. For once the monks, nuns and the public were together in the main part of the Abbey – usually they occupied separate areas. I could see Prospero near the front, next to Andrew. He was slightly taller than most of the others, and his striking dark head was bent over some sheet music. As I watched, he stepped forward, turned to face the congregation and started singing, unaccompanied. I hadn't known what a beautiful voice he had. It sounded like a rainbow, like the voice of hope; I could have listened to him for hours. As the service ended, I took the opportunity to slip from my hiding place into the crowds of people and then back to my room.

***

I woke early on Christmas morning and headed over to assist Pedro in the kitchen. I took the outside route and found there was a layer of snow on the ground and more in the air. In the past, snow had been a problem for me; it made keeping warm and dry much harder. I suddenly realised I wouldn't have to worry about that now so I spent a few minutes just enjoying it instead. It was still early, so there was no one to see me dancing and catching snowflakes. Pedro smiled at me as I entered the kitchen.

"You've got snow in your hair," he said.

I just grinned back and got on with my work. About twenty minutes before breakfast was due, Pedro turned to me.

"I can manage fine here now—you go and get changed into your new clothes."

"You know about that?" I asked in some surprise.

"Of course," he said. "Edward's been working hard to get it finished. Now, go on, shoo!"

I went. When I returned to the dining hall, Lord Gabriel beckoned to me to sit next to him. I didn't recall having seen him at breakfast before today but maybe we'd just not overlapped. There were only a couple of tables in use anyway, with so few people around.

"You look beautiful," he said. "Merry Christmas."

He passed me a small box. I was already flustered by the compliment and I didn't know what to do or say. He smiled. "Open it."

Inside was a necklace, silverwork set with blue stones, which matched my dress perfectly. I looked at him, speechless, shaking my head.

"Indulge me," he said, understanding. "It's been a long time since we've had a daughter to treat." He lifted it from the box and fastened it round my neck to compliments and murmurs of approval from those nearby. "There's one slight catch, though," he said.

I should have known there would be. Was this it, the catch I hadn't been able to spot? I glanced around the room, making sure of my path to the exits. Lord Gabriel touched the silverwork gently.

"This is in the form of the crossed keys of St Peter," he said. "That's the symbol for our House. If you wear this, it will mark you as belonging to us, part of our House. I hope you don't mind."

Do I mind? Belonging? That was the opposite of trapped. I'd be there because I was wanted, not because I couldn't leave. If that was what he meant—a welcome as a person, as an equal, then I thought that perhaps I'd never take it off. But some people used belonging to mean ownership; that I did mind. If he meant that, then I was out of here.

As I hesitated, I looked around and I realised for the first time that most people wore the symbol in some form. For the monks and nuns it was embroidered on the breast of their tunics, as it was for those who were dressed in hospital uniforms. Others wore it as a brooch or a badge. They seemed relaxed about it, and surely they were here because they wanted to be, and free to leave if they wished? For now, I decided to give them benefit of the doubt and wear the necklace with pleasure.

Pedro wouldn't let me help clear up breakfast, and he did have plenty of help. Not knowing what else to do, I curled up in a chair in his small office checking out a couple of recipe books he had there. He'd said before I was welcome there anytime and I'd spotted a couple of variants to bread recipes that I wanted to study. After a while he put his head into the room and said I should get over to the Abbey for the service because it would be filling up and I might not get a seat.

I put my book away, then ran across the courtyards to the side door of the Abbey. Pedro had been right; it was packed with people from the town, a number of whom I knew, but I soon found somewhere to sit. It wasn't a particularly long service but I enjoyed it and afterwards I found myself chatting to someone I knew from the town. I told her about my change in circumstances and she seemed pretty pleased for me. She spoke very highly of the House and monastery. Maybe, just maybe, I'd landed on my feet here and there was no hidden agenda. I found that difficult to believe.

Pedro wouldn't let me help with the preparations for lunch either, but he did send me into the dining hall with Edward to set the tables. Edward was enjoying himself with festive cloths and decorations and I found his enthusiasm infectious. It wasn't just him, either. The meal itself was an informal, relaxed and happy event, loads of food, and loads of laughter too. And everyone was allowed into the kitchen to get involved with clearing up afterwards.

I stood with Pedro as he watched all these people invading his kitchen, doing things wrong, putting things away in the wrong place. I couldn't believe how relaxed he was.

"Nothing's going to happen that can't be put right," he said to me. "And I always find everything again in the end." I shook my head in disbelief, but he just grinned. "It's God's kitchen, not mine. Everyone here has as much right to be in it as I do."

That seemed like a very strange perspective to me.

Once the meal had been cleared, Lord Gabriel rounded everyone up for what he called 'healthy fresh air and exercise'. In practice this meant a walk through and around the whole campus

– monastery, House, college and hospital. It had been snowing whilst we'd been eating and clearing up, and it was perhaps ankle deep, or a little more. Everyone spread out, groupings of individuals changing from time to time as we walked. I stayed somewhere in the middle, quite happy to amble along without necessarily talking to anyone.

We had covered most of the campus and were heading back to the main courtyard when something shot past my ear and hit someone a few yards in front of me on the shoulder. Without thinking, I gathered the power around me, turning and forming it to defend us and attack whoever was attacking us. Almost in the same instant someone put their arms around me from behind, pinning my wrists to my sides and using their own gifts to dampen my power.

"Just a snowball, just a game," they whispered in my ear and then I was released again, the power gone.

I looked round, but couldn't work out who it could have been; it had all happened so quickly I thought I could almost have imagined it. Around me all these serious, senior, respectable adults were gathering snow, forming snowballs, starting to throw them, ducking to avoid their colleagues' missiles. Struggling with the aftermath of thinking we'd been attacked, I watched, bemused, for a few moments until Andrew nudged me.

"Come on," he said. "You'll be a target if you stand still. Attack's the best form of defence."

He pushed a snowball into my hands and indicated Prospero some distance away, with his back towards us. Now that was a temptation I couldn't resist, no matter what the consequences. I got him square on the back of the head then ducked round Andrew, giggling at the look on Prospero's face as he turned. After that, the only possible choice was to join in wholeheartedly, so I did. The game continued until everyone was breathless and laughing and most people had snow in their hair and clothes.

Lord Gabriel herded everyone back towards one of the smaller recreation rooms near the main dining hall. I hung back a little, still trying to work out who had grabbed me earlier. I knew it wasn't Prospero simply because I'd have known if it was and anyway he'd been ahead of me. Neither Edward nor Pedro were gifted so it couldn't have been them; I realised that I didn't know who else was or wasn't gifted. Nobody gave me any clues by their reactions to me, so I followed the others indoors.

By the time I had dealt with my coat and boots and outdoor clothing, Pedro had arranged a table full of cold meat and bread and cakes for anyone who might be hungry. Lord Gabriel was making sure people got hot drinks after the cold outside. I collected something to eat and drink and sat down on the floor by the fireplace to watch over the chestnuts roasting there. Prospero came and sat next to me.

"Have you enjoyed the day?" he asked.

I nodded, touching the necklace, which he seemed to be staring at. "Lord Gabriel's been very generous. I didn't expect that."

He smiled. "It suits you. You should wear it all the time—it looks much better on you than in a vault. Jewels are meant to be worn, the stones are happier that way."

That seemed very fanciful to me and I must have looked at him oddly because he went on. "The touch of skin and the warmth of a body makes them glow, that makes them look better."

I thought I was probably starting to glow at such comments and turned back to the fire in some confusion.

He passed me a paper bag and a toasting fork.

"Marshmallows," he said but I looked at him blankly, never having heard of them before.

"What are they?" I asked.

"Sugar, mostly," he replied. "You can eat them like this, but they're even better toasted."

He stuck one on a toasting fork and held it over the fire, twisting and turning the fork so it cooked on all sides. Then he held it out towards me, warning me it was hot. It was sticky and sweet, not quite solid and not quite liquid, and I liked it – I could eat a lot of these. Everyone else could too and we were kept busy for a while toasting marshmallows and roasting chestnuts. After the rush had died down Prospero stayed beside me talking quietly.

"We used to do this when I was a child," he volunteered, indicating the marshmallows.

He seemed relaxed, willing to talk, so I asked him what Christmas had been like for him then. His faced tensed up a little and his eyes went dull for a moment. Clearly there was some reason he didn't like to talk about his family. Maybe it was whatever that was, rather than Andrew, that was why he didn't visit them at Christmas.

"I suppose it was pretty similar to this," he said slowly. "There'd be worship, small gifts, plenty to eat, extended family all around. And in the afternoon we'd go for a long walk across the farm, have a snowball fight if there was snow – I've lots of brothers so it'd be a pretty good fight. Lots of fun."

"So did you start the snowball fight today, then?" I asked him though I knew the answer. He'd been ahead of me and the first snowball had come from behind.

He grinned. "No, that wasn't me, not this time, and it

wasn't Andrew either. I think it was Edward."

I looked at him in disbelief.

"Edward's a terrible troublemaker, you know," he told me. He seemed to be struggling to keep a straight face.

Anyone less like a troublemaker than Edward would be hard to imagine, and I looked around to see where he was. He was close by and he spotted me looking.

"Prospero telling you stories, is he?" he asked.

"Just what a troublemaker you are, and how you must have started the snowball fight," Prospero told him with a grin.

Edward smiled back. "Don't believe everything he tells you," he said to me and then carried on, "It wasn't me. I thought it was Benjamin."

That was equally unbelievable, and the banter travelled around the room, through a group of people comfortable and at ease with each other. It was entertaining to see who denied it outright and who parried the question. I was beginning to think it must have been Lord Gabriel himself who started it so I looked across at him. He winked at me and touched his finger to his lips.

As the conversation died out, Prospero turned back to me. "What about you?" he asked. "What's Christmas been like for you before?"

I shrugged. I didn't want to talk about me. "With the Traders it was pretty much like any other rest day."

"What about before you jointed the Traders?" he persisted.

"I don't really remember that time," I said. "But I do remember Christmas being happy and warm and not hungry for once."

"Were you often hungry?" he asked.

"I'm used to it," I said shortly, annoyed with myself for having revealed more than I'd meant to.

"Are you still hungry?" he said quietly.

I deliberately misunderstood him. "After all the food there's been today? No way."

He just looked at me, like he was waiting for more.

I felt almost compelled to answer. "There are plenty worse off than me."

"Maybe," he acknowledged. "Do you go hungry because you share what little you have with those who have less?"

I didn't answer; I hadn't meant to let him get that close.

"You don't have to do that here. Anyone who hasn't enough food can come here and we'll help them."

I looked at him. "Why would you do that?" I asked.

"I've told you before," he replied. "We're here to help those who need it."

I shook my head. "Even if that is true, it'd be far too dangerous for them to come."

"There's nothing dangerous about it," he insisted. "We're not going to hurt them, or demand anything from them. Just help them."

"They still won't come," I said.

"Bet they will. You tell them and we'll see."

Prospero was so certain, there didn't seem to be any point in arguing further, even if I knew he was wrong. He leaned back a little and called across the room. "Pedro, Leonie has some friends who need more food. Make sure she knows where they can get it, would you?"

Pedro nodded at him, and Prospero turned back to me.

"Tomorrow," he started, then corrected himself, "No, not tomorrow, the next day. We'll have a session starting to work out exactly what you can and can't do."

Instead of responding I yawned, which rather took me by surprise.

"Am I boring you?" Prospero asked.

I tried to explain but I got caught by another yawn, blushed and got all confused.

He smiled at me. "I'm teasing you. Don't worry about it. Besides, just look around the room."

I did—at least half those there were asleep where they sat.

"Warm, comfortable and well fed," said Prospero. "You could sleep, too, if you want. You'd be quite safe."

I shook my head, I wasn't sleepy despite the yawns. I didn't know quite what I felt like doing but it wasn't sleep.

Chapter 12

Prospero

Sitting by the fire with Leonie, Prospero found that he didn't want the day to end, although he knew it had to. This was unusual; normally the similarities between Christmas Day here and that of his childhood reminded him too much of his family. Even if it was his choice not to be with them, Christmas accentuated how much he missed them, which in turn reminded him of the damage he'd done. As a result he would be eager for the day to be over.

Now his mind drifted back over a day he had enjoyed from the moment Leonie had arrived at breakfast – was he perhaps seeing things afresh as she experienced them for the first time? She'd almost danced into the dining hall, radiating pleasure at her new clothes without realising it. The sight of her had taken his breath away again. Of course he'd seen the outfit already. All the monks had because Edward had brought his work into the private area in the evenings to be sure he would complete it on time. But seeing it then on Leonie, he had realised how well Edward had crafted it to suit her. And with just a few days of eating properly, sleeping, and being accepted as herself, she'd started to relax, put on weight, and she really was very beautiful.

Her blush and confusion when Lord Gabriel had given her the necklace had been delightful, and had added to Prospero's enjoyment. He hadn't spoken to her at breakfast, contenting himself with watching her. In fact, he'd been so intent on watching her, Andrew had had to nudge him twice to get him to pass the toast.

"You're being obvious," Andrew had whispered to him, "Stop staring at her."

He had taken Andrew's advice, at least until they were in

the Abbey for the morning service. Then his eyes had been drawn to her again, to the point of being a little distracted from the service which Andrew had noticed and which had earned him another sharp nudge.

The people Leonie had sat with in the Abbey were Settlers, Traders who had chosen to give up the nomadic life and stay in one place. That tied in with her story. She had inferred that it had been the leaders of her caravan that chose to leave her behind, but everyone knew that Traders took care of their own. If she was known to be connected with them, she'd probably be safe enough whenever she left the Abbey campus.

He was under no illusions about her potential behaviour; she might have agreed to stay but he expected her to push the boundaries to the limits, if not beyond. His mind drifted to a conversation he'd had with Gabriel about her.

"I think we should require Leonie to stay within the campus boundaries," Gabriel had said. "She'll be safer that way."

Prospero had disagreed, "No, she's already worried about being a prisoner. If we limit her movements, she'll just run away."

Gabriel had sighed. "Very well, then. But if she does disappear, it'll be your job to find her and bring her back. Understood?"

Prospero had accepted this and decided that he'd have to get to know her better, partly to discover any clues as to where she might go if she disappeared, and partly to find a way of reassuring her and making her feel safe so the she didn't feel the need to leave. That had been his motive when he'd moved alongside Pedro on the after-lunch walk.

"After something, are you?" Pedro had asked, with a grin.

Prospero had nodded. "Have you got any marshmallows? I

just fancy some, toasted over the fire, later."

Just as Pedro had agreed to find some, a snowball had whacked Prospero on the back of his head. He had turned sharply, to see Leonie giggling and ducking behind Andrew. Andrew had held up his hands in denial, then grinned, ducked and hurled another snowball straight at him. That had meant war, and Prospero had thrown himself enthusiastically into the fight. Leonie had targeted him successfully at least once more, and he knew he'd returned the compliment. But she had proved surprisingly difficult to hit.

Thinking about it now, he realised she must have used telekinesis to divert his ammunition and the thought brought him both admiration and amusement. That pulled him out of his day dream to look at her once more, and his eyes rested again on the necklace Gabriel had given her. He'd recognised it immediately, although he thought he was perhaps the only person in a position to do so. At breakfast he'd assumed it was a copy; this close he knew it for the original. Either way, it was significant that Gabriel had chosen to give it to her, and even more so that he'd chosen not to tell her anything about it. If that was Gabriel's choice, Prospero would follow his lead.

They'd been chatting on and off for a while, but now Leonie seemed to be fidgeting a little, unsettled and not sure what to do with herself. To be honest, he was feeling a bit restless himself. He stood up and held out his hand to her.

"I've got some chores to do over in the Abbey. Want to come over and help me?"

She hesitated for a moment, but then nodded and took his hand helping her up. Together they left the room and headed towards the Abbey.

They carried on chatting, about nothing very much as they

fulfilled his chores in the Abbey – mostly checking on the floral arrangements and a little bit of tidying up.

Leonie touched the central jewel of her new necklace. "Why did Lord Gabriel give me this?"

He smiled and shook his head.

"I don't know. He didn't discuss it with me. Perhaps because he thought you'd like it? Or to welcome you as part of our family? Or both?"

"Does everyone have something like it?"

"Oh yes," he said. "Everyone who belongs to the House has it in some form or another. Look—"He pointed to the logo on his tunic, then bent his head and lifted off the cross he wore around his neck and handed it to her. It was a simple design but it did incorporate the cross keys symbol.

"All the monks and nuns wear one of these, which symbolises both our calling and our House. Others might wear a brooch, or a pin, or a necklace or a bracelet."

At the word bracelet, she rolled up her sleeve to reveal an intricate Trader bracelet.

"Like this?" she asked.

He nodded, taking hold of her arm to turn it this way and that to look at the workmanship and design, eager for the excuse to touch her.

"That's beautifully made," he said. "Does it represent the caravan you were with?"

He looked up at her as she nodded and then back at the bracelet. "Yes, just like that, then. A sign of where you belong. You don't have to hide your bracelet round here, you know. Traders are welcome here; there are plenty in the community, even some in the monastery."

He wondered if she was worried about that. He'd only ever lived in places where Traders were held in high regard, but he knew there were any number of places where they weren't welcome.

She smiled shyly at him, lifted her arm from his hands and rolled her sleeve back down. But he noticed she didn't worry about pushing the bracelet back up her arm, instead leaving it round her wrist, where he could still glimpse it as they worked. It wasn't long before their activities were interrupted by Andrew, coming to help, or so he said.

Chapter 13

Early January

Gabriel

Gabriel thought it would be very useful to discover a little more about Leonie. He was very much concerned that his visions meant she would turn his whole House upside down. On Christmas afternoon, he had been sleeping with one eye and both ears open, and had noticed Prospero and Leonie leave. Andrew had got up to follow them but Gabriel had gestured to him to stay put.

"Prospero was making some progress in getting her to talk to him," Gabriel had said quietly. "Give him half an hour or so then go and find them."

Unfortunately, Prospero had found out very little that they didn't already know, and they hadn't added to their knowledge in the few days since.

His thoughts were interrupted by a knock on the door. The Porter ushered in a boy in his teens, with a package he would not hand over to anyone but Lord Gabriel in person. Recognising the boy as a Settler and also the handwriting on the package, Lord Gabriel sat the lad down and closed the door behind him.

"What's your name?" he asked the boy.

"Simeon, sir. I was sent by Merchant Tobias," the lad answered, his voice wavering with nerves.

That made sense to Gabriel; Tobias was the leader of the local Settler community and no doubt knew all about Leonie.

"And do you know where he got this letter?"

This time Simeon shook his head. "I don't know where he

went but..."

"Is it something you aren't allowed to tell me?" Gabriel asked him, knowing that the Settlers guarded certain secrets very closely.

"Oh, no, sir. Uncle Tobias told me that I could tell you anything. I'm just not sure where it started."

Gabriel understood. "Let me help. I should think it started when your family came to the Christmas service at the Abbey and your uncle, or possibly your aunt, talked to Leonie. Am I right?"

"It was my aunt. And then we all went home and there was, there was a Calling."

Most people knew that Settlers were Trader families who had decided to leave the traveling life and stay in one place. Very few knew that this was rarely their main motivation. Whilst other Gifts were rare amongst Trader people, Trader women were almost all telepathic. By placing their strongest telepaths in key towns on their major routes, and in each caravan, they had established an extensive communications network. A Calling directly linked one or more community or caravan leaders. It took a great deal of energy; the most powerful telepath in a group would link to the others for additional power, but they would also link to, and draw energy from, other non-telepathic members of their community. Hardly anyone outside the Trader community and caravans knew anything at all about their ability to communicate like this. Gabriel's knowledge had been acquired many years ago in circumstances he chose not to think about.

"I assume it was Katila's caravan you Called? To speak with Merchant Ethan?"

Katila had taken over the caravan on Katya's death. Ethan had remained the Merchant within that caravan.

"Yes," Simeon agreed. "And then they arranged for Uncle Tobias and Merchant Ethan to meet up. I don't know where that was, just that it was a long, hard ride for both parties. Uncle Tobias set off the morning after Christmas Day and got back this morning. He sent me to you straight away."

"He must trust you very much."

Simeon nodded and shrugged at the same time, showing a flash of silver from the bracelet at his wrist. "I hope so."

"Will you take a message back for me?"

"Of course," Simeon agreed.

"Give Merchant Tobias my thanks. Tell him that Traders and Settlers are always welcome in House St Peter. And ask him to pass the same message onto Merchant Ethan."

Simeon repeated the message back, and then left. Gabriel shut his office door again to ensure that he would not be disturbed as he investigated the contents of his package. It contained a letter in the same handwriting as on the address, a small leather drawstring bag such as might contain coins or jewels, and another envelope in a different handwriting, but one which Gabriel again recognised. He smoothed the first letter out on his desk and read it.

Lord Gabriel,

Katya told me to ensure that you received the enclosed letter as soon as possible after both we and you knew that you had Leonie in your care. Katya considered the girl in the light of a daughter, as do I. As such, she has a substantial portion which we will bring to you when we next pass through. As a small token of this, Katila sends the enclosed. The Sight has told her that you may need them before we arrive. It is my prayer that you do not need them all.

With every blessing,

Ethan, Merchant

So, thought Gabriel, this little waif we've taken on is all but a Trader princess. He'd wager a fair bit that she had no idea and wondered why not, why Katya and Ethan would have kept this from her. With her colouring, it seemed unlikely that she was born a Trader – that red hair meant it was likely she was some by-blow from the House Chisholm – and maybe that made a difference? He wondered whether it made a difference to what he had to do. No longer was she an abandoned orphan with no one to care and few to mourn her loss. Now she was at the centre of a large extended family even if she didn't know it. Obviously one life was not worth more than another, but the consequences could be vastly different. He sighed, opened the bag and tipped three small bundles into his hands. He unwrapped them and stared at them for several minutes before carefully replacing two of them in the bag. They were very much what he'd expected and a confirmation of his fears. Like Ethan, his prayer was that he would not use any of them, his fear that he would need them all. He turned to the second letter and opened that with some trepidation.

Dearest Gabriel,

You now have in your keeping my most precious and unusual jewel, a rare merge of two opposing forces. I can no longer guard her, and can think of no one I would rather entrust her to. There are others that seek her, for their own gain. My jewel is damaged; I do not know whether this is a flaw or simply a past bad setting. I did what I could to remove the damage, but my time, options and abilities were limited. I hope that you can place her in a setting where, damage or flaw, it becomes an asset, an essential part of her purpose. I trust her to you because you will do what is right, no matter how dire the consequences.

Please ensure she is loved and valued, as I love and value you.

Until we meet again, eternally.

Katya

For a while Gabriel sat with his head in his hands. Katya had called Leonie a jewel, which tied in with his dreams about her, but Ethan had sent jewellery that indicated a potential close relationship with someone, probably Prospero. And Katya had called her a 'rare merge' yet in his dreams he saw her as a single ruby. Or was that something to do with the emerald he had seen?

He was very concerned that he would not live up to Katya's trust that he would do the right thing no matter what. And if he did what Katya asked and grew to love the child, what then? How would he be strong enough to do what would be necessary whilst knowing that his actions would lead to her death? He was already troubled about the extent to which he had involved Prospero, and his uneasy dreams and unsettled nights had been reflecting this.

He very carefully folded up the letters and put them away safely with one of the small bundles, leaving the little drawstring bag out. He sent for Brother Edward, and when he arrived, gave him the bag and indicated that he should open it. Edward unwrapped the contents and stared at them, nestled in his hands.

"Beautiful," he breathed. "Exquisite. Such workmanship.

They must be unique."

"I should imagine so," agreed Gabriel. "Please put them somewhere safe, but close to hand. I have a feeling we may need them soon."

Edward looked up. "Soon?" he asked. "Should I prepare?"

"Yes, I think you should. And ask Pedro, too. But involve no one who is not essential."

"May I ask who they are for?"

"Do you need to?"

Edward shook his head. "No, not immediately, but I will need a couple of days' notice."

"You'll have that."

Impulsively, Gabriel reached into his desk and pulled out the third small bundle, handing it to Edward. "Do you know what this is?" he asked.

Edward unwrapped it and nodded, again admiring the workmanship.

"It's a Deathstone," he said turning it over in his hands. "It's not actually a stone, of course. The Traders place them on the body before they cremate their dead. Originally, if the fire burnt hot enough to melt the Deathstone, then it was hot enough to have destroyed any germ, virus or plague that might have caused the death. That's not so important now, of course, but they still do it. The setting contains the stone somewhat as it melts, and when it cools they keep it as a memento of the deceased."

He looked up at Gabriel. "Do you wish me to put it with the others?"

Gabriel shook his head. "No, not this one. I'll keep it. But please don't speak about it to anyone else."

Gabriel was left with his thoughts as Edward took the little bag to a place of safety. Something was nagging at his memory, something he'd seen and forgotten, something that he knew was significant, but he couldn't remember what. He sat back in his chair, closed his eyes and let his mind freewheel in the hope that it would come back to him. It was to do with the boy, Simeon, and connected with the Calling but not directly. Something he'd seen and expected to see that made him think of something he hadn't seen and should have done.

He sat up suddenly as it came to him; he'd seen a flash of silver when the boy had moved his arm and known it for his Trader bracelet. Formed of fine silver and semi-precious stones they were given to Trader and Settler children on their sixteenth birthday. The design showed which caravan or community they belonged to, and the stones were power stones, facilitating the energy transfer needed in a Calling. If Katya and Ethan had considered Leonie as a daughter, then she should have a bracelet but he'd never seen it. He made a mental note to ask her about it. Given the history of the necklace she now wore almost all the time it could be important.

Chapter 14

Leonie

Brother Prospero kept to his plan to assess my abilities; he and Brother Andrew put me through a whole series of tests. Actually, we had several sessions, and to my surprise it was Brother Andrew who led them. Then I remembered that Brother Benjamin had told me that it was Andrew who specialised in the development of gifts rather than Prospero so perhaps that made sense.

I found the sessions exhausting, but exhilarating; never before had I been able to use my abilities like this purely for the sake of using them and it was a real challenge to find out just what I could do.

We started with telepathy. I sat facing Andrew and he explained that Prospero was in contact with a series of telepaths each of whom would give me a code word which I was to repeat back to them and then say out loud. The code word would tell Andrew how far away the telepath was, and so measure my range. That was easy.

"Red."

"Orange."

"Yellow"

"Green."

And it was boring. There was a pile of little foam blocks behind where Andrew was sitting. I started to arrange them in patterns and piles, ignoring the wave of amusement I could feel from Prospero behind me. Then the code words changed.

"Eighteen."

"Minor."

"Caught."

"Trapped."

"Freedom."

I forgot about the blocks as I concentrated on not giving Prospero the satisfaction of me turning round and glaring at him. Then the words just stopped. Andrew looked up at Prospero, raising his eyebrows questioningly. What I felt from Prospero now was more like annoyance than amusement, although that wasn't quite the right word.

Andrew just made a huffy sort of noise. "That'll do for that," he said.

I guessed there must have been a word I hadn't heard; I must have reached my limit, whatever that was. We moved on to perception – knowing where people are without being able to see them. That was pretty easy, too. I just had to reach out with my mind in a set direction and describe what I could sense until I couldn't reach any further. Prospero – who I could still feel behind me – was doing the same thing to check my accuracy. Every time I said anything, he made a non-committal sound so I couldn't tell how well I was doing. In the end, I turned round and glared at him. He just stared back, cool as anything and indicated I should carry on.

Then, suddenly he called a halt. "She's getting pale, she needs a rest and something to eat," he said to Andrew. "I'll be back in a few minutes."

With that he left the room. I looked at Andrew in some annoyance and bewilderment. Prospero was right which was annoying; I was tired and I was hungry and I knew those were making me feel irritable, but his attitude had definitely wound me up.

"He's gone to find you something to eat," Andrew said calmly.

"But he doesn't know what I want or what I like!" I snapped.

"Well, maybe not," Andrew conceded, still calm. "But he does know what you need."

Despite Andrew's placating tone, that didn't make me feel any less irritated and I fumed until Prospero got back. Andrew just ignored my sulking and got on with making notes, presumably about how well or badly I'd done.

Even more annoying when Prospero did get back – and he was pretty quick – it looked as though he did have a fair idea of what I liked. He'd included my favourite type of cheese and a choice of fruit, all of which I liked, and Pedro's special chocolate-chip cookies, which were my all-time favourite. He'd brought way more than I'd eat but he just sat down and started eating himself, as did Andrew. I looked at him in surprise but he claimed that he'd been working hard too, which I supposed was true. I was still irritated at him but the food was too tempting and I felt much better once I'd eaten. Now I felt calmer, I challenged him on what he'd chosen and how he knew about my likes and dislikes.

"I just got a variety," he said. "Mostly things that Andrew and I like so I knew we'd eat what you didn't choose. Except for the cookies – Pedro told me those were your favourites."

"They are," I confirmed. "And that's my favourite cheese."

He smiled. "Mine, too. It was stupid of me not to have snacks here already. We were bound to get hungry with all these tests. Next time we'll be prepared."

He was as good as his word. In the sessions that followed he always made sure that we stopped, rested and ate before I got hungry and irritable. He could be so nice and thoughtful but at the same time he could be so annoying, particularly because he was nearly always right. I found I was thoroughly confused; I'd look forward to his company and then end up irritated and unsettled.

Prospero

Testing telepathy was supposed to be easy, Prospero thought. He had a list of contacts and he knew how far away they each were. He alerted each one in turn, and they gave Leonie his choice of code word. Leonie had grown bored and started playing with the telekinesis practice blocks behind Andrew's back, much to Prospero's amusement.

"What?" Andrew asked him, telepathically.

He shook his head slightly, *"It doesn't matter."*

So he started changing the code words, just to see what reaction he would get. And it had been worth it to watch Leonie trying not to respond. But she had the last laugh, even if she didn't know it. Suddenly, they reached the end of his list of contacts. Andrew looked up sharply at him.

"What?" he asked telepathically again. *"Why have we stopped?"*

"I've reached the limit of my range. I can't go further."

Even if telepathy couldn't convey emotions, Prospero struggled to keep the shock off his face. Only one person had ever been able to reach further than he could. He hadn't thought of her in years, and he didn't want to now.

"Well, there's nothing more we can do about that then,"

Andrew replied prosaically, and moved on to testing Leonie's perception.

That hadn't done Prospero's ego any good either. This time, when they reached his limits before reaching Leonie's, he made an excuse and left the room quickly to compose himself.

"Further than you again?" Andrew asked in his head as he left.

"Yes," he answered shortly, *"Give me a moment."*

By the time he'd found food and they'd eaten he was feeling more in control of himself again. They moved on to testing the accuracy of Leonie's perception. This time, with her hearing and sight blocked, she was supposed to point to where he was in the room. Again, she must have grown bored because she picked up one of the soft foam blocks, using telekinesis and held it over his head wherever he went.

"She can perceive where objects are, not just people," he told Andrew telepathically. That was unusual to say the least; Prospero had read of cases, but never known anyone who could.

"I can tell," Andrew replied.

Prospero swatted the block with his hand to see what would happen. It bounced out of the way and hovered just higher than he could reach. He jumped for it, and it dived, circling him at waist level a couple of times before settling at shoulder height, again just further than he could reach. He put his hands down by his sides and the block returned to float about a hand's width above his head. Whatever he did, it stayed there unless he reached for it when it whisked, teasingly, just out of reach. He could see Andrew having a hard time not laughing out loud.

"Enough," Andrew said to his relief.

He must have said it telepathically to Leonie because the block returned to its companions and she removed her blindfold. That had been the end of that whole session, too. Later sessions hadn't been quite so bad for Prospero. He'd beaten her in telekinesis, and in precognition, although he'd only been a witness in pyrokinesis as he had no ability at all in that area.

Overall, he'd enjoyed both the sessions and her company, and thought they had been getting on remarkably well.

Chapter 15

Mid January

Prospero

Prospero had just finished breakfast and was heading for the library to do some research when Lord Gabriel called after him.

"Leonie's missing. Eleanor says she hasn't appeared for breakfast and her bed hasn't been slept in. Can you see where she is?"

Gabriel's ability to perceive others was limited to about the size of the campus but Prospero had little difficulty in spotting Leonie outside it.

"Yes," he said, sighing with disappointment. "She's perhaps a couple of miles away, maybe less, in the woods. She's not moving. I can't tell if she's hurt or not."

"What did I tell you? I knew we should have stopped her leaving the campus," Gabriel replied.

"I don't think she's running away," Prospero insisted. "If she was, she'd be long gone by now. I think she's stuck for some reason."

"Well, you can go and get her. I'm far too busy today. You can deal with whatever you find however you see fit."

Gabriel turned away and Prospero went to find Andrew and prepare for their outing. It was a pleasant enough walk despite the cold weather and Leonie didn't appear to move as they made their way towards her. Andrew carried food, spare clothing and blankets, whilst Prospero took a range of medical supplies. They reached the point where Prospero's senses told him they would find her, but saw nothing and no one as they looked around. Andrew looked towards Prospero and raised his eyebrows in mute question.

"She's here—I can feel her, right here, we just can't see her!" Prospero's frustration was clear in his voice.

Andrew was about to suggest that, just this once, Prospero could be wrong when both men jumped as Leonie landed in front of them.

"You woke me up!" she accused them and indeed her eyes still looked full of sleep.

Taken aback by her accusation, Prospero responded in kind, "What are you doing sleeping here anyway?" he snapped. "You've got a perfectly good bed back at the House. What's wrong with that?"

Leonie's face went blank and she turned away, only to find Andrew now in front of her.

"Don't run away," he said, gently.

Leonie looked at him, surprised. "I wasn't running away. I was just running to get my thoughts straight. And then I was tired and it was night so I slept." She turned back towards Prospero. "Did you think I'd run away? I agreed to stay."

"No," he replied, regretting his earlier tone, "I was afraid you were lost, or hurt, and needed help or couldn't get back for some reason."

"I don't get lost."

"Hurt then. Accidents can happen to anyone."

Leonie looked at him for a moment, clearly unwilling to concede the point but unable to argue against it. He stared back, and, in looking at her properly, realised that she was wearing neither shoes nor coat, a fact which he then pointed out.

"I was running," she explained again, carefully, as if he was forgetful. "I didn't need a coat and shoes just get in the way."

Andrew smiled at that and Prospero grinned too. Leonie looked at them both, puzzled until Andrew confessed that he also preferred to be bare foot, although not in winter. Andrew remedied the lack of a coat with a spare fleece from his pack, but was unable to do anything about the shoes, which Leonie didn't seem to mind. She was quite willing to go along with their suggestion that she should walk back to the House with them, all but dancing along between them as she kept up with their longer strides.

Prospero felt the dry static crackle in the air almost as soon as it started but for once it was Andrew who identified it first.

He whispered to Prospero, "She's generating!"

They stopped in their tracks, Leonie dancing on a couple of steps before she realised and turned to face them. Prospero looked at her. "Leonie, how are you feeling?"

"I'm fine." She looked puzzled.

"Does your skin feel tight, tingling, like it's crawling with electricity?"

"Well, yes, but I often feel like that."

"What do you do about it?"

She looked at him as if he was stupid and again spoke very slowly and carefully, "I run. That's what I was doing."

He nodded. "Of course. Do you want to run now? You can go on ahead and we'll catch up with you or you can double back when you are ready."

She nodded, shrugged off the fleece, handed it to Andrew then set off. Prospero watched her go. *Honestly*, he thought, *I deserve to be considered stupid.* Generating energy tended to happen at times of high emotion, stress or confusion, all of which were pretty much the normal state of affairs for teenagers, especially the Gifted ones. Using Gifts burnt up the body's energy in the same way that physical activity did. Sometimes, the mind and body converted more energy into the form accessed by the Gifts than was needed at the time, and this was known as generating.

He should have been looking out for it anyway, and when Leonie had said that she was running to get her thoughts straight, that should have sounded warning bells in his mind. Despite everything he'd seen her do he still kept expecting her to have the Gifts more common to females and now the differences were catching him out. She fascinated him, and drove him crazy in about equal measure and somehow his brain always seemed clouded, addled when she was around. Even as he thought all this, he turned to Andrew.

"Watch her feet!"

Andrew looked as closely as he could at the now disappearing Leonie. "They aren't touching the ground!" he exclaimed.

"No, that's clearly how she burns off the energy, levitating, using telekinesis on herself."

"That's impressive, but it's an awful lot of power. No wonder she's so thin."

Prospero considered, "I wonder if I could do that, for that long?"

"Why would you want to?" Andrew glanced back at him. "I

can't believe you! You're seriously considering it, aren't you? Just because she can do something you don't know you can do!"

"She can do a fair bit I know I can't do," Prospero replied ruefully. "Look what happened when we were testing her abilities."

"That doesn't mean you have to try! You're not in competition with her."

"I suppose not," he conceded. Then he smiled. "At least I'm better than her at precognition."

"That's not saying a lot, is it? Given that you have hardly any ability and she has none."

"And I can shield better. And teleport."

"Her shields are strong, just not sophisticated. She'll learn. We picked the right classes for her. As for teleportation, who'd teach that to a first year student?"

Prospero conceded that point, but then Leonie came running back to them.

"It's getting busy at the main entrance already," she said. "We should go round the back way."

Prospero nodded. "That'll be everyone returning after the break." He took a moment. "You've been all the way there and back already?"

"Not all the way, just to where I could see the gate."

He took a deep breath. "But before we get caught up in all that we need to come to some agreement so we're not worrying about you and searching for you when we don't need to."

Leonie

I should have known that was coming. Here was another detail he'd not thought to tell me about before – rules as to where I should be and where I could go.

I really had gone out the evening before intending to come back to sleep. I'd needed to run to get my thoughts straight about all that was happening. And to see if I could work out the catch in this deal – or even if there was one. I still couldn't believe there wasn't. I'd had some food to take to my friends out of town, too. Whatever Prospero said on Christmas Day, they wouldn't come to the Abbey. Pedro had understood without any explanations.

"Whatever they need – food anyway – just ask me and I'll help," he'd said.

So I'd taken them a big basket of provisions and a few other things I'd got hold of. And I'd left them my coat because it was cold, and I didn't need it. It had been both late and dark after that and I'd decided it would be easier to sneak back onto the campus early in the morning. I'd headed for my place in the woods, a large tree, where I had a few things stored that made sleeping out that bit warmer and more comfortable. I must have been more tired than I'd thought because I hadn't woken until I'd heard Prospero and Andrew looking for me and it was much later than I'd intended.

Now I squared up to Prospero. "You said I wasn't a prisoner!"

"You aren't," he confirmed. "But we're still responsible for you and if you aren't where we expect you to be we worry that something has happened to you."

"So I'm not a prisoner, but you still want to restrict what I can do and where I can go?"

He took a deep breath. I could see him trying to control his reaction and I knew I was irritating him again. Good.

"No," he said, "I just want to agree some ground rules, so that we know when we need to come looking for you. Common sense things, the sort of precautions we all take."

I was still on the attack, even if I suspected that he might well be being quite reasonable about this.

"So, what did you have in mind?" I shot back.

He took another deep breath. "Be back on campus every night before the Shields are switched on, and don't leave again until morning. Be at all your classes and work shifts on time. If for some reason you can't, then make sure someone knows where you are – you'd better tell Lady Eleanor. If you are going off campus, tell her when you expect to be back. If you're not in the dining hall for one meal, that's okay, but don't skip two in a row without telling her."

I stared at him while I thought about this and what leeway it gave me for the things I needed to do. Classes and work shifts and meals were fine; I'd be doing that anyway. Even telling someone when I expected to be back was okay as long as I didn't have to tell them where I was going. The catch here was having to agree to spend every night on campus and risk the effects of the nightmares. I thought fast; I could stay awake at night and sleep off campus during the day and I could still sleep in the Abbey or the Old Chapel. And maybe I could find one or two other out of the way places that still counted as on the campus. I decided to agree. Arguing the points would raise suspicions and lead to questioning and explanations that I didn't want to have to give.

"Okay," I said.

Prospero narrowed his eyes as he looked at me. He clearly

hadn't expected it to be that easy. Good, again. Perhaps he was wondering what he'd forgotten or what loophole he might have left. There was one I could use even if it felt a bit dishonest. He'd said I shouldn't leave campus until morning, but technically morning started just after midnight so if I sneaked out after that I'd not be breaking any agreement. I decided to keep that in reserve as an idea in case I needed it. For now I gave Prospero my best innocent look, which was a mistake because that made him look suspicious, and decided to be on my best behaviour for the rest of our journey back to the campus.

That resolution lasted about a minute before it was overtaken by curiosity. "Why did you come looking for me?" I asked.

Prospero answered, "You weren't where Lord Gabriel expected you to be, so I looked for you and then he sent us to fetch you."

"Am I in trouble?"

"Not with Lord Gabriel." Prospero grinned wickedly, and I realised this was his revenge for my innocent look earlier, but he relented. "Stick to our agreement and it'll be fine."

Still I was curious. "You could tell it was me all the way out there?"

"I can see further than that, and you're pretty distinctive. At least to me."

Well, I knew he could see further than that, but not that he could recognise me. I could see people much further away than I'd been, but I wouldn't have known who they were. At least, I didn't think I would. I'd never been in a position to find out. I'd have to try it sometime.

But that meant he could check up on me pretty much

anywhere I went. I was going to have to be very careful about remembering to shield my presence.

"I'm not going to spend my time tracking you, not even spot checks," he said. "It takes too much energy and I have other things to do. And I'd rather you didn't feel you need to spend the energy on hiding from me. Either you keep our agreement or you don't, it's up to you. I'll just look for you when you're not where you're supposed to be."

Ouch! So he was going to trust me. Somehow, whilst the lack of checks would make it easier to break some of the rules, the fact that he would trust me without checking made me far less willing to risk it. It wasn't far back to the campus now, but I thought about that for the rest of the way. And I wondered what made me distinctive to him because I'd spent years trying to be unnoticed.

Chapter 16

Late January

Prospero

As the first weeks of the year progressed, as far as Prospero could tell, Leonie was keeping to their agreement. Not that he was checking up on her, but he did keep an eye out for her at mealtimes, often choosing to sit next to her given the opportunity, and there were no complaints that she'd missed classes or work shifts. It was Eleanor's role to make sure that she was where she should be. He was sure he'd have heard if she hadn't been because he'd have been asked to look for her. He found he was missing their assessment sessions and thought that he should suggest to Andrew that they set up a further meeting, or a series of sessions, to see how she was progressing and if there were any problems.

So, when he needed to search the House library for an obscure medical textbook, Prospero was both amused and surprised to find Leonie there. Surprised because he'd never thought of her as a bookworm; amused because she was curled up asleep on one of the window seats, book still in her hand, something he'd done himself on more than one occasion. He left her to sleep while he continued his search and then took his find to one of the comfortable chairs by a low table. He sat with his back partly turned towards her, so that he didn't appear to be watching her, but where he could still keep an eye on her and make sure she wasn't disturbed.

She looked like a sleeping cat, her legs tucked beneath her, one arm under her head, the other hand resting on the seat, holding the book she'd been reading. Her hair was longer now, copper-red corkscrew ringlets nestling round her ears. What would it feel like to twist his fingers into those curls, stroke her warm soft cheek?

Resolutely he pulled his attention back to his book. Almost immediately the hairs on the back of his neck rose, as he felt tendrils of power and fear reach out for him. Knowing it for the start of a nightmare he moved quickly to Leonie's side taking her hand in one of his and placing his other hand on her temple. He whispered to her, concentrating on trying to calm the nightmare, rather than where his hands now were, just as he'd imagined only moments ago. The words he used didn't matter; it was the tone of voice that was key. He'd used this technique many times in the past, though this time it worked faster than he expected. The nightmare dissipated and Leonie settled back into a peaceful sleep. With any luck when she woke she might not even remember it starting.

Once he was sure she was calm, he returned to his chair utterly shaken by the feelings he had experienced as he'd soothed her. He tried to ignore them, to pass them off as his imagination, but really he was just fooling himself. Her hair had been soft and silky, claiming his fingers. Her hand had relaxed in his, warm and trusting. And just touching her skin had sent shivers of pleasure through his whole body.

Of course, she'd fascinated him from the start, but he'd assumed that was because of her multiple Gifts and the skill and power she'd demonstrated. His mind always felt clouded and slow when she was around but again he'd decided that was because she was so quick, always on the defensive, always trying to throw him off balance. And he'd told himself that the reason he enjoyed her company so much, even sought it out, was because he enjoyed the challenge she posed him.

But none of that was true, was it? Or at least it wasn't the whole story? However much he tried to deny it, there were other reasons altogether for his reactions. He hadn't felt like this about any woman in many years; despite his past, celibacy itself had not been the major issue for him.

He told himself not to be so stupid. She was a ward of the House, a student, and he was a monk, for goodness sake. He was in a position of responsibility towards her. Any feelings he might have were entirely inappropriate and irresponsible and he should work at squashing them. He resolved to avoid Leonie, other than when unavoidable, and, if his feelings persisted, to discuss them with Lord Gabriel. The thing to do now would be to take his book and leave Leonie here in the library, undisturbed. Except that someone should keep an eye on her in case the nightmare returned and there was no one else around. He sat, undecided, trying to lose himself in his book, and then realising that he had no memory of the last few pages he'd read. It wasn't exactly a good choice of book to distract himself with anyway because he'd been looking for references to the development of multiple Gifts in females. He sighed, put it down, and chose an alternative, a recent publication on social history, one of his other interests. That worked a little better, although he still struggled to concentrate. He was aware as soon as Leonie woke.

Leonie

When I woke, for just a moment I didn't know where I was. I kept my eyes closed while I worked it out. I could remember feeling the edge of fear that meant the start of a nightmare, but I had no memory of the nightmare itself. Then I realised I was in the House library, a large, warm and welcoming room, stuffed with shelves and books, but also with comfortable armchairs, low tables and best of all, a number of cushioned window seats looking out over one of the courtyards. This afternoon, I'd found the books I was looking for and curled up on a window seat. But I was warm and safe and I must have dozed off.

As I stretched my mind out across the room, I spotted that Brother Prospero was there too, sitting with his back to me. I decided that I was safe to open my eyes, sit up and collect my books together. He turned round as I moved and smiled at me. He was more than good-looking enough already, but the smile lit up his whole face.

"Did you sleep well?" he asked. "I've dropped off just there before, it's very comfortable."

Without thinking I headed over to him. "I like it here," I told him.

"Me, too," he agreed. "What have you been reading?"

He reached towards my pile of books, which I'd put on the table. I felt a need to explain and defend them. "I wanted to know more about what's important here. I've read the Bible, but I don't understand it. Pedro suggested that one would help. And that one's about the history of here, the Abbey and the House."

He looked at both books. "They're good choices," he agreed. He tapped the first one. "If you want something after this or have any questions, Brother Matthew would be a good person to ask though anyone would help. And if you want a wider background to the history one, I could find you something."

I murmured some thanks but he'd moved on to my other two books – one was romantic fiction, the other a children's book.

"And these two?" he asked. "Pedro didn't recommend them?"

I shook my head, amused at the thought as he appeared to be, too. "No, there are so many books I didn't know where to start. I saw Lady Eleanor reading one by that author so I thought I'd try it."

"Our powerful Seneschal likes romantic fiction, does she?" he asked, with a wide grin.

Had I given away something I shouldn't? I moved on

quickly to my final book. "That one just looked familiar. I thought perhaps I'd seen it as a small child."

He nodded. "I wouldn't be surprised. It's a classic bedtime story book. I used to enjoy it when I was a kid." He looked at me. "Is that what you were reading when you fell asleep?"

"No," I said slowly. "But when I was asleep, I thought I felt a nightmare. But I don't remember it, and I'm still here."

He leaned back in his chair, relaxed, like it was an everyday thing. I suppose maybe it was for all I knew.

"I felt the power at the start," he said. "There's a technique you can use to stop it then, if you're in the right place at the right time. It's not much use normally because you've only got about a minute, if that, before it's too late. I just happened to be here at the right moment."

Perhaps that was the answer to my nightmares – only sleep within arm's reach of Prospero. I dismissed the idea as utterly impractical, if very attractive.

"You didn't do anything," he reassured me. "The nightmare never reached that stage."

I was going to ask him more about the nightmares but I heard a clock chime and realised I was supposed to be in the kitchens, so I made my excuses and left. I was relieved in a way; I liked being with Prospero but I always felt that I was going to tell him too much without thinking, things that were safer kept secret.

Chapter 17

Andrew

It took Andrew less than eighteen hours to realise that Prospero was hiding from something. The most telling sign was that Prospero stayed within the restricted area for breakfast. Lord Gabriel almost always did that, and so did several of the older monks, but Prospero normally ate in the main dining hall. As soon as they had a private moment, Andrew challenged him.

"It's Leonie," Prospero confessed. "How I'm starting to feel about her. I have to keep away from her."

Andrew struggled to keep his face relaxed and his voice even. "I'm sure it's not serious. It's just because she's new and challenging you. It'll blow over."

"It's not just that. I stopped her nightmare as easily as it started."

"So? That doesn't need to mean anything."

"She remembered it starting. That means high power. So I shouldn't have been able to stop it that quickly, unless..."Prospero's voice drifted off.

Andrew did his best to stay calm, but he was very concerned. Being able to stop a nightmare almost as soon as it started was an indication of a strong connection between two people. Prospero had never before had this level of connection with a woman without sleeping with her and this had been the danger Andrew was afraid of when Gabriel had first involved him in these plans to put Prospero and Leonie in close proximity. He spent the next two days following Prospero around, making sure he was never alone anywhere there was the slightest chance of meeting Leonie. What worried Andrew most was that Prospero didn't object to being shadowed.

Seeing no other choice, he took his worries to Gabriel again, not in any way seeking to disobey, but to alert Gabriel to the now very real danger. He dragged Prospero with him, again concerned that he raised no objections.

"Staying in the restricted area is simply running away," Gabriel told Prospero. "You need to face up to this and address it once and for all."

"In that case, Father," Prospero asked formally, "may I request time away from the Abbey to pray and meditate on what I should do?"

"You can go to Father Stephen. Four days," Gabriel conceded.

Andrew heaved a – quiet – sigh of relief. Father Stephen led a small, satellite monastery, far enough away that there was no chance of Prospero making any contact through use of his Gifts. But best of all, Father Stephen was also familiar with Prospero and his background.

***

Two or three nights after Prospero had left for his retreat, Andrew, as the duty doctor, was called to treat a patient. He found Lady Eleanor with an almost unconscious Leonie.

"Pedro found her in the kitchen," Eleanor told him. "She's burning up, and she's cut her arm."

Andrew inspected the long and recent gash down Leonie's right forearm. Although it had been cleaned and well looked after, it had become infected. Now angry and red it was almost certainly the reason for the fever. This was a common problem; adepts were particularly vulnerable to infection and fever, but equally tended to recover quickly. With Eleanor's help, he managed to clean and treat the injury, despite a lack of cooperation from Leonie. As he worked he struggled with his own feelings about her and he knew it was affecting his professional detachment. This injury was typical of those suffered by adepts during a nightmare, yet he knew there was no record of her having had a nightmare recently enough. That meant she'd been sleeping outside the campus again, which irritated him as it meant the injury, infection and consequences had almost certainly been avoidable.

He was also disappointed that she'd chosen to do this; he'd believed they could trust her to keep to the terms of the agreement that he and Prospero had made with her. And thinking of Prospero, this girl was the reason that he wasn't here, and the cause of all the issues and stresses he was facing. Andrew was indignant on Prospero's behalf, and although he didn't want to admit it, he also blamed Leonie for the fact that he was missing his friend. He pushed the thought that he might be jealous of her ability to evoke feelings within Prospero to the very back of his mind.

He'd almost finished dressing her arm when she made a sound, and he looked at her in some surprise to find she was staring intently at him. He could see in her eyes that she was fighting the confusion of the fever to try to communicate and for the first time it struck him that this language they spoke might not be her mother tongue. She spoke slowly.

"I need Prospero."

He shook his head. "He's not around right now."

Again she tried. "When?"

"When will he be here? I don't know. A few days perhaps."

Now there was panic in her eyes. "Can't stop nightmares."

She reached over and put her good hand on his arm, and for a moment, a fraction of a second, he was overwhelmed by her emotions. Predominantly he saw fear, fear of the nightmare, fear that she couldn't control her Gifts, fear that she'd hurt someone, but behind that he sensed loneliness, rejection, loss, abandonment. Those feelings were so close to the ones he had experienced as an orphaned teenager himself, that in that moment his heart went out to her – which didn't help the conflict he was feeling.

"It's okay," he said. "I'm going to give you something that'll stop the nightmares for tonight. And something for the fever and the infection. You'll be able to sleep undisturbed, you don't need to worry."

"And I'll stay with you through the night," Lady Eleanor added. "You'll be quite safe."

Leonie just looked back and forth between them, leaving him unsure whether she'd understood. Andrew reached into his bag and extracted two small packets, which he gave to Eleanor to mix with a little water and he coaxed Leonie into drinking it. It wasn't easy. Andrew reverted to techniques he'd not had to use since…since…well, not for a very long time. Those were memories that certainly didn't help under the current circumstances.

Lady Eleanor noticed his actions. She looked at the sleeping Leonie and then back at Andrew.

"Is Leonie the reason Prospero's gone on retreat?" she asked.

Unsettled by having felt Leonie's emotions, Andrew let his guard down and poured out his problems.

How Leonie was the cause of the problems that Prospero was having, and which were therefore also affecting Andrew. How Gabriel was pushing Prospero and Leonie to work together, how she was everything that Prospero found attractive – beautiful, intelligent, Gifted to the point of challenging his abilities, competitive, strong willed but in need of care and looking after. How he'd been concerned that this was putting too much temptation in Prospero's path, how he'd been right and Prospero had fallen for her, how Gabriel seemed unsympathetic to this problem.

Eleanor listened and seemed to understand his worries.

"Surely," she said, "if Prospero's feelings are simply infatuation or lust, and unreciprocated he's well enough protected, here in the monastery? It might be hard for him, but he's got people all around him, like you, who will care for him and support him. And, he must have grown and developed in his time here. Maybe we're not giving him the credit he's due?"

Andrew nodded, just a little relieved. Of course he'd support Prospero, help him in whatever he needed.

Lady Eleanor continued, "On the other hand, if his feelings are genuine and Leonie feels the same, and this is where God is leading them both, what is it that's particularly worrying you?"

That question required Andrew to be very honest with himself, and he had a strong suspicion Lady Eleanor knew exactly what he needed to be honest about. And if he were honest, what concerned him, almost to the point of panic, was the risk, the fear of losing Prospero to this girl. That was something he needed to work on, it was neither Prospero's fault nor Leonie's. Fortunately, Lady Eleanor didn't expect an answer, at least not then and there.

Very gently she made a final point, "You can't blame Leonie for Prospero's feelings, you know. She's only responsible for her own feelings and actions."

***

When he returned to check on Leonie the following morning, Andrew supposed that one of the good things about night duty was that at least he'd not spent a sleepless night fretting over her and Prospero. He'd fretted, of course, but he wouldn't have been sleeping anyway. He'd spent the night working through Lady Eleanor's comments in his head. Now it was time to try to put his conclusions into action, and the first would be to try to control and change his attitude to Leonie as he checked her condition. She was already awake and he tried to be gentle with her as he inspected and redressed her arm.

"How did you do this?" he asked.

She looked puzzled. "I don't know. I had a nightmare and it was there when I woke. It's happened before."

He nodded. "That's not uncommon. But it must have been recent. When was the nightmare?"

Again she seemed a bit confused. "The other day, a couple of days ago?"

"Where were you?" he asked. "Were you sleeping out in the woods?"

She nodded without looking at him.

He sighed with disappointment. "We could have taken better care of you if you'd stayed here, you know."

She protested, "I took care of it, I cleaned it properly, it's just, I didn't realise I had so little ointment. I ran out, I need to make some more."

He was curious about her reference to ointment, and she indicated a little pot on the table. He picked it up, noting that it was empty, all but wiped clean, in support of her story. He sniffed it.

"Hmm, aloe, comfrey, yarrow and perhaps something else I don't recognise. You made this?"

She nodded again. "It varies depending on what I can get hold of. I didn't realise I had so little left."

Andrew was impressed. The ingredients she'd chosen and the fact that she could make the ointment at all suggested quite a knowledge of medicinal herbs that he hadn't expected her to have. Still, much as such remedies were used extensively throughout the hospital and beyond, he'd prefer her to use something that was provided by trained medics.

"It's a good mix of herbs," he said. "But you've run out so I'll leave you something in its place. I want you to come and see me at tomorrow afternoon's clinic at the hospital, please. In the meantime, Lady Eleanor will keep an eye on you today – no classes, no workshifts."

Leonie nodded so he assumed she'd understood. Whether or not she would obey was another matter altogether.

Chapter 18

Leonie

I really did intend to go to the clinic. I didn't like hospitals at all, they scared me silly for reasons I didn't understand. I couldn't remember any incident or experience involving a hospital but all the same I was terrified of going inside one. Despite that, I tried; not only did I feel obliged to do what Andrew had asked of me, I found I actually wanted to. I got as far as the plaza outside the main entrance to the hospital but I couldn't make my legs walk across it. I sat on a bench at the far edge of the plaza, staring at the door, shaking and trying to summon up the courage to walk up to it.

How have I got myself into this mess?

The rules Prospero had set for me were not restrictive. Sometimes I chose to stay awake at night and then head off the campus to sleep during part of the day. And I was pretty sure Prospero had kept to his word about not checking up on me but I'd often see him at mealtimes. I'd usually sit with Sister Chloe. She was only a few years older than me but she'd wanted nothing more than to be a nun from her early teens and she was just so happy about it you couldn't help but be happy with her. She was the most amazingly organised person, so she mostly ran Lord Gabriel's office for him. We were frequently joined by Prospero – and invariably Andrew. That hadn't happened for a couple of days, though, and Prospero hadn't been around at all.

Prospero's absence had made me feel unsettled, and I'd had that shivery feeling that meant a nightmare was coming. So a few days ago I'd headed out into the woods to find somewhere to sleep, during daylight, where I wouldn't put anyone else at risk. The nightmare had come, sure enough, and when I'd woken from it I'd found I had hurt my arm, a long but quite deep scratch from inner elbow to wrist. I'd treated it and kept it covered the next day, working in the kitchen. Towards the end of my shift I'd felt all hot and achy, so instead of going back to my room I'd curled up at the back of the office in the dark and quiet to give it a chance to pass.

I must have dozed a little because then I hadn't known where I was. The memory of the night took over.

I was hot, I was cold, there were people around making me move. I didn't want to. I could feel the power lurking, waiting for its chance to attack, for the nightmare to start, and make me do things I couldn't control. I had to concentrate on blocking it, not on whatever these people around me wanted. But I knew I was losing the battle, I needed someone to stop it. Prospero, I needed him, he'd stopped it before. I had to tell someone to get him.

I concentrated hard, trying to pull the right words from the confusion in my head and yet still hold the power back. It was Andrew in front of me; that was good, he'd be able to get Prospero. When he said Prospero wasn't there the panic came rushing back, I didn't know what to do, I couldn't handle it and in the terror I couldn't make out what Andrew was saying. Then he held something for me to drink. Again, I didn't want to, I was afraid it would make me sleep and then I'd lose control. But I was being held firmly even if I couldn't see how; I could smell the cup under my nose, hot and spicy and the scent got into my head. It wrapped itself around my mind, soothing the confusion. In a moment of calm I found myself drinking the liquid, syrupy and smooth against my throat. Even as I swallowed I could feel it bringing the power under control, making it disappear. Words started to be easier to find again; I tried to say something to Andrew but I found I was lying down and then sleep overcame me before I could finish.

I pulled myself back from the memory; remembering that fear certainly didn't help me now. I went on staring at the hospital doors, the people coming in and out. It should be easy to go into the clinic, just a few short steps.

Surely I can do it?

I didn't make it; I just sat there and the time ticked by until the clinic had finished. I carried on sitting there, letting myself down and knowing that Andrew would be disappointed in me – I got the feeling he disapproved of me anyway.

Prospero

Prospero rode back from his retreat to the Abbey concentrating more on what had happened than on his horse and his journey.

He had found the retreat confusing as much as clarifying. The one thing that had become clear through his prayers, study and meditation with Father Stephen was that he needed to return to the Abbey. Whatever problems he might be experiencing there, it was where God wanted him to be. As Gabriel had told him, he would have to address his problems head on. Father Stephen also felt that Prospero was coming to a crossroads in his life. He had broached the thought that Prospero might be at the point where he should consider whether or not to continue in the Order.

The thought of facing his problems terrified Prospero. The thought of leaving the Order was worse. He had experienced a number of issues in his late teens as a result of expectations laid on him by others, and had deferred facing them by coming to the college to progress his studies. At college there had been further problems – including those with women – which had escalated beyond the point at which he could cope. Through a process which was traumatic both for him and for those around him, God had called him into the Order. That had protected him from the expectations laid on him outside, and provided him with a safety net of vows and rules when interacting with the issues that had caused problems during his college years. Leaving the Order would remove his safety net and might well resurrect the previous expectations of his family.

Father Stephen had understood his fears.

"Let's just take it one step at a time," he'd suggested. "We know that you must return to the Abbey, so we'll put in place some strategies to help you cope with the situation you are in at the moment."

They had done so, creating a set of practical guidelines to protect both Prospero and Leonie. Fleetingly Prospero had been reminded of the rules he had set up for Leonie and was somewhat amused that he was now the subject, with someone setting rules for him.

"As for the other matters," Father Stephen had continued, "whilst they may be interconnected, your feelings for Leonie should be secondary. First you need to establish just what God is calling you to do next, and then I feel the rest will become clear." He had paused and corrected himself. "Or at least a little clearer."

He had put together a series of studies and readings for Prospero to continue to meditate on and pray about as he sought guidance from God.

As he rode, Prospero realised that while he was scared of what he might have to face and how it might affect him, he was also both pleased and excited to be returning. He arrived in time to fulfil his duties in the afternoon clinic alongside Andrew. Between patients, during interludes and indeed whilst with patients, he and Andrew had a continuing verbal and telepathic conversation about his retreat and its consequences. Towards the end of the clinic Andrew seemed a little distracted and after his last patient Prospero asked him why. Andrew shook his head with disappointment.

"I told Leonie to come today. She hurt her arm and I wanted to check it. Never mind, I'll catch her later."

Prospero heard only that Leonie was hurt. "When, how, what happened?" he asked urgently.

"Nothing too serious. She was sleeping out in the woods and had a nightmare during which she cut her arm. She kept quiet about it all and by the time we found out it was infected and she was feverish. She recovered quickly enough; I just wanted to check it."

"You're sure she's okay?"

"I'm sure she's fine. I'm just disappointed that she broke the curfew to sleep out in the woods, and that she hasn't turned up today. I'd hoped for more. I'll find her later."

Prospero thought that Leonie would have had good reason for her actions and scanned the area around for her. He spotted her without any trouble.

"Come on," he said. "Bring what you need, she's outside, at the far edge of the plaza."

He set off, assuming Andrew would follow. Prospero spotted Leonie again as soon as he was outside and saw her take flight. Without thinking twice, he followed her. She shielded her presence from him but he could still hear her and follow her trail. Intermittently he sensed snatches of her presence which meant she was struggling to maintain her shield, which was in itself a sure sign that something was wrong. Although he couldn't see her, he could tell when she stopped only a short distance ahead of him.

Remembering that last time she had been up a tree, he looked up, spotting her lying along a branch just above his head height. He stretched up, took hold of her and swung her down to stand in front of him, not letting go in case she ran.

He was struck by the feelings emanating from her.

"You're scared. Is it us?"

Again without thinking he reached to touch her mind gently as he looked in her eyes.

"No, it's not me," he said. "It's the hospital. You're terrified of the hospital. That's why you didn't come into the clinic."

Leonie

I moved as soon as I saw Prospero coming through the main hospital entrance, closely followed by Andrew. Then I shot off the bench, across the campus boundary and into the woods as fast as I could in the hope that they hadn't seen me. I didn't want to meet up with either of them right now, not until I was more in control of myself.

They had seen me and they were following me. Panicking, not thinking straight after being upset by the hospital, I left the path, ducking and weaving through the trees, wincing at every crack of a branch underfoot. I leapt up the next tree, climbing into the shelter of the leaves. I lay along one of the branches, not moving, scarcely daring to breathe. I hadn't been quick or quiet enough, nor far enough ahead; they arrived underneath my hiding place within moments.

I was shielding; I knew Prospero couldn't sense where I was even though he was standing right underneath me. I could have stretched out and touched the top of his head. Then he looked up, reached out and lifted me straight down in front of him before I could resist. I was even more thrown when he worked out what was bothering me but before I had time to respond he had his arms around me and was moving us both.

By the time I gathered what was left of my wits – not much

– we were sitting on the ground. Prospero had his back to the tree and I was sitting with my back against his chest, his legs either side of mine. He had his left arm around me, both holding me against him and restraining me. His right hand was holding my right arm at the wrist, and my injured arm was stretched out, resting along our legs.

"No reason why you need to go into the hospital," he said. "We've come to you. Come on, Andrew, you can do whatever you need to here."

Andrew gave him a look; I don't think they were in agreement about this, but he sat down too, pushed my sleeve up gently and started to check my arm.

I suppose I could have argued, fought or tried to get away, but Prospero was definitely physically stronger than me. His gifts seemed more powerful too, or at least more practiced. I decided to relax and accept the inevitable. Being so close to him was making me feel a little dizzy but it was also reassuring and I guess I didn't really want to get away. One of the things I remembered about my early childhood was that my aunt and I always shared a bed and there were lots of hugs. After that, wherever I'd been, there were always warm bodies to sleep with. And with the Traders, space was at a premium so it was never less than two to a bed. Since then I'd missed close physical contact with another human and I had to admit – at least to myself – I was enjoying being held so closely by Prospero. He was watching Andrew over my shoulder and commented on my injury.

"That was nasty, wasn't it? How—"

Andrew interrupted before he'd finished speaking. "She doesn't know how she did it, any more than you ever did."

I twisted my head to look up at Prospero questioningly.

"Yes," he confirmed, "I've injured myself a time or two sleepwalking. Want to see the scars?"

He started to move his arm from around me but Andrew almost snapped at him.

"At least hold still until I finish this!"

"Sorry," Prospero said unconvincingly.

He put his arm back round me. I felt both safe and reassured, though I wondered whether they were my feelings or Prospero acting on my mind as I knew some adepts could do. Actually, that wasn't strictly true; what adepts did was to project their own feelings. Anyone close enough would sense those feelings without realising and might act on them. It only worked if someone was close to the adept. Of course I couldn't move away from Prospero right now, but mine or not, they were good feelings, and they made me feel better, so I didn't mind.

Andrew didn't take long to finish. "It's healing well," he said. "You don't need to come back to the clinic, just leave the dressing for another day or so and it'll be fine."

Reluctantly, I started to get up, but Prospero held me back.

"Sit a while," he said "There's no hurry."

That got him another look from Andrew; maybe they were arguing telepathically. There was definitely something up between them today.

Their relationship puzzled me anyway. They were invariably together and seemed as close as any married couple, but I didn't think they were a couple. I was pretty certain pair-bonding wasn't permitted within the Order. Besides my instincts were telling me that Prospero's orientation would be women, whilst Andrew's wasn't exactly men. No, I thought Andrew's orientation was simply Prospero. I could understand that; whilst he could wind me up without even trying I still thought Prospero was very attractive. I'd concluded they were what the Traders called a dyad—a couple who are emotionally and domestically close, but with no active romantic or sexual involvement. It's more than a close friendship and they function fine as individuals, they are just more complete as a team.

I stayed sitting where I was, quite happily. I didn't want this time to end.

"I didn't know you were back," I said to Prospero, twisting my head round and up slightly to look at him.

"Did you miss me, then?" he asked cheerfully.

Andrew interjected before I could reply. "Yeah, 'cause it's always so much more quiet and peaceful when you're gone."

He was smiling, teasing Prospero, so I guess his mood was improving. He had a point, though. It wasn't that Prospero was loud or noisy, but I did notice whenever he was in a room, and it felt like there was a hole when he wasn't there. I had a question for him, something that I now realised had been puzzling me since I'd seen them coming out of the hospital.

"What happened to your hair?"

All the monks and most of the nuns had short hair. Right now Prospero had almost no hair, just stubble across his head. He ran his hand over it before answering then looked at Andrew who shrugged.

"It's symbolic," Prospero explained. "We shave our heads completely when we take our vows. After that, we repeat it whenever we plan to spend time specifically dedicated to prayer and meditation and seeking direction. It's about commitment and purification and it's a visible representation of setting ourselves aside for God."

"Is that what you were doing when you were away?" I asked.

He nodded. "Yes. I went somewhere with fewer distractions."

I waited to see if he added anything, like what he'd been praying or meditating about, but he clearly wasn't going to.

Instead Andrew changed the subject. Leonie," he asked, "why were you sleeping out here anyway, when you got hurt? I thought we'd agreed you wouldn't leave the campus at night."

Briefly I wondered if Andrew also thought attack was the best form of defence. But what would he be defending Prospero from, anyway? He sounded disappointed, and I didn't want Prospero to think I'd broken the rules, especially when I hadn't.

"It wasn't at night, it was during the day. I didn't do anything wrong," I protested.

Andrew glanced at Prospero so I figured they were discussing me telepathically.

He spoke again almost immediately, so it can't have been a long discussion. "But why do you need to sleep outside the campus? Or deeply enough in the day time to have nightmares?"

That's the sort of question I didn't like answering, it got too close to things I've found it safer to keep secret. But I was feeling reassured and safe leaning against Prospero so my mouth started answering before my brain thought about it.

"When the nightmares come, the stuff I do in them happens in real life too and I can't stop it. Damaging things is bad enough, but I can't risk hurting people. So, when I know one is coming, I find somewhere to sleep where there aren't people so I won't hurt anyone. When I agreed not to go out at night that meant it had to be during the day."

Prospero held me closer. "You don't have to do that," he said. "That's part of what the watch team is for. If you stay on the campus, we'll spot the start of a nightmare, and come and help. We won't let you hurt anyone or do too much damage to anything."

Andrew was nodding agreement.

I looked between them doubtfully. "It's not that I don't believe you, exactly. It just seems too big a risk to take. I can't control what happens and sometimes it starts so fast."

"We've had a lot of practice," Prospero said. He sounded a little amused. "And we were there when you had that one before Christmas. No one's been hurt by a dreamer yet beyond the odd bruise."

I was still unconvinced but he seemed very confident.

"Put us to the test. Stay on the campus to sleep. At night. Next time you have a nightmare, we'll be there to help and no one will be hurt."

I didn't exactly agree but it was certainly something to give some thought to.

Andrew spoke then, "Did you say you know when a nightmare is coming?"

I tried to explain that I never know that they aren't coming – they could easily take me by surprise – but sometimes I knew for sure that they were. He was quite impressed; apparently there were only about half a dozen people in the whole House who'd ever had any idea whether their nightmares were or weren't going to happen. Prospero was one of them, of course; I should have known he would be.

He shrugged. "I only ever knew occasionally that they wouldn't come that night, which is different," he said. "And it's a long time ago now."

I was going to ask him how long ago and when the nightmares might stop but Andrew said we needed to get back or we'd all be late so I stored it up for another time. I had plenty to think about anyway. If I knew for sure that I wasn't going to be able to hurt anyone or damage anything, and that there would be someone to wake me soon after the nightmare started, then maybe I wouldn't need to be so worried about them and they might not be so bad. I just didn't know whether I could take the risk.

Chapter 19

A few days later

Leonie

I was feeling happy and relaxed as I headed back towards the campus one evening after visiting the town. I had plenty of time before curfew and it was a clear night so I stopped near the river and laid back to watch the sky. It was tranquil and peaceful, the only sound the rustling of the trees in a gentle breeze.

The Them were coming for me and the only thing I could think of was that I needed to get back to the campus. I needed to find Prospero to help me stop them. The Them swirled around me, cloaks and hoods billowing in the breeze. I had no weapons, nothing I could use and they were coming towards me, getting closer and closer, surrounding me. I took my courage in both hands and charged into the Them who were directly in my path. They melted away like mist as I reached them, but now they were behind me and chasing me. I ran and ran but somehow they appeared ahead of me. I grabbed a sword which turned to a javelin in my hand so I threw it. Now the weapon melted away but the Them were still there. I gathered the power, throwing it directly at them as I ducked sideways. I was running through treacle; I struggled against it knowing they were closing in on me and I couldn't get away. Suddenly I smacked into a wall I hadn't seen.

Prospero

It was a quiet night in the control centre, so Prospero was sprawled across one of the couches reading when Lord Gabriel and Lady Eleanor came in. He sat up sharply, aware of his rather casual position and concerned that their presence might involve Leonie.

"Leonie isn't in her room, nor anywhere else on the campus." Lady Eleanor said.

Immediately, Prospero scanned the campus with his mind, but with no success.

"Do you know her well enough to recognise her?" Nick – the team leader that night – asked him.

"Yes, but she'll be out in the woods." He pointed on the monitor at the boundary between the campus and the woods. "Switch off the containment shield on this side," he suggested. "That's where she's most likely to be and I'll be able to check."

Nick turned to the control panel and switched off the shield as asked. "There you go," he said. "Try now."

"Found her," Prospero said. "She's not far away, heading this way, but I think she's asleep, which means a nightmare."

"Okay," said Nick. "Let's go and get her."

She was just outside the campus boundaries, running and fighting shadows with the typical movements of an adept having a nightmare. Nick took the lead, attempting to distract and engage her. It didn't work; she threw a bolt of mental power at him and veered off to find a hiding place deeper in the woods. Prospero placed himself directly in her path but she seemed not to see him. He braced for the impact and used his mind to slow her as much as he could before she cannoned into him. She looked up at him, her eyes clear for a moment.

"You are here," she whispered sounding surprised and then crumpled.

He caught her just in time and lifted her into his arms, the nightmare gone, at least for now. He wasn't sure whether she was asleep, awake or faint but he was immediately surrounded by the rest of the team.

Nick took her wrist to check her pulse. "I want to admit her," he said. "With that much power, I'd be more comfortable with her in the hospital."

Only Prospero was anything like prepared for Leonie's reaction to that last word as she started struggling in his arms, lashing out with her mind, desperate to get away. He gripped her more tightly, using his mind to contain and restrain her power, feeling Nick duck away from Leonie's blast and then move in to assist him both physically and mentally.

"I don't think that's a good idea," he replied once she was immobile again, his voice sounding much calmer than he felt. "Hospitals terrify her for some reason. She couldn't even manage to walk into the clinic the other day for Andrew to check a dressing. It'll stress her and make things much worse."

Despite being held still by his mind, Leonie managed to lift her head from where it was tucked into his shoulder.

"No hospital, please. I won't fight, please not there," she begged.

"I'll do what I can," he reassured her, "but you have to help us. Nick's worried about how much power you're using, so ease back, stop fighting and trust me to work something out, okay?"

She looked at him with huge scared dark eyes, hid her face in his shoulder, and then he felt her just give up. Nick felt it too and backed off carefully. She didn't react at all, so Prospero eased back his own mental restraint of Leonie, but remained ready in case she was tricking them. He didn't think she would but he wasn't going to take any chances.

He was struggling with his own feelings. The sensation of his arms around her, her body against his, her face against the skin of his neck – he knew he was finding too many opportunities to touch her, however innocent it appeared. He was finding her almost addictive. Now he was worried about the look of fear and defeat he'd caught in her eyes before she'd given up. He knew just how terrifying the nightmares could be and he wanted to protect her or at least help her through them. He knew one way, and then he was shocked at himself for even thinking of it.

He told himself firmly to concentrate on the one thing he could do for her right now, which was to keep her out of hospital. He turned towards Nick who was speaking to him.

"The ward is better resourced to deal with this much power," Nick argued. "The team doesn't have enough staff." He paused for a moment. "She looks all but asleep, but it's still a risk. Anyway, Gabriel's waiting for us, we might as well see if he has any good ideas."

He pointed towards the nearby gate onto the campus where Gabriel was standing with Lady Eleanor. Prospero carried Leonie. It occurred to him that if it had been one of the male students they'd be encouraging him to walk, ensuring they woke properly from the nightmare. She was just so much smaller and somehow more fragile, and anyway there was no way he was going to put her down. Nick might think she was asleep, but Prospero could sense the tension in her body as she clung to him. She had to be hating this. He had always hated this stage – adrenaline flooding through his body, yet exhausted and totally vulnerable, utterly dependent on others to take care of him. That would be just as hard for Leonie who was so self-contained and independent.

And he'd always felt a failure for being unable to handle the nightmare himself, when others much less Gifted didn't seem to have the same problems. It had taken him months to understand that the power of the nightmares rose exponentially with the strength and range of the Gifts. The more Gifted ones were those who would be less able to cope. Despite his own experiences, he didn't know how to reassure Leonie, how to make her feel better, but he had to try. He angled his head so his mouth was close to her ear and started whispering to her, just telling her that she was doing well, that she didn't have to worry, that he'd keep her safe. He thought he felt her relax a little but it was difficult to be sure.

Nick had reached the gate and explained the problem to Gabriel and Eleanor. Gabriel nodded, understanding.

"There's a day bed in my outer office," he said, "and that office is staffed around the clock in case of emergencies. Put her there, Prospero can sit with her, he seems to be able to manage her best, and Chloe'll be with them all the time in case he needs help or if you need to call on him for something else."

Prospero and Nick took Leonie off to the office as suggested, whilst the others returned to the control centre. Prospero lowered Leonie until she was sitting on the edge of the bed, but she clung to him, keeping her face buried in his neck, afraid to look.

"Not a hospital?" she asked, still pleading with him.

"Not a hospital," he reassured her. "Just an ordinary bed. Slip your coat off, and tell me, do you hurt anywhere?"

She wasn't convinced and asked again, "Not a hospital?"

Patiently he repeated, "No, not a hospital."

Satisfied this time, she answered his question, "Don't hurt."

"Good," he replied. "Now drink this. It'll help. You've had it before."

He suited actions to words, holding the cup that Nick

passed him so that she could drink. She drank without protest, and again he was concerned at her lack of fight; was she feeling that defeated, or was it that she trusted him, just a little? The medicine acted very fast. She was swaying against him almost before she'd finished swallowing and asleep as soon as he laid her down. He pulled her boots off and covered her with a blanket whilst Nick checked her pulse, breathing and temperature.

"She seems okay for now," Nick said. "Good luck watching her. Rather you than me. I hadn't realised just how strong she is."

Prospero nodded. "I think she'll be fine now."

Shortly, Prospero was left with the sleeping Leonie. He made himself comfortable on a nearby couch and took the opportunity to rest.

Asleep, Leonie looked even more vulnerable and he desperately wanted to protect her. The nightmares would ease with time, as her Gifts developed but they could last another three or four years which seemed a long time for her to continue to suffer. Their frequency and severity – at least those he knew about – suggested that not only was she very Gifted, but also that there were some horrific experiences in her past and he didn't like to think what they might be. Her intense fear of hospitals also concerned him; again he was afraid of what might have happened to her. He found the thought of what she might be reliving in her nightmares bad enough; her experience would be worse and that led him to thinking of ways to alleviate it.

The trouble was he knew several ways and none of them were acceptable. One involved using drugs, similar to those they used after a nightmare, but stronger. The downside was that using that much medication stopped the development of any Gifts and after using the drugs for a while the user would lose any ability at all. Sleeping under a dampening shield every night would have the same effect – prevent nightmares but at the cost of losing all

Gifts. Whilst some people did choose this, he knew it would be unacceptable to Gabriel and, he was equally certain, to Leonie.

The other method didn't have this problem, but that led his thoughts down paths he was trying to avoid. It was to share a bed – just to sleep, nothing more – with someone you trusted and cared about, who cared about you, preferably someone who was also Gifted. Such close contact promoted the production of oxytocin in the body. That had a major impact in reducing both the frequency and severity of nightmares with no downside or loss of ability, though they'd never been able to replicate it artificially. It had worked for him; there had been people who'd had this effect on him, and he on them, until one of them had betrayed his trust. After that, he'd turned to other methods to try to blunt the nightmares – with mixed results – which had nearly destroyed him. If it hadn't been for Andrew… He pulled his thoughts back to Leonie. She was a very private person; he doubted that there was anyone she trusted enough for this to work. Actually, he realised he didn't want her to share a bed like that, or in any other way, with anyone but him. And that was wrong on so many levels it was no wonder his thoughts were troubled. Even if it was entirely innocent it was impractical to the point of impossibility and he was being possessive rather than protective; he should have no problem with her benefiting from sleeping with someone else. His thoughts weren't innocent, though, far from it.

The desire he felt for her as a woman threatened to overwhelm him. And it wasn't just lust, he was sure of that; it was far more than he'd felt for any of the other women who'd been part of his life, a different quality altogether. He wanted to protect her, care for her, ensure she didn't have to hurt or suffer again. It hadn't taken him long after discovering her to recognise how she made him feel, or to acknowledge it could be a problem but he had yet to truly accept that he needed to do something about it. He had tried to in leaving the Abbey to spend time away in prayer and reflection, confession and discussion with Father Stephen. Away from the Abbey he'd felt that he'd be able to cope with the difficulties on his return. Father Stephen had also believed that this was the right path and they had discussed strategies to help him cope. Indeed if Father Stephen hadn't been confident in him he wouldn't have been allowed to return.

Whether he had underestimated the effect Leonie had on him or overestimated his own abilities he wasn't sure, but he had been back only hours before he'd realised that the planned strategies weren't going to work. And he knew Andrew was concerned about him; that was what they had been arguing about when Leonie had run from the clinic. Prospero couldn't believe he'd offered to show Leonie his own scars. Most of those had come from a night that he was deeply embarrassed by, that he'd much rather forget. Even Andrew had been rather thrown by hearing that offer.

He ran through some of the strategies in his head, trying to work out what he could recover from the mess he was in. Plan A had been to keep away from her as much as possible; that one had flown out of his head the moment he'd discovered she'd been hurt. He'd tried it since then, yet here he was now. Something always happened that drew him back to her like a moth to a flame. Besides, it wasn't exactly compatible with the fact that he was probably the only one strong enough to contain and calm her during or after a nightmare.

Plan B involved not being alone with her in private, which was pretty much a given anyway, and keeping his distance from her when they were together. He could work on that, he supposed, except that his ability to stop her nightmares and calm her down relied heavily on touch and so required him to hold her closely.

Plan C was more about attitude; he needed to work on thinking of her as off limits. But how could he do that when she needed him?

Really, all he could rely on was what should come even before Plan A – continued prayer for strength to do what he should do, and guidance as to what that should be. Taking that as good advice from himself, he settled down to pray.

Undisturbed, his prayers drifted into sleep and some very pleasant dreams. As dawn approached, he was woken by Leonie tossing and turning in her own sleep, then calling out for someone. It sounded like Angus to Prospero as he moved towards her, sitting on the edge of the bed and stroking her head to calm her. That worked; she curled herself around him, muttered another name – this one sounded like Jimmy – in a satisfied tone and settled into peaceful sleep again, with her head on his leg and one arm draped across his lap. So much for keeping his distance, he'd blown that one again already.

Chloe walked over to them. "Who are Angus and Jimmy?" she asked.

"Is that what you heard, too?" Prospero queried. "I don't know, she's never mentioned them. Can you see anything?"

Chloe was a strong telepath, but she also had the very unusual Gift of being able to see other people's dreams. She shook her head.

"She's not really dreaming at the moment," she said, "but I get the impression that they are from a long time ago, when she was a very small child. They represent safety and security to her but she may not even remember them consciously."

Prospero continued to stroke her hair. "I guess right now she thinks I'm this Jimmy."

"Maybe," Chloe conceded, "but like I said, she's not really dreaming. She just feels safe and she's associating that with a previous time that she felt safe. I think it's you doing that, not some age-old memory."

"I'm not sure she trusts me – or anyone for that matter – enough for that." Privately he was awash with hope that Chloe was right.

Chloe shrugged. "I'm just telling you what I think from the little I can see. I caught a little of her nightmare, too, but it just seemed to be a standard being chased, running, fighting type, nothing out of the ordinary." She sat down on the couch that Prospero had just vacated. "Your dreams, on the other hand…"

Prospero looked up at her in alarm. "You looked?" he asked accusingly. "Is nothing private?"

"You were broadcasting, I didn't have to look. You know I don't tell. And anyway you don't have to worry, there was nothing improper. I thought it was sweet, caring."

Prospero blushed. "I'm sorry, it just took me a little by surprise."

Chloe nodded. "That's okay. No one can control their dreams. I assume you've tried keeping away from her?"

"Yes, but then something always happens, and I forget all that in the need to make sure she's okay. Or Gabriel assigns me a task that involves her, like watching her tonight."

"Lord Gabriel knows how you feel?"

"Of course. I wouldn't hide this from him."

"And yet he still gives you tasks which involve her? Interesting," Chloe rested her chin on her hands for a moment. "I wonder if trying to avoid her is the right approach?"

Prospero was curious. "What do you mean?"

"Well, there doesn't seem to be any problem with your actions with regard to Leonie. Whatever your feelings may be, you've done nothing improper, nothing that you wouldn't do for any other student in the same circumstances. And Lord Gabriel must be confident that situation will continue, even if you aren't, or he'd not take the risk of involving you so closely with her."

"It isn't what I do, it's what I feel. I shouldn't be feeling like this, not about anyone. And it's what it leads to. You're too young to have been here, you won't know, but I got in such a mess before, hurt so many people. I can't risk that happening again. I should stay away from the temptation."

"That's not working, though, is it? So you're adding feelings of failure to the mix. Perhaps you should relax about it, accept that inevitably you're going to spend time with her as Lord Gabriel and circumstances require, without feeling guilty, but concentrate on ensuring your actions are only those of duty and friendship whatever your feelings might be. You may even find that familiarity eases the feelings, makes them more manageable."

Prospero smiled at her. "That's certainly an interesting approach. Or do I think that because it gives me an argument for doing what I want to do anyway?"

Chloe smiled back. "Only you can work that one out! She enjoys your company too, you know."

She helped Prospero tuck Leonie back into the bed and returned to her desk to continue her work. Prospero carried on praying and watching Leonie who slept quietly for the rest of the night.

***

Leonie woke earlier than Prospero had expected though it was a few moments before she opened her eyes. He assumed she was checking out the situation before showing that she was awake. She sat up, and swung round to sit on the edge of the bed.

"Why?" she asked.

He smiled at her.

"Which why do you want the answer to? Why here – because you were distressed at the thought of the hospital and we didn't have enough people spare to watch you in your room. Why me watching – because you seem to calm down better for me than anyone else. Why the nightmares at all – because they are part of your Gifts developing. Or do you have another why?"

He thought for a moment that she did, but then she shook her head.

"Okay," he said. "What do you remember about last night?"

She shrugged. She could exasperate him in no time flat whatever his feelings were.

"Leonie, I wasn't making small talk, I was trying to assess the impact of the nightmare on you."

This time she answered though she neither looked nor sounded abashed. "You said once that a team watches for the nightmares and when they happen you come to help?"

He nodded. "Yes, that's right."

She carried on, "I didn't mean to fall asleep there. When it started I tried, I was trying to get back here even in the dream world. And then you were right, you were there. I didn't expect that, I wasn't here."

"We knew you weren't around so we were looking for you."

"But then someone said about the hospital and I knew I'd been trapped, tricked, when I thought I was safe. And I couldn't fight you, not then, you were too strong."

"I was barely strong enough, you still managed to move. Is that why you gave up, why you stopped fighting?" He tried to keep his voice calm, to let her explain, and not to leap in defending himself.

She nodded, looking at him with those huge dark eyes again. "If I wasn't safe here, if I'd been tricked and trapped here where I thought I was supposed to be, there was no point in going on, nothing left to fight for, nowhere else to go. But then you were on my side, you stopped them, and I was safe again, at least while you were there."

"You were always safe," he replied gently. "We're all on your side. They didn't know how you feel about hospitals or no one would ever have considered it. They were only trying to work out what would be best for you."

"It didn't feel like that." She wasn't complaining, just stating a fact.

"No," he conceded, "I don't suppose it did."

His head was full of the fact that she had chosen to believe him, to act on that, and to trust him out of any of them.

"That was the why," she said. "Why were you on my side? Why did you stop them?"

"Because I know you better than they do. Right then you needed someone to tell them how you felt or they'd have made things worse without knowing, and you weren't in any state to speak up for yourself. I remember, I know, probably better than anyone else here, what it's like immediately after a nightmare."

She looked at him curiously, then nodded her thanks before looking around the room. "Where is everyone?"

"It's early still. Most people are at the first service."

She looked concerned. "You couldn't go because of me?"

"It doesn't matter. Prayer and worship aren't limited to a particular time or place. Sometimes there are other, more urgent needs, and right now taking care of you is one of them." Leonie seemed bewildered by this idea so he changed the subject. "We've got about twenty minutes until breakfast. Do you want to go back to your room and freshen up?"

She nodded and stood up but seemed a little surprised when he escorted her there. There was a small sitting area nearby, where he waited for her. Although she wasn't supposed to be left alone this soon after a nightmare, at this close range he could sense her presence without trying and he was sure that he would be able to tell if there were any problems. Not only was he now hyper-sensitive to her presence – he'd be able to pick her out over several miles, even in a crowd – he was finding that she'd started to glow in different colours in his mind, depending on her mood. He just hadn't matched all the colours to the right moods yet. She was the only person he saw like this which was something new for him, and he wondered what it meant. Most people were just a point of light; a few were specific colours – Andrew was blue, Gabriel yellow, and Benjamin green – but no one else changed colour. While he waited, he amused himself by trying to deduce what colour meant what mood, and vice versa.

Leonie

I knew I didn't have long but I stood under the shower for a few moments, letting the water pour over me while I tried to sort out my thoughts and feelings.

When I'd woken from my nightmare, out it in the woods, I'd known it was Prospero holding me but I'd been totally unable to comprehend what was going on. Someone had mentioned the hospital and I'd been terrified of what was going to happen. Then Prospero had stood up for me, defended me against his colleagues. He'd put me, my well-being, what I needed, ahead of everything else. I'd have expected him to side with his colleagues over me and he hadn't. I didn't remember anyone else ever putting me first like that. Katya had valued me, I was sure of that, but the welfare of the caravan and the Traders always came ahead of the welfare of an Outsider, like me.

Somehow, without me consciously realising it, this place, this community, had become my haven, somewhere I was safe and could be me. I thought it had been torn away from me, that I was no longer safe, and I had given up. But Prospero had been there and had given me my haven back, and along with it, my reason for going on.

I owed him, deeply, and it had changed how I felt about him. I was sure he'd still drive me crazy and his touch still felt like electricity crawling across my skin but I now knew that if he asked anything of me, I would give it, willingly, whatever it was. My feelings for him were getting deeper; I wouldn't be able to refuse him anything. I was in big trouble, and so was he, whether he knew it or not.

I was afraid of what would happen to him if I stayed. Really, I should leave to protect him, but how could I? I'd promised him I wouldn't. If I broke that promise, he'd despise me. I couldn't handle the thought of that, and anyway, I had nowhere to go. I wasn't going to be able to solve this problem now, so I tried to put it to one side. I'd be in far more immediate trouble if I took too long and he came looking for me. Instead I raced to get ready, took a very deep breath and went out to meet him.

Chapter 20

Prospero

Prospero and Leonie were late for breakfast in the end and so did not sit at the high table. Andrew joined them at one of the other tables as did Nick.

Nick spoke cheerfully as he sat down. "You gave us a bit of a challenge last night. How are you feeling now, Leonie?"

"I'm fine," she replied, her voice little more than a whisper.

"You're scaring her, Nick," Prospero said, trying to keep his voice unemotional despite the flare of protectiveness in his head. "Or rather, you scared her last night and now she's not sure she can trust you." He turned towards Leonie. "There's nothing to worry about," he said, hoping to reassure her.

Nick looked concerned. "Did I scare you, Leonie? I'm sorry, I didn't mean to. I didn't know how you felt about the hospital but I've put it in the watch book now."

Leonie looked at Prospero, and now he felt triumphant that she turned to him.

"What's the watch book?" she asked.

"It's a reference book, I suppose," he replied. "We keep a record of each person's nightmares so we can see how often they happen, how they are likely to behave, what helps calm them or stop them, that sort of thing."

"Are you in it?"

He smiled and gestured round the table.

"We're all in it somewhere," he admitted. "What you're experiencing isn't that unusual round here."

The others murmured agreement.

Leonie turned to Nick. "I know you were helping me. I'm sorry I was difficult."

"Not difficult, rather much stronger than I was expecting," he answered kindly. "We'll be better prepared next time."

Leonie shuddered at the thought of next time and Prospero tried to reassure her.

Nick was more interested in the cause of her fear. "Why are you afraid of hospitals?" he asked her.

Prospero glared at him, afraid he would distress her further, but Leonie answered quite calmly.

"I don't know. I know there's things I can't remember. Maybe they're why."

Nick nodded. "Prospero's the one you want for missing memories. He can look in your mind and help you find them," he told her.

She looked at Prospero, her eyes widening in surprise but he spoke before she could question him. "Your mind is hiding them to protect you. When you're ready to deal with it, you'll remember."

It didn't distract her sufficiently.

"You can look at people's memories? Even what they can't remember?"

"I can," he said. "It doesn't mean that I do, or even that I will. It's not something to be done without a lot of preparation and counselling, and even then it's something of a last resort."

"Is it just you, or can lots of people do it?" Leonie asked, her eyes still fixed on Prospero.

Nick answered, sounding a little amused, "It's not just Prospero, but there aren't many who can."

There was a look in Leonie's eyes that Prospero was beginning to recognise as trouble.

"Don't even try it," he warned her. "It won't do you any good."

She faced him with a look of such wide eyed innocence that he was immediately suspicious.

"I mean it," he said, trying to sound severe, and she dropped her eyes.

"Melanie could," said Nick.

That did distract Leonie somewhat. "Who is Melanie?"

Thankfully, Andrew answered quickly, before this conversation also went the wrong way, "Melanie's Lady Eleanor's daughter. She trained as a doctor here, but married and moved away about ten years ago."

"Lady Eleanor can as well," Nick said.

"She can," agreed Prospero, very eager to move the conversation away from Melanie, "but she won't. She says she's not trained to deal with what she might find, and she'd rather leave it all well alone. I think she's got a point."

Andrew

Andrew took the opportunity to divert the conversation. "You're remarkably cheerful and relaxed for someone who's been up all night, Prospero. Nick looks like he needs sleep, but you don't."

Andrew had been watching both Prospero and Leonie

since he'd sat down at the table. He had immediately noticed a change in Prospero. Up to this point Prospero had been tense whenever he was in Leonie's presence, a result of the conflict between how he thought he should feel and how he actually felt. This morning the tension seemed to have eased. Leonie, too, seemed different – today she seemed to be turning to Prospero for reassurance.

Prospero grinned back at Andrew. "I was assigned to look after Leonie, who was no trouble, so I did get some sleep. And I've still got several hours to watch her, which pretty much equates to a morning off with good company so I have every reason to be cheerful."

"I have classes," Leonie interjected.

"No, you don't," Andrew corrected her. "No one has classes or work assignments for at least twelve hours after the end of a nightmare. Nick will have sorted that out for you."

"But..." said Leonie and then stopped as she thought better of it.

"But," mimicked Prospero, clearly understanding, "you've had any number of nightmares in the past, or that we don't know about, and you've got on with things the next day and been fine. Is that it?"

She nodded but he didn't wait for her confirmation before carrying on with, "You've been very fortunate. There are a number of fairly nasty after effects and we don't take any risks with them. Each time, you'll spend a minimum of twelve hours with someone who knows how to recognise them and what to do. They don't have to be Gifted or a doctor, just experienced. Today you've got me."

Andrew watched her to see how she was taking this. To his

relief she seemed to accept it, although he could see a hint of rebellion in her eyes.

Prospero continued, apparently oblivious to the rebellion, "Is there anything you'd particularly like to do, or anywhere you'd like to go? Or shall I show you one of my favourite places on the whole campus?"

She nodded. "I'd like that."

Concerned about what Prospero might be up to, Andrew spoke to him telepathically, *"Your favourite place is the roof garden."*

"I know."

"You can only get there through the hospital."

"Ten metres of corridor and four flights of stairs at the shortest route. I'll give her a choice, but she'll choose to do it."

"You're not being fair to her."

"I know what I'm doing. Trust me."

Out loud Prospero spoke to Leonie, "You'll need a coat—it's outside. Andrew, are you coming with us?"

Andrew said that he would, it being the direction he was going anyway. At least if he joined them he might be able to help deal with the consequences if things went wrong. And he could get Prospero to tell him more about what was going on.

It took some time to sort out coats and ensure Leonie was warmly attired to Prospero's satisfaction. He'd insisted she had a hat, gloves and a scarf as well which had led to considerable conflict. Andrew had been amused; Leonie had refused to wear a hat unless Prospero did, but as Andrew well knew, Prospero never wore a hat if he could possibly avoid it. Prospero had pointed out that Leonie was the one who'd had a nightmare and was therefore under his care; she'd countered with the fact that she had a lot more hair to keep her head warm than he did. Somehow, they'd both ended up without hats, although Leonie had given way on the gloves.

Andrew had been concerned as to how subdued Leonie had seemed at breakfast and this little episode reassured him as well as amused him. Whatever else might be going on, Prospero had clearly met his match for stubbornness in Leonie.

Prospero led them across the courtyards in the general direction of the hospital. They entered one of the buildings at the corner tower – Andrew noticed that Leonie removed the gloves and scarf as soon as they were indoors, stuffing them in her pockets – and went up a floor and along a corridor before reaching a covered footbridge over a road. At the far end of the bridge, Prospero stopped by the locked double doors and turned to Leonie.

"Right," he said. "Look through the window in this door. Can you see the door on the left about ten metres along?"

She nodded mutely.

"We go through that door and up four flights of stairs and then we're outside again, okay?"

Again she nodded.

"Now this is entirely your choice, we don't have to do this, we can go somewhere else, but to be fair I have to tell you, that corridor and the stairs are inside the hospital."

Now she shrank into her coat, her eyes wide in fear but Andrew saw that she leaned towards Prospero, very slightly.

Prospero continued persuasively, "What do you think? I

reckon you can manage it. I'll be right with you all the time, and Andrew will be there too. It'll be worth it when we get there."

She inched closer to him; Andrew knew then that she would agree. Prospero placed his hand on the sensor plate, opened the door and shepherded her through, heading for the second door and the stairs.

Andrew watched Prospero and Leonie as he followed them up the stairs. He didn't think that either of them realised that they were holding hands. He could feel the slight fizz in the air that indicated an adept was broadcasting their feelings. Although he knew he shouldn't, that he was invading someone's privacy, he stretched his mind out to see what he could identify. He was right that Leonie had no idea she was holding Prospero's hand. She was broadcasting fear and had unconsciously reached out for the nearest source of comfort and reassurance.

Prospero should have known better than to broadcast his feelings. Andrew could tell that he was trying to exude feelings of calm and reassurance, but what was coming across most clearly was his delight that Leonie trusted him enough to take his hand.

Andrew withdrew his mind as they reached the top of the stairs, and Prospero leaned forward to open the door. Prospero was slightly ahead of Leonie and he turned back so that he could see her expression when she got her first look at what was outside. Even from where he was standing, further back, Andrew could see that she was entranced.

This section of the roof was a herb garden, full of aromatic plants. Leonie moved towards them instinctively, reaching out to touch them and then withdrew her hand and looked at Prospero as if for permission.

He nodded. "Yes, you can touch them. Go ahead, explore, go where you choose."

She did just that, venturing further away as she was lured from one plant to the next. Prospero leaned on the parapet wall to watch her, and Andrew went and stood beside him.

"Okay," he said quietly, "you win. Now tell me just what is going on between the two of you because something has changed since yesterday."

Prospero gave him an innocent look. "Leonie had a nightmare. I got assigned to look after her."

"That much I know already. Now tell me the rest of it."

Prospero grinned back at him. "We were short on people and she freaked out about the hospital, so we put her on the bed in the main office and Chloe was there too. Something Chloe said made me think. All the time I've been fighting how Leonie makes me feel, trying to beat it and yet I can't avoid her and Gabriel's requirements don't help. Chloe suggested that I accept how I feel rather than fighting it but concentrate on how I act instead."

Andrew nodded. "I can see that would make sense." Of course it would, he thought. It was pretty much his own approach to his feelings about Prospero. "That explains why you're more relaxed, but her attitude has changed too. What about that?"

Prospero was still watching Leonie as he answered. "I don't know for sure, but I think she's starting to trust me, us even. Last night she was off campus, but she hadn't meant to be and even in the nightmare she was trying to get back to us. And then Nick suggested the hospital and she was terrified, and she considers that I was the one who saved her from being taken there."

Andrew didn't have to reply as Leonie came bounding back towards them, all signs of fear and apprehension gone.

"It's beautiful," she said. "How far does it go on?"

Prospero smiled at her and stepped away from the parapet, indicating that she should look over.

From the outside, the hospital appeared to be a huge square block some five storeys high. From this vantage point, the reality was very different. At ground level the hospital was built around several interconnecting courtyards, with roofs at every level. It looked haphazard but Prospero explained that it was designed so that every ward, clinic, staff room or public place had access to outside space whether that was a courtyard, roof garden, terrace or balcony. Every roof at every level either formed part of that outside space or housed solar panels to contribute to the hospital's energy needs. From this high point, the garden wound its way down to ground level through a series of slopes and steps, although it was not a short journey.

Leonie looked up at him in clear delight. "Can we see it all? Can we walk through it? I never knew it was here."

"Yes, we can walk through it. Only, I'm not having you overexert yourself today, so once we get to the bottom we're not coming back up which means the way out will be through the main reception hall."

Her face dropped a little at that. "But will you be there all the time?" she asked.

He reassured her, "Yes, I'll be there, I won't leave you alone."

"So I'll be safe?"

"Yes, you'll be quite safe."

She nodded her consent and then turned to Andrew. "Will you be there too?"

He shook his head. "I'll walk with you part of the way, but

I'm on duty later. I won't have time to come all the way down."

Telepathically, he spoke to Prospero. *"Not overexert herself! That's rich given you're the one putting extra stress on her."*

"All the more reason to be careful. I told you, I know what I'm doing."

"Yeah? And what about not being alone with her?"

"You're here with me."

"Not for that long."

"This is a public garden, well overlooked."

"I seem to remember you knowing all the private spots!"

"I don't plan to show her them!"

Andrew shrugged and accepted that. There was no changing Prospero's mind when he was in one of these moods. The three of them ambled through the gardens, Leonie distracted frequently by the different plants. Andrew and Prospero both had a good working knowledge of common medicinal herbs, but Leonie's knowledge of the rarer ones was far more extensive.

On the other hand, Andrew was amused by Leonie's surprise at Prospero's detailed knowledge of the wide range of flowers and greenery used to decorate hospital, House and Abbey.

"While everyone in the House has a job – you're a student, we're doctors, Pedro's the chef," he said. "We've all got a domestic role, too, to keep everything functioning. You work in the kitchens, I work in the stables, but Prospero works in the gardens, so naturally he knows about the plants."

Leonie frowned. "How can the kitchen be Pedro's job and my domestic role? Aren't they different things?"

Andrew agreed, "Yes, they are different. But everywhere, gardens, kitchen, stables, the workers will be a mix of those for whom it's their job and those for whom it's their domestic role. But those for whom it's their job tend to be more senior, and in charge in each area."

That satisfied her and she went charging off to look at another plant that had caught her eye.

About halfway down they reached the point where Andrew had to leave them for his hospital duties.

"Be careful," he told Prospero telepathically, still concerned.

"It'll be fine," Prospero replied the same way, his body language emphasising his confidence, even if telepathy couldn't convey it. Then he pointed over to the outdoor terrace seating for the hospital's restaurant a short distance away and spoke out loud. "We're going to go and sit over there, and get something to eat and drink."

He turned and smiled reassuringly at Leonie. "It's too cold to sit outside, but we'll sit right by the doors and I'll go over to the counter and order for us both."

Still not convinced the rest of the journey would be trouble free, but constrained by the need to fulfil his medical duties, Andrew left them there.

Chapter 21

Leonie

I watched Prospero as he went over to the restaurant counter. After our sessions at the start of the year I figured I could trust him to find something I liked to eat and I really didn't want to go any further in. When Prospero told me we were going through the hospital itself, I'd been terrified but I hadn't been able to say no to him. And I'd survived. So far.

The gardens were amazing and I wondered, if I'd known they were here and how to get to them, would I have been brave enough to try it? Would I be brave enough to come back, on my own? I had an idea there was far more to them than Prospero was showing me and I was longing to take the time to explore them in real depth. I was enjoying Prospero's company too. Okay, he was bossy and thought he knew best but I'd won on the matter of the hats and he'd looked after me at breakfast time and he was working hard at making sure I felt safe and relaxed now. Which I did, I realised, as he came back with hot chocolate, fruit and muffins.

I decided to take the opportunity to ask Prospero about the nightmares, particularly when they might end.

"I don't know," he said heavily. "I'm sorry, Leonie, I just don't know. I've been researching it and I just can't find anything helpful. It's more Andrew's area than mine but he can't come up with anything either."

He'd already been looking for something to help me? I couldn't believe anyone would take that much trouble over me. I must have looked puzzled because he went on.

"There's a biological sex bias in Gifts. In males, Gifts tend to start to develop around sixteen or seventeen, the nightmares peak around nineteen or twenty, and then peter out by about twenty one. Male Gifts tend to be based around telekinesis – moving things – and pyrokinesis – setting fire to things – which is what makes their nightmares dangerous to others. Although a few may have telepathic or clairvoyant based Gifts, males practically never have these unless they already have one or more of the others."

He paused and looked at me. "In females, the Gifts start to develop younger, maybe fifteen, and reach their peak around eighteen. But because their Gifts are normally those associated with telepathy or precognition, the nightmares only affect the dreamer and aren't dangerous to others. I can't find any records of females with your range and strength of Gifts at your age. There are a few who have telekinetic Gifts at fifteen which fade within a year or so, and a few who develop them later, after their other Gifts and that's it."

He sighed and continued, "So I don't know whether yours will be over soon because you're female, or last longer because of what they are, or something in between. I'm sorry."

I hadn't known about how gifts divided between male and female but that made a lot of things clearer. It explained why Katya had told me about here rather than the convent, why Lord Gabriel had chosen to keep me in an environment geared to male students, and why Prospero himself had thought I was likely to cause chaos anywhere. But there was something I hadn't told Prospero and it wasn't going to make things any easier.

I started hesitantly, "You said gifts develop around fifteen in girls?" He nodded confirmation, so I went on, "I can't remember a time when I couldn't do this stuff. It's got easier and better and stronger and just more as I've got older, but I've always been able to do some things."

He looked at me; I couldn't read the expression on his face.

"I've never come across anyone whose Gifts developed before puberty," he said. "I don't know how that would affect things. When did you start having nightmares?"

"You mean the ones where I do stuff?" I'd always had the more conventional nightmares, still did, but I didn't think he meant those. "Two or three years, perhaps a little more. Some before the Traders left me here. More since then."

He looked a little more positive. "Two or three years already could mean they'll be over sooner. How often are they happening? I know of the one in December, one when you hurt your arm, one last night. Have there been any others?"

I looked down at the table, fiddling with my mug, knowing I would have to confess. "A couple of others. I wasn't sleeping here. They happen at least every couple of weeks now."

He shook his head, but there was concern in his eyes. "That's too many. Even I only had about one a month, and that was too many. You must find them very draining."

I shrugged. "It's not like I have a choice about it."

Inside I was overwhelmed that he was concerned about the impact on me, rather than what I might do to others.

He sighed again. "There are options, you should know that."

I looked up sharply and he must have seen the hope in my eyes as he continued, "Don't get your hopes up. They aren't particularly good options, but there are drugs you can take or shields you can use to stop them. The only thing is, they'll cause your Gifts to fade and eventually disappear."

I shook my head. I didn't have to think about that. "I couldn't give them up. They're part of me. I wouldn't be me without them. I'd rather take my chances with the nightmares."

"I thought you'd say that. It's what I'd say if I were you," he said, smiling slightly. "It's what I did say, when it was me."

I found that interesting. He'd been asked to make this choice, too, so he must have an idea of what it all felt like. I wondered how he'd coped with the nightmares. He didn't answer that, but he did speak again, "I'm going to tell you this because I don't want you to make a mistake that could destroy your life. Some of the older students are bound to tell you that you can stop the nightmares with drink, or by having sex, or taking recreational drugs. Don't try it, it's not worth it."

I didn't understand why they'd say that, if they didn't work.

"It's not that they don't work exactly," he told me. "They'll each buy you a night's sleep free of nightmares. Only each time you'll need a bit more to achieve the same effect and pretty soon they'll take over your life and destroy your health. You only get the one body, you need to respect it, look after it, not abuse it."

He sounded as if he was speaking from experience. I'd been told he was pretty wild as a student, lots of girls and parties, but that didn't seem to tie in with him being a monk. Anyway it didn't change my choices.

"So, I can put up with the nightmares, or give up my gifts, or choose drink, drugs and sex? That's not really a great set of choices, is it?" I said, somewhat bitterly.

He looked as if he was trying to make up his mind about something, then he spoke. This time he was the one fiddling with his mug, not looking at me. "There's another option. It's better than the rest, but it's not without its own difficulties. You need to find someone you trust, someone who cares about you, and share a bed with them. I mean just to sleep, nothing more. If you find the right person, it stops most nightmares and reduces their impact when they do happen."

That was also pretty interesting and probably explained why the nightmares had got worse when the Traders had left me behind. Before that, I'd hardly ever slept alone. I wondered if this was how Prospero had dealt with his nightmares and that must have shown in my face because he answered my unasked question.

"Yes, I had someone like that. It helped a lot."

I thought it must have been Andrew, but I didn't say so.

Prospero had sort of closed up and there clearly weren't going to be any more revelations. Instead he stood up. "Are you ready?" he asked.

I nodded and we continued our journey through the rooftop gardens. Much as I loved the gardens, I became more and more hesitant as we got closer to the bottom and the moment when I would have to face walking through the building itself. Lower down I felt more closed in, as if the walls were hovering above me, trying to trap me. As we stepped into the bottom courtyard I found I was shaking and having difficulty breathing.

Prospero realised immediately how I was feeling and made me sit down on a bench in the courtyard.

"Breathe slowly," he instructed then he squatted in front of me so our eyes were at the same level. "Do you think you can drop your shield and let me into your mind so I can help you?" he asked.

I tried, I really did, but I couldn't bring myself to drop it, and I couldn't find the words to tell him that I was trying but that I couldn't do it, so I just shook my head.

"Never mind," he said. "It was a lot to ask under the circumstances."

He sat down next to me, close so that his body was touching mine, with one arm along the back of the seat behind me. I could feel he was trying to radiate calm and reassurance, which did help a little as did the contact with him. My breathing eased, even if I was still shaking. We sat for a while and then he told me to look through the doors into the main reception hall.

"Look," he said, "you can see right the way through to the exit, so you'll be able to see the way out all the time. And it's just full of ordinary people, children and parents, young and old, staff and patients, probably even some people you know." He went on and although I didn't take in all the words, his voice was soothing and calming too. "Now," he said, "see if you can feel any shields between us and the exit."

I found I could try that, and there were no shields in the direct path, just one or two small ones off to one side which I told him I'd found.

"That's right," he agreed. "There's no shields over the main part, but any patient can ask for the shields to be switched on in the individual consulting rooms to the sides if they want. That won't trouble us."

Next, he got me to listen telepathically to the superficial thoughts in everyone's minds – not pinpointing thoughts to individuals, just the general mass of chatter.

"There's nothing threatening or frightening there, is there?" he asked me.

I shook my head.

"So, ready to go?" he asked, standing up and offering me his arm.

I was pretty sure I wasn't ready but it was now or be stuck here so I took a deep breath and we set off. I concentrated on putting one foot in front of the other and remembering to breathe. Part way through I started to feel even more panicked. My vision blurred, colours swirling around me. I could hear my heart beating so loud it threatened to deafen me. I couldn't breathe. I was trapped in the middle. The exit was too far away. Prospero moved so that my hand was in his and his other arm was round my shoulders, his body against mine protectively.

"You're okay," he said. "You're doing really well. Only a few more steps to take, you can do it."

I found I could. A few moments later we were through the front doors and out onto the plaza in front of the hospital.

He let go of me slowly and I turned to look at him.

"I did it! I did it."

He was grinning as widely as I thought I must be. "You did. Well done."

In my excitement I flung my arms round his neck without thinking, and he can't have been thinking either because he put his arms round me and spun me around before standing me down. He was still smiling as he spoke.

"Come on, it's nearly lunchtime and I reckon we've earned it today."

Prospero

Prospero watched Leonie as she ate lunch. Lord Gabriel had welcomed them to his table, seating Leonie next to him and Prospero on her other side. After a shy start, Leonie was now talking to him about the roof garden and the uses of various herbs, her hands moving as she emphasised some point.

Privately, Prospero was feeling relieved that the morning's activities had gone as well as they had. Sitting with her in the lowest courtyard, he'd realised that he didn't have a contingency plan and at that point he hadn't been at all sure she'd make it through the reception area. Taking her to the roof garden and out through the hospital had been an impulsive act and with someone so scared there should have been planning, preparation and back up. But she'd made it, and he'd got away with it so he wasn't going to dwell on what might have gone wrong.

His supervision of her would end with the end of this meal and she'd be fine to return to everyday life and duties as he would also have to. He found himself thinking about and trying to plan when he could next spend time with her and then thought that was probably going rather further than Chloe's 'accept it when it happens'. Still it wouldn't hurt to check up on Leonie in a couple of days, and he could also suggest to Andrew that they have a session reviewing how she was doing with the development of her abilities. And Leonie's birthday was coming up, her eighteenth; maybe he could suggest to someone that they make something of that.

Lord Gabriel turned to him, and Leonie twisted slightly in her seat so that she was facing him too. She had that gleam in her eye that suggested she was up to something, probably mischief.

"You and Andrew need to keep an eye on what Leonie is learning about the use of her Gifts," Lord Gabriel said. "I think she may be racing ahead of some of the other students and we might need to adjust her classes."

Now Leonie's look was positively smug, though she wiped it off her face before Lord Gabriel could see it. Prospero agreed with Gabriel immediately, but that idea was so close to what he'd been thinking he now worried that Lord Gabriel might be reading his mind. Then he told himself not to be so silly. He should know that wasn't possible. Their thoughts must just have been going along the same tracks, probably because Leonie was sitting between them. He looked up and saw Lady Eleanor glancing at him from further down the table. He'd have to be careful. He wouldn't want to raise her suspicions about how he felt about Leonie. On the other hand, she might be a very good person to talk to about Leonie's birthday.

Chapter 22

Gabriel

Lord Gabriel returned to his office after lunch and sat back in his chair, contemplating the last few weeks. He was feeling very much better today despite the papers on his desk containing yet another report of unrest between Houses. Over Christmas and the early part of the new year he had pushed Leonie and Prospero into each other's company and then fretted about the potential consequences and whether he was doing the right thing. Then he had worried that they weren't spending enough time together and that this might derail his plans, whilst being relieved that he wasn't placing Prospero in a dangerous situation he couldn't cope with.

When Prospero had come to him, asking for a retreat, he had kept his pangs of guilt to himself. He had toyed with the idea of telling Father Stephen about the whole situation but in the end had decided not to. Father Stephen was a good and godly man; Gabriel had trusted to God that Stephen's direction and work with Prospero would fit with Gabriel's understanding of God's purpose. In some ways, he had hoped that it would not, because that would relieve him of this burden that he felt sure he was handling inadequately.

But Prospero had returned and Gabriel had spoken to Stephen, and clearly he was going to have to continue along this difficult path. Reports of fighting and skirmishes between other Houses kept coming, putting more pressure on him. None of this had done his ability to sleep any good at all. He had prayed for help, and waited for an answer.

Last night, when he'd consigned Leonie to Prospero's care, Eleanor had touched his arm.

"I would sit with her, I'd be happy to," she'd said softly.

"I know," he'd confirmed. "But she's already disturbed you one night recently and you have duties during the day. Prospero and Chloe were expecting night duty, they'll manage this way."

She'd looked at him sharply. "You're up to something, Gabe, I can always tell. I don't want anything happening to Leonie."

He'd sighed. "Are you growing that fond of her, Ellie?"

"Yes, I am. She's a lovely girl that's been badly hurt. She's good company and I want her to feel safe. And I think you need to be careful with Prospero. It's my opinion he's falling for her."

Gabriel had smiled. "You've always had a soft spot for him, too, haven't you?"

"He was good for Mel," she'd replied. "I think it's time you told me what's up."

He'd looked at her in some indecision and then agreed. They'd found somewhere quiet – one of the small chapels within the Abbey where they were very unlikely to be disturbed. Gabriel realised, with a huge sense of relief, that of course he could utterly trust Ellie, and indeed she had all the manipulative skills that he needed. Clearly, her involvement was the answer to his prayers. He had told her everything – dreams, visions, letters, jewellery, and his fears, worries and guilt.

"Oh, Gabe," she'd said, and he still wasn't sure whether her tone had been sympathetic or reproachful. "Why didn't you tell me at the beginning? You've had to deal with this on your own for a couple of months when I could have helped. Honestly, Gabe, you still need to learn when to ask for help."

"Sorry, Ellie," he'd said, "I thought... No, I don't know what I was thinking. I should have told you much sooner."

"You've done pretty well so far, at least for a man," she'd told him, with a smile. "This really isn't your area at all, is it?"

He'd shaken his head and then confessed the likely outcomes. The possible death of either or both of Leonie and Prospero had shocked her into momentary silence. Once she'd recovered her voice, she'd told him off severely and he'd hung his head and accepted it as a minor penance for his actions. Whatever else, though, he knew Ellie had a real deep faith. She understood and accepted why he was doing what he had to do although he wasn't entirely convinced she agreed.

"I'll help you all I can," she'd said, "but there's a condition. You have to do all you can to make whatever time they have as good and as comfortable and happy as possible."

He knew Ellie would help him no matter what but he had agreed because he wanted to do that anyway.

"Right," she'd said, "we need to make this easy, but not too easy. Remember, forbidden things are always more attractive. Prospero's already all but fallen for her and he can be very charming when he chooses. You need to make sure they have the opportunity to spend time together. I'll have a think, but first off you should make sure it is always Prospero who deals with her after a nightmare."

"I thought of that and did that tonight. Aren't you proud of me, Ellie?" He'd smiled back at her. Ellie was the one person in the world whose good opinion mattered to him and she knew it.

"I'm always proud of you, Gabe, but that's just a first step. I think it would be a good idea if you arranged for Prospero and Andrew to reassess Leonie's abilities. She's had six weeks or so of classes and that one soaks up information like a sponge. She's probably way ahead of her class already, and that's another excuse to bring them together. By the way, who else knows?"

"I've only discussed it with Benjamin. I don't think he will forgive me if we do lose Prospero. I think Edward suspects something."

"I wouldn't be surprised. He knows nearly as much about what is going on round here as you and I do. Anyone else?"

"Pedro might have an idea. And I asked Chloe to make friends with Leonie, which she seems to have done."

That had interested Ellie. "Chloe? Now she might be very useful indeed."

Gabriel had been a little alarmed. "You're not to corrupt Chloe! It's bad enough what we're doing to Prospero and Andrew."

"Who said anything about corruption? And anyway, I doubt Chloe is half as innocent as you think."

Having engaged Ellie's support Gabriel had slept better last night than he had in days. This lunch time he had accomplished his first task and told Prospero to reassess Leonie.

He leaned forward and picked up the top report from the pile on his desk. He could safely leave Prospero and Leonie in Ellie's hands and await her instructions as to what he should do next. He had plenty else to occupy him. Glancing at the report, he smiled to himself; he wasn't going to be able to forget about Leonie quite yet. This report was from Lady Sarah on Leonie's academic progress.

When Sarah had assessed Leonie, early in the new year, she'd found Leonie's knowledge typical of a Trader youngster. She was fluent in both the common language and the Trader one. Her reading was good, her handwriting appalling through lack of practice, and her maths limited to basic arithmetic. Her knowledge of history, geography and politics were only what a Trader would need to plan a good trading route. Gabriel hadn't wanted to overload Leonie academically, but to keep the emphasis on training her Gifts. So he'd limited her classes to maths, handwriting and early Post Devastation history. She appeared to be doing well in all of them. Good, that was another thing he didn't have to worry about.

The next report he picked up was from one of the watch team technicians. They had spotted a signal being broadcast from the campus over the last few months and couldn't find the source. That was easy to deal with too. It would be one of the wealthy non-adept students over in the college with some gadget provided by their High Lord. He'd pass it over to Lady Sarah to sort out.

If only all his paperwork was this straightforward.

Chapter 23

Mid February

Leonie

The Them surrounded me, wafting towards me, stretching cloaked arms towards me. I ran, desperate as always to get away. But this time, some part of my mind was outside the nightmare, telling me that the watch team would be on the way, that all I had to do was stop and wait and hold the Them off until they got there.

I tried it; I stopped, turning towards the Them behind me. They stopped too, and I pushed power hard at them to keep them away. They moved, again surrounding me, reaching to grab me. I lit a circle of fire; the Them backed away, unwilling to cross the fire. Where was the watch team? I couldn't see them; I didn't know what they'd look like in the dream. Surely they should be here by now? How long would the Them be afraid of the fire? How long could I risk waiting to be rescued before I had to take more action?

Then someone seized me from behind, turned me round, and I woke to find myself standing in front of Prospero, his hands on my arms.

He looked down at me. "Well done," he said. "You trusted us. You stayed and waited and we came."

I could smell smoke, burning, and I looked around. We were on the grassed centre of one of the courtyards; a number of the plants looked the worse for wear and there was a ring of burnt, scorched earth around us. Several people were tidying up.

"Well done?" I said bitterly. "Look what I've done, the damage I've caused."

"No one was hurt," he said. "And this is nothing, it'll be put right in no time. We've seen much worse before. I've done worse myself."

I wasn't consoled. "I could have hurt someone."

He pulled me close against him and put his arms round me. "No, you couldn't. And you didn't. It's okay, it's all over now."

I didn't believe him. I just leaned against him, shaking and sobbing with the aftermath of the nightmare.

Prospero

The watch team had struggled to get to Leonie. Prospero had approached her from behind, using a bucket of earth to dampen the fire in his path. She hadn't seemed aware of his presence so he'd simply reached out for her. Now he held her close trying to offer peace, reassurance and safety whilst she came to terms with waking up.

He was trying to deal with his own feelings of guilt about her nightmare.

At his insistence, he and Andrew had had a couple of sessions retesting Leonie's abilities the previous week. They'd both been surprised how much easier she had found all the tests that Andrew had set. She had to have been working hard in class, and it had paid off.

After one session she'd asked them if there were any more rooftop gardens like the one over the hospital. They'd glanced at each other for a moment or two, discussing telepathically whether they should tell her about the other one.

"I know when you're talking about me," she'd said. "You might as well say it out loud before I work out how to listen in on your conversations."

Prospero had been alarmed. No way could he risk her listening in on his thoughts. "That's not possible," he'd said.

Andrew had been amused by it. "Want to bet Leonie won't be the one to discover how, if anyone does?" he'd asked. Then he'd turned to Leonie. "Most of the courtyard buildings and the Abbey itself have solar panels for heating and energy on the roofs but there is one other roof garden. I'm sorry, though, you can't go there, it's restricted to those in the Order."

Leonie had had that look in her eyes. The one that said she was planning some mischief.

"I can tell when you are planning trouble," he'd said. "Don't go looking for it. If you want to go back to the hospital roof garden, I'll come with you anytime I'm free. Or Andrew will."

He'd found a couple of opportunities to take her to the roof garden. He'd made her pay for it by also making her explore more of the hospital each time. She'd definitely been getting more comfortable with the hospital, but he hadn't taken her near the wards, or the clinics or anywhere that she couldn't always see windows and a door and a way out.

But such activities – both stress and using her Gifts a lot – made nightmares much more likely and now she was paying for it.

Benjamin was the duty doctor tonight and he came over to them whilst the others put out the remaining fires and picked up the various items of debris.

"Let's get you back to bed," Benjamin said to Leonie.

Prospero wasn't sure she'd heard, but he turned her towards the buildings to get her moving, keeping his arm close around her. She flinched against him and he looked down, realising she was barefoot and had trodden on the embers of one of the fires. He lifted her straight into his arms.

"Benjamin," he said urgently. "Her foot, she trod on the fire."

Benjamin took a quick look. "It's okay, nothing serious. Bring her back to her room and we'll deal with it there."

Prospero carried her, unaware until they reached her rooms that they'd picked up something of an entourage including Gabriel, Eleanor and Chloe. He looked around with curiosity, it being the first time he'd been there since she'd moved in. He thought the space was not exactly bare, but rather blank, not really reflecting her personality. There were study books and classwork on her desk in the outer room, a small Bible and a library book by the bed but little else. He tried to put her down on the bed but he could feel the power rising in her along with her panic, and she clung to him so he sat on the bed himself and continued to hold her close. Benjamin shooed the entourage into the outer room and came back with the sedative for her to drink.

She refused, burying her face in Prospero's shoulder. "It'll come back," she whispered.

"No, it won't," he said, deciding firmness was called for. "Would you rather do this the hard way?"

She shook her head, assuming he meant the hospital. Actually, he wasn't quite sure what he meant because he had no intention of subjecting her to the hospital.

"So drink," he instructed. "The nightmare won't come back."

"Promise?" she asked.

"Promise," he confirmed, and she drank.

He held her for a few minutes longer while she fell asleep and Benjamin dealt with the minor burn on her foot and then he placed her in the bed. Gabriel decreed that Lady Eleanor and Chloe should sit with Leonie. Prospero was sent to get some sleep and assigned to supervise her the next morning. Benjamin and Gabriel went back to their duties.

***

Prospero had a feeling that he been pulling more than his fair share of night duty but it meant he had a better chance of being around if Leonie needed him so he wasn't going to call attention to it. Sent back to his room, sleep now eluded him. He tossed and turned, concerned over how worried Leonie had been about the damage she'd caused, and afraid it would put her off sleeping in her room. He wanted to be there when she woke to reassure her again but at least he'd have an opportunity during the morning. In the days since her last nightmare, his head had been all over the place. Most of the time, as Chloe had advised, he'd coped by concentrating on his actions rather than his feelings. When his feelings got too much, he tried to avoid Leonie and bury himself in work and worship. He never managed it for very long. With the exception of prayer, Father Stephen's strategies, however sensible they seemed, had proved pretty much unworkable.

He had spent considerable time praying and meditating over the studies that Father Stephen had set him and discussing them with Lord Gabriel. He decided he had two options. Either he could choose to stay in the Order, in which case the only fair thing for both him and Leonie would be for one of them to be transferred to another location. Or, it was time for him to leave the Order and deal with whatever God had for him outside. Now his problem was to face up to which was the right option – to determine the one God was directing him to. At night, waiting for sleep to overtake him, as he was now, he was tormented by fears of opening up all the issues that had almost succeeded in destroying him in the past. He chose to pray and eventually he slept.

Eleanor

Lady Eleanor decided to take advantage of the night to talk to Chloe and see what information she could glean. She was in no particular hurry, but Chloe gave her an opening early on.

"Do you know why Brother Prospero is so afraid of how he feels?" Chloe asked quietly.

"What makes you say that?"

"Well, obviously he's in love with Leonie, and clearly she feels the same, yet he's trying to deny it."

"You don't think his vows have something to do with it?"

Chloe shook her head. "We all take our vows expecting them to be for life, but we all know that there may come a time when we're called to leave the monastery. It seems to me that's what God's doing with Brother Prospero, so why is there a problem?"

"You're going to make a very good Abbot one day." Lady Eleanor told her, smiling. "I agree with you and I don't really know the answer. I don't know much of Prospero's background, but I think there were expectations placed on him that he couldn't fulfil and he came to college to avoid them. Then joining the Order also protected him from them. Once he leaves, it may be possible those expectations are resurrected. If he couldn't face them once, maybe he's concerned that he can't face them again?"

"I suppose that's possible. But it seemed to me to be more about being afraid to be close to Leonie, worried about having a close relationship, about something that had happened in the past."

"Ah," said Eleanor, understanding, "that'll be about what happened here before he joined the Order."

Chloe looked at her expectantly, and she carried on, "It's quite a story. When he started at the college the combination of those external pressures and his Gifts gave him nightmares. Early on, he had a girlfriend, I'm sure he slept with her, and that helped keep the nightmares under control. Then something happened and she left, not just him, but the college, too. After that he tried other methods to stop the nightmares."

She sighed. "My daughter didn't help him. She was trying other methods, too, at the time, mostly to rebel against me. I know they both slept around, I know they drank, I don't know if there were drugs but I suspect there were. That, and Brother Andrew, got Prospero through most of his studies, but then Andrew was called to join the Order. Prospero didn't take it well and then he had one nightmare the likes of which I hope we never see again. He ended up in hospital, quite badly hurt – it'd been almost as if he was trying to hurt himself. It marked a change in him. We had two or three very traumatic weeks as he recovered and stopped his abusive behaviour and then Gabriel accepted him as a novice in the Order. It wasn't easy for him for a long time after that but he's always been very committed." She paused again. "He'll be worried that without the boundaries of the Order he'll revert to his past behaviour. He won't, he's changed a lot since then, but I can see how it might concern him."

"I've always thought of Brother Prospero as finding things easy. He seems so strong, so secure in his faith, so sure of the right thing to do. You never realise just what might be behind what you see, do you?"

Lady Eleanor agreed, "No, you don't. I think there's a lot behind what we see of Leonie, too. You said you thought she was in love with Prospero, too?"

Chloe nodded. "I'm sure of it. But she's afraid, too. And she doesn't think she's good enough for him, of course."

Lady Eleanor thought for a moment. "Do you know, Chloe, I think that's been very helpful. Perhaps we need to help them both get over their fears. I shall have to give that some thought."

They continued to chat, on and off, through the night. Eleanor ventured one or two ideas, Chloe had some of her own, and they refined their plans as the night progressed.

After breakfast the next morning, once Leonie had been consigned to Prospero's care, Eleanor hurried to Lord Gabriel's office.

"We're making good progress, Gabe," she told him. "But they're both too afraid of what might happen if they take things further. We need to make Prospero more afraid of losing Leonie than of leaving the Order. What is it that he's afraid of, outside?"

"I can't tell you, Ellie."

She glared at him. He told her everything, confessing all the secrets of Prospero's background. Once she looked at him like that he knew there was no point in holding out. "But I'm working on it," he added. "It's just rather delicate, interfering in the workings of another House."

She accepted that. "We'll have to work with it, then. I'll help you."

He shook his head. "I'm still having visions, Ellie." he said, despondently. "And I don't think anything's getting any better out there, whatever I do."

Eleanor was as aware as Gabriel of the reports of trouble and discord across the world, and that they seemed to be increasing.

"Show me the visions then," she said gently. "Let me help with them, too."

He did so, linking their minds as they had often done before. In the surreal nature of dreams, both timelines seemed to run together. The war took place in one, vicious and destructive. In the other, he now knew the monument as a memorial and it varied who he saw there. Mostly it was just Andrew, sometimes Prospero was with him. Eleanor understood the torment immediately.

"It's the hope, isn't it?" she said softly. "That's the hardest bit. The hope that the worst won't happen. If it was certain that it would, you could deal with it. It's the hope that it might not."

They were together later that day, their minds still linked, when Gabriel had a particularly tantalising version of his vision. Andrew, Prospero and Leonie were all by the monument and Andrew was carrying a small child, a boy with Leonie's colouring and Prospero's smile. It shook both Eleanor and Gabriel so much they had to go sit in the Abbey chapel for a while to recover.

Chapter 24

Leonie

As I always did when I woke, before opening my eyes I reached out with my mind to see where I was and who was around. My last conscious memory was of clinging onto Prospero because he was the only way to keep Them at bay. I tried to find him so I could be sure I was safe, but he wasn't there. Instead I found Lady Eleanor and Chloe. I was in my own room, so I figured I was okay to open my eyes and admit to being awake. As soon as she realised that, Lady Eleanor was business-like, making me get up and wash and get ready for breakfast. Chloe was just Chloe, reassuring and helpful and happy. It was difficult to be either scared or miserable around Chloe because she just radiated contentment, whatever she had to face.

The three of us headed to the dining hall together and sat at one of the smaller tables, rather than the high table. Prospero joined us.

"You've got me keeping an eye on you again this morning," he said cheerfully. "Where would you like to go? The roof garden again?"

I shook my head. I wanted to share somewhere I liked with him this time. "How far can we go? There's somewhere up in the woods."

"I'm afraid we need to stay on or near the campus—the wood is too far for today," he said.

I didn't feel like arguing. "Then can we go to the Old Chapel and down by the river?" I asked.

He nodded. "Of course, no problem."

The weather was still cold and he made me wrap up well

again, although he didn't even try to make me wear a hat this time. Andrew didn't come with us which surprised me but Prospero said he was busy. I supposed he was working. I wandered into the Old Chapel and, as I always did, walked along the side wall, running my fingers over the memorials, feeling out the engraved letters.

"Are the stories true?" I asked Prospero, idly. "The ones about the Devastation?"

The Traders had said that once our world had been home to ten billion people. The demands of its inhabitants had been too much for the world and it had responded with earthquakes and volcanoes, hurricanes and tsunamis, floods, drought and famine. The first memorial commemorated those who had died as a result of these natural disasters and included a pledge to take care of the earth and live sustainably upon it.

The first time I'd heard this story I'd expected the survivors to work together to help each other. But instead they'd fought each other. Traders told of weapons that could kill millions and leave the land around unusable for generations. I had my doubts. If resources had been scarce why would anyone use weapons that destroyed them further? But I'd seen the edges of the Badlands, even now only just being reclaimed, and the ruins of what were said to have been cities housing millions of people. The second memorial was to those who had been killed in the Final War, with a pledge to try to live at peace with each other.

The natural disasters and the War had been followed by disease and plagues, which had killed more billions. That was the subject of the third memorial and this one pledged future generations to respect and care for each other.

"True enough, I guess," Prospero said. "Every legend has a grain of truth at the centre. The important thing isn't always the facts but what we learn from them."

I supposed that was right; the important thing here was not the events but the pledges to do better. The first communities rebuilding the world tried to establish an environment where they kept those three pledges. Now we had the Great Houses, whose leaders met in Council over matters which affected the world, but they didn't interfere in each other's jurisdictions. Each Great House had any number of High Houses pledged to it which it represented and similarly the High Houses had Low Houses pledged to them. And individual farms and homesteads and businesses and crafters all pledged themselves to a Low House.

My mind drifted elsewhere. "Is the Bible true, then?" I asked him.

He smiled. "Have you brought me here to interrogate me?"

"No, I just wanted to know," I told him.

"I believe that the Bible is the word of God," he said. "I happen to believe that it is factually and historically true, but again, what is really important is the message it has for us, how we use it to inform and change our lives and behaviour. Facts and legends and stories can all have important lessons for us."

"Does it mean the same to everyone?"

"No, that's what I find so fascinating. The same passage can have different messages for different people depending on their circumstances. The same passage can even have different messages for the same person at different times. What we read is a translation and sometimes you get different translations which seem to have different messages. I like to think that each version has its purpose as a message for someone, at some time."

That satisfied me for now. I went across to the other wall, the fourth memorial, my favourite, commemorating the early adepts. I reached out, touching and stroking some of the names there.

Prospero pointed to one of them. "She was my ancestor, many generations back," he said.

I looked at him in amazement. "You know who your family was, that far back?"

"There are records," he said shortly. His face closed up and he turned away for a moment. He recovered quickly though. "You never know," he said, "one or more of them could be your ancestors, too. In fact, with you being so Gifted they probably are."

I'd never thought of that and I liked the idea. It gave me a sense of belonging. Prospero seemed relaxed so I chose to push him a little to see if I could find out any more.

"You said you have brothers. Do you have a lot of family? Are they all gifted?"

He looked at me and I wondered what he was thinking.

He came back with a question himself. "Is family important to you?"

Was he joking? Of course I wanted a family, I wanted to belong. I should have known better than to ask him such a question; it was always like this with Prospero and it was so easy to end up telling him more than I meant to. I shrugged. "I guess. I think it must be nice to have one, to belong."

He smiled. "Yes, it is."

I thought that was going to be all I got, but he carried on, "I've got five brothers, all younger than me. My parents are farmers and Matt, the oldest of my brothers, really loves the land, the farm. Sam, who comes next, is very good with animals and then there's the twins, Jack and Eddie, who train horses. There's a bit of a gap to Jonny, the youngest. He's Gifted, but he's only eighteen so we don't know how Gifted yet. The others, not so Gifted."

"Do you miss them?" I thought I was being very daring but I got an answer.

"Matt and Sam, yes, especially at first, but it was my choice and it's been a long time. I'm used to it. The others were that bit younger so I don't really know them the same, especially Jonny. I write to them, and they write to me, almost every week."

I couldn't understand how he could stay away from them. I knew I wouldn't be able to if I had a family. I was silent for a moment and now it was Prospero's turn to ask the questions.

"Do you like it here?"

I nodded. "It feels safe. And it's so quiet and peaceful. I come here when I need to think."

"I used to do that, too," he said. "I should do it more often. Mostly these days I go into the Abbey, but there's often someone else there."

We ambled out again and walked alongside the river. There were several places where rocks and boulders went right out into the water. In some of those places, you could climb all the way across the river. We chose to stop at a place where the river curved, giving a broad low grassy bank. To one side of the curve was a line of boulders and I walked and climbed out along it until I could stand on a large one right in the middle of the river. Prospero watched for a moment and then followed me. He stood behind me and I leaned against him, feeling the wind as it blew along the river, listening to the sound of the water as it flowed.

"Okay," he said quietly, and I could hear the rainbow in his voice, like when he was singing. "I can see exactly why you like this."

We stood a little longer and then clambered back to the bank. Prospero had brought hot drinks and snacks so we had a picnic. I sat, leaning back against him again and thought that I'd never felt so happy.

"Talking of legends," Prospero said, "some of those boulders we walked on are remnants from before the Devastation."

I looked at him in surprise.

"Have you heard of the Badlands?" he asked.

"I've been to them," I told him, feeling a little smug.

Now it was his turn to be surprised. "You can't have. They're dangerous, no one goes in."

"There are people reclaiming some of them," I said, very pleased to know something he didn't for once. "They're working from the edges in and the Traders deliver to them. I've been a few times, and once I went more than a mile in as they showed us their plans and what they were going to do next."

He shook his head in disbelief. "You never fail to surprise me. Anyway, you'll have seen the ruins there then?"

I nodded, and he carried on, "The people then didn't just build where the Badlands are, they built all over, roads, bridges, huge buildings. Some of the boulders in the river are the ruins of what they built near here. Probably a bridge."

We sat there for a while quietly. I didn't want this morning to end and Prospero seemed reluctant to go back, too.

"It's an escape," he said. "A few minutes or an hour away from life's day-to-day pressures. We can take our time."

Chapter 25

Late February

Leonie

We might have taken our time, that day, down by the river, but one thing I couldn't put off any longer was thinking about everything that had been happening, especially my feelings for Prospero. I left the dining hall after lunch one day and walked down to the Old Chapel. It was empty as usual but I couldn't risk anyone disturbing me, so I curled up under the altar table where any other casual visitor wouldn't spot me.

Amongst the Traders, men and women would normally pair-bond around my age, certainly not a lot older. So I'd been involved in a few conversations about how the brides-to-be felt about those they'd chosen. What I was feeling for Prospero wasn't a whole lot different from what they'd described.

But I didn't dare fall in love with him; people I loved left, or more often, died. I didn't want that to happen to him and I couldn't face it happening to me, not again. I didn't know what to do. Once again I was back to the choice of leave or stay, and neither seemed a good option. If I left, where would I go? This was where I was meant to be. If I couldn't be safe here, if I couldn't be here at all, I had nowhere else to go, and no reason to carry on. I wasn't a Trader, nor a Settler and I never would be; there was no point in returning to them.

Yet, if I stayed, how could I deal with my feelings for Prospero? Avoiding him wasn't an option. I bumped into him for one reason or another every day. Obviously my feelings couldn't develop into anything given his vocation. But in that case did the fact that I cared about him put him in danger in the same way that everyone else I loved had been? Or did that mean he was safe?

And how safe was I from him? I'd already recognised that if he asked anything of me I'd give it. Look how I'd agreed to walk through the hospital when I was terrified.

Most Trader girls would be pregnant when they pair-bonded. That was part of the point of the bond – every caravan wanted sons to add to its strength and daughters to add to its prestige. If Prospero asked anything physical of me, I knew I couldn't, wouldn't resist, far from it. I wanted him to want me like that. I ached for the touch of his hands on my skin, daydreamed about the softness of his lips on mine. And far, far more – which potentially could put another life at risk. The Traders weren't ignorant of contraception even if they rarely used it, so I knew of herbs that I could use, but I didn't know where to find them round here.

Briefly, I contemplated discussing the whole thing with Chloe, or even with Lady Eleanor. But how could I? Chloe was a nun, she wouldn't possibly understand. Lady Eleanor would just tell me I was being silly, and not to worry about it. And I didn't think I could tell anyone without letting on it was Prospero who concerned me. That wouldn't be fair on him because he'd done nothing wrong.

In the end, I remembered that I'd heard of clinics in the lower part of town where I could get contraception, no questions asked. And they were nearly always in a community hall, so there were no worries about going into the hospital. That decision made me feel just a little bit more in control. I would stay for now and see what happened. After all, if I left before the end of the month they'd just come looking for me anyway.

I headed off to town the next morning. I knew the clinics were frequent and it wouldn't take me long to find out where it was today.

Andrew

Andrew enjoyed clinic duty, particularly the variety of things he had to deal with. The town surrounding the Abbey attracted migrants and refugees from harsher regimes who tended to be poor in both money and health, and untrusting of those in authority. The Great House and hospital tried to arrange frequent free clinics in unthreatening locations to assess migrant needs and to encourage improved health. Today's was based in the town in a room off an old hall, and many, but by no means all, of the patients had been there for antenatal care and the extra vitamins and food the clinic provided. He called for the next patient, and then continued with some paperwork as he waited. He heard the door open and someone enter.

"Andrew, I didn't know..."

He looked up in surprise.

"Leonie, what are you doing here?"

She started to back towards the door.

"No, don't go," he said, trying to make his actions match his resolution not to blame her for Prospero's issues. "If there's something you need, I could help, you don't have to leave."

She allowed herself to be persuaded to sit down, but she was unwilling to look at him.

He asked gently, "What's the problem? How can I help?" And then he realised that he meant it, that he no longer saw her as the root of Prospero's problems, but as someone as vulnerable as any of the refugees, in need of care and support. "Anything you say to me will be confidential."

Suddenly, she looked him straight in the eye. "I need contraception."

That did surprise him; he thought he would have known of anyone that close to Leonie. He kept his face blank. "Would you prefer to see a female doctor, or have someone else with us?"

She shook her head. "No, this is fine."

He looked down to make some notes. "Okay, then," he said. "I can help you with that. I didn't know there was a young man on the scene."

At her silence he looked up again and saw her face. In that moment her feelings became clear to him.

"Oh, Leonie, no," he said sympathetically, understanding now.

She spoke hesitantly, "I wouldn't be able to say no to him, I couldn't, I wouldn't want to anyway. But I can't risk a child. I want children, I'd want his child, but I couldn't take care of one now, I can't risk it."

"You're not in any danger. He won't ask."

"You can't be sure."

"I know him, better than he knows himself. However he feels, he can't and won't break his vows."

"I have to be sure, I don't expect anything from him, he can't know how I feel, but I can't take a risk because I can't trust me. You of all people must understand."

Andrew sighed. That was much sharper, much more perceptive than he'd given her credit for. He hadn't realised she'd worked out so much about his relationship with Prospero.

"Yes, I do understand. I'll help you, and it will be confidential." He looked at her. "You understand that he doesn't know how I feel either?"

She nodded. "Slow, isn't he?" she said with a weak grin.

That made Andrew laugh. "There's a few things I need to check before prescribing anything, okay?"

They carried on talking while he checked her blood pressure and listened to her heart, their conversation interrupted from time to time for medical queries and issues.

"He's no prize, you know," he told her.

"He is who he is," she replied. "You can't help who you have feelings for. He irritates me beyond measure sometimes, and other times he can be so nice, so understanding, but it doesn't make a difference which."

"It doesn't, no."

She was curious. "How do you deal with it? Early on, I was confused, I thought you were a pair, a couple except that he…"

She clearly didn't know how to describe it so Andrew stepped in.

"Except that he appreciates women rather than men?" he said with a smile. She nodded and he continued, "How did you pick all this up? It's a monastery, we are all celibate. It shouldn't be an issue nor obvious."

She frowned for a moment, thinking. "I don't think that changes what you are, what you feel, and I could sense that. I think it changes what you do about it. At least here it seems to. I've come across other places where it doesn't always."

He was impressed. "I think that's very well put. And it's your answer. I don't indulge how I feel. Instead I take it to God and leave it with him, and put that energy into other things. And I try not to get into situations I would find difficult. I'm not saying it's easy, though it has got much easier with time, but it does work.

We're friends, we care about and support each other. It doesn't need to be more."

Leonie was doubtful. "I don't know how to make that work for me. I haven't got anywhere else to go and I don't think I could keep out of his way, not for long, not if I stay."

"No, perhaps not. It would be difficult on a day-to-day basis. And anyway, he'd come looking for you, unless Lord Gabriel ordered him to stay away. Even then, he'd find it difficult. Your abilities fascinate him. He's very competitive and no one has challenged him like you have in a very long time, if ever."

That pleased her, as he knew it would, and he paused for her to take it in before carrying on. "But, Leonie, please don't leave because of this. I'm starting to think of you as very much part of our family. You belong here just as much as he does, and I'd hate to lose you."

"I suppose I'll just have to work out my own way of dealing with it," she said.

"Yes," he agreed. "But if there's anything you think I could do to help, you just have to ask."

She nodded, obviously a little overwhelmed by this offer.

He understood. He passed her a box of tablets. "We're all done for now. You're free to go when you're ready. These tablets will last a couple of months. Just come and find me again about a week before they run out."

She smiled her thanks at him and headed for the door. Impulsively, he called out to her as she was about to leave, "He's struggling with his feelings, too, if it helps."

She looked back over her shoulder. "It does. Thank you. For everything."

Then she was gone. Andrew paused before calling in the next patient, wondering what he was supposed to do. This was way past the 'encourage a friendship between them' that Lord Gabriel had asked of him. Gabriel should know how things were developing so he could take any necessary action. Yet he had promised Leonie confidentiality, just as he would for any patient. He sighed and concluded that he'd just have to find a way of dropping a hint to Gabriel without actually telling him. As for Prospero, it wouldn't be fair to tell him anything, he was finding things difficult enough as it was.

Leonie

I escaped from the clinic and headed off to find somewhere private to recover. I hadn't even thought that the doctor would be someone I knew, let alone Andrew. I shuddered at the thought that I might even have walked in on Prospero. When I saw Andrew, I'd nearly run then and there, but he'd been so kind and caring when I'd thought he disapproved of me – and he'd said he didn't want me to leave. I'd misjudged him badly.

On the downside, he now knew exactly how I felt about Prospero but he had said everything would be confidential, so I'd have to trust he wouldn't tell. Did that promise override his loyalty to Prospero or not? It was too late to worry about it, if it did. On the plus side, I'd got my contraception, and there was someone who understood how I felt and was willing to help me when I needed it. And, if he could manage his feelings and stay around Prospero, then there was some hope for me. When I thought through everything that Andrew had said, it seemed to me he'd dropped several hints about how Prospero might feel about me. Hugging those particular thoughts close to myself I set off back towards the Abbey.

I felt a bit awkward the next time I saw Prospero and

Andrew in the dining hall, given what Andrew now knew about me but it turned out to be okay. Andrew was much friendlier than he'd been before – not that he'd been unfriendly before, just sort of neutral. He whispered the odd funny comment to me when Prospero's back was turned – usually about Prospero – and once or twice I struggled not to laugh out loud. It felt like we had something of a bond and I realised that I now had a real ally in what I faced.

Chapter 26

End of February

Prospero

In the end it was Lady Eleanor, not Prospero, who suggested a birthday celebration for Leonie. They settled on a simple cake and a small gift after the evening meal on the last day of February. However, Prospero was involved in the discussions about the choice of a gift. Pedro suggested jewellery, which Gabriel vetoed. Chloe suggested that she be given a Bible. Eleanor was horrified to think that she didn't have one.

"She does," Prospero said, "But it's just an old one from the pile in the Abbey. I saw it in her room the other night."

Edward disappeared to search in the depths of his stores and came back with a pocket sized Bible in the latest translation, bound in soft blue leather. He passed it to Lord Gabriel.

"That matches her necklace," Prospero said.

"And the dress she had at Christmas," Eleanor agreed. She took the Bible from Gabriel and stroked it. "I love the smell of new leather," she said, inconsequentially.

It was that comment that gave Prospero the idea for the plants.

"Leonie loves herbs," he said. "Especially aromatic ones. And her room's really bare. We could pot some up for her."

Andrew had some good suggestions about which herbs and plants to choose, and then Prospero had to negotiate with Sister Soraya in the gardens for the supplies he needed. Lady Eleanor assisted them with the final execution.

Somehow, despite being sent to fetch Leonie for the

evening meal on her birthday, Prospero didn't end up sitting next to her. Andrew managed that honour, with Lady Eleanor on her other side. Prospero was on the other side of the table, and a seat further away than Andrew. Frustration and jealousy competed for control of his emotions.

"You don't need to protect me," he said privately to Andrew. *"I was fine looking after her the other day. I can handle it."*

Andrew stared at him calmly.

"Can you?" he asked, equally privately, *"You shouldn't be using telepathy here. Someone will feel the power."*

Prospero all but growled back before he subsided, but he did glance along the table to check who might feel it. Fortunately, those on either side of him weren't Gifted, and it was Chloe opposite Leonie. Even if she felt something she wouldn't say anything. And that glance meant he realised that he was in a good place to watch Leonie throughout the meal even if he was a little far away to talk to her. She looked relaxed, chatting with those around her, which puzzled him. She had to be aware that from today they couldn't hold her, that they wouldn't come after her, didn't she? If she was so afraid of being trapped, shouldn't there be a sense of anticipation around her today, in contemplation of the freedom ahead?

He forced himself to relax, aware of tension in his shoulders, generated by his own fear that she would leave them, that she would leave him. Towards the end of the meal, Leonie got into a dispute with Andrew about the medical uses of a couple of herbs. That made Prospero smile, although he tried to keep it to himself; both those herbs were ones he'd planted up for her. He picked up the dispute as they left the table, manoeuvring so that he was now beside her, and saying something provocative just to get a reaction.

It worked as a distraction, and she followed him into the neighbouring room where they had cake and the gift ready. Her face was a picture as she realised, but he felt a sense of unease emanating from her, and made it his business to stay close by her, radiating calm.

He followed Leonie back to her room after the birthday celebration, telling himself that he just wanted to make sure she was alright and not overwhelmed by what they'd done. In fact, he wanted to be close enough to be able to sense her reaction when she saw the planters in her room. Lounging on a bench in the courtyard outside, he achieved that and her joy and pleasure brought a satisfied smile to his face.

Although he was pleased with himself, once night came sleep eluded him again. He couldn't help but dwell on the fact that Leonie was now eighteen and he'd have no excuse to go after her if she left at any point. Somehow she lit up his life. It seemed as though up to this point it had been grey and now it was all the colours of the rainbow. Perhaps that was related to how he saw her in different colours, he thought, amused for a moment. He struggled to imagine life without her or without the Order and he couldn't manage either. What he wanted was both, which was clearly impossible. How was he supposed to know which way God was directing him – was Leonie a test of his commitment and faith, or was she the path he should take now? Was what he wanted – or what he feared – clouding his vision?

And suppose he left the Order and she didn't want to be with him, didn't feel the same way about him, what then? He would be at the mercy of his fears, having lost everything. And if he wasn't with her, how could he be happy not knowing how she was faring? He continued to turn these thoughts over, tossing and turning until sleep eventually found him.

Leonie

I'd followed Prospero into the small lounge next to the dining room without thinking. What I'd found there was a group of people, all the ones I'd come to know and trust, wishing me happy birthday, and a cake, specially made by Pedro. And Lord Gabriel had a gift for me.

"Just a token to mark your eighteenth birthday," he said, as he passed me a small package, neatly wrapped and decorated with a small bow.

I didn't know what to say, I was so overcome I was tempted to turn and run but there was someone between me and the door. Then Chloe touched my arm and I could feel her calm so I took a deep breath and faced up to it all. I unwrapped the gift to find a Bible, all my own, and Lord Gabriel had also inscribed it. I would treasure that. To my surprise, I actually enjoyed the time although we weren't there for long as everyone had duties and responsibilities to get to.

I wandered back to my room, thinking about what my birthday meant. I had vague memories of celebrating it from when I was a small child and then it had become irrelevant. When I was with the Traders anybody's birthday was an excuse for a rest day; it just didn't matter whose birthday it was. The big problem was that if it wasn't a leap year I didn't know whether to have my birthday on the last day of February, or the first day of March. Here, I'd decided it was just easiest to ignore it, at least publically. But privately, to me it meant freedom. After my birthday, I could choose to leave and nobody would chase after me. Not that I planned to leave yet, I just wanted it to be my choice whether I stayed.

When I got to my room I had a further surprise. Placed around the room were at least a dozen small pretty planters containing herbs and there was a message on the desk, which simply said 'Happy Birthday'. I had to look at each planter to see what was there. They included several of my favourite aromatic herbs, as well as ones that I used most frequently. I wasn't sure who was responsible. Prospero had had quite a smug look on his face all evening, but he couldn't have done this without help. And I suspected the influence of Andrew in some of the choices of plant. I moved them around a little so each came as close to its ideal growing conditions as possible, and put a couple of the sweet smelling ones in my bedroom. I drifted asleep with the scent of them in my nose. When I woke, it would be March and I would be eighteen.

Chapter 27

Early March

Gabriel

For Gabriel, the next stage of Ellie's plans involved an interview, or at least a conversation with Leonie. He found he was dreading it, more nervous than he'd been about anything in a very long while.

She's an eighteen-year-old girl, he told himself. *You have nothing to be nervous about.*

Yes, he'd answered himself, *and the fate of the world hangs on the actions of this eighteen-year-old girl. You want to send her to her death. Be nervous, be very nervous. If you get this wrong...*

There was another occasion where the fate of the world hung on the answer and actions of a teenage girl, he thought. *Had the Archangel Gabriel felt this nervous when he was sent to tell Mary of the coming of the baby Jesus? Or didn't Archangels get nervous? What would have happened if Mary had said no? Was she the first or only one the Archangel visited, or the first one to say yes?* Pushing these thoughts aside as distracting and irrelevant, Gabriel geared himself up to face Leonie.

She appeared promptly at his door, stopping on the open threshold and looking around, clearly uncertain as to whether she should just enter. *She's as nervous as you are.* He came round from behind his desk, smiling at her.

"Come in and sit down," he said, gesturing at the comfortable seating area. "I had Brother Pedro send up some cookies. Would you like one? And something to drink?"

Leonie smiled at him shyly, nodded, helped herself and sat down, although she perched on the edge of the seat. Gabriel lowered himself onto an armchair nearby and forced his body to relax. He took a deep mental breath. *Here goes.*

"Both Lady Sarah and Brother Andrew tell me you've been progressing well in your studies. Have you been enjoying what you've been learning?"

***

Sitting at the head table at the start of the evening meal, Gabriel was starting to grow concerned that Leonie was nowhere to be seen. *Did I say something wrong to her earlier?*

He thought back over their discussion. After a hesitant start, Leonie had chatted happily and she hadn't seemed either antagonistic or scared. After her academic progress they'd covered her plans for the future (uncertain, she'd not really looked past completing her studies) and how she felt about marriage (open to it, with the right person). He'd pointed out that as her High Lord and guardian he could arrange a marriage for her if she wished (no, and he'd coaxed out of her that there was someone she felt like that about who wasn't available).

"Tell her very subtly," Ellie had instructed, "that, even though you'd never force her, some High Lords and parents have the authority to arrange their children's marriages no matter what. And make sure she knows that God can just as easily call someone out of the monastery as into it."

I did that, I know I did.

In fact, Leonie had looked quite interested at that and he realised that, by his phrasing and conjunction of subjects, he'd insinuated there was someone amongst his monks who felt strongly about her. Whilst that might be true, he hoped he hadn't given too much away. He'd finished by saying how welcome she was as part of the House and how he hoped she'd stay once she'd finished her studies because he valued her very much. He didn't quite understand what Ellie was up to, but he was sure he'd played his part adequately, at least. *So why isn't Leonie here?*

Out of the corner of his eye he could see Prospero, fidgeting, and continually looking around the room and at the doors, not paying any attention to his food. Andrew was beside him, a hand on his arm, whispering quietly in his ear, a calming influence. Eleanor looked unconcerned, eating and conversing as though nothing was wrong.

"Ellie," he said to her telepathically as the meal ended, *"she hasn't turned up. I've done something to scare her away."*

"Calm, Gabe. I expected this. Prospero is about to come over and ask permission to go and find her. Let him, but be reluctant. Don't seem eager and don't make it too easy. You can send Andrew with him."

Just as Eleanor had predicted, Prospero came over to Gabriel.

"She doesn't miss meals," he said, "at least not the evening meal. And she's not on campus."

"She's over eighteen, she's allowed to leave if she chooses. We're not committed to fetching her back," Gabriel told him.

Prospero protested, "I don't think she's run away. She's a few miles away, but she's not moved since I spotted her. If she was running away she'd be shielded, trying to hide from us. And she doesn't feel right, there's something wrong but I can't tell what. She could be hurt. Let me go get her, this time at least."

"Oh very well then," Gabriel conceded, "If you think she's hurt then you'd best go. Take Andrew in case you need help. And if she's that far away, take horses. Only two, mind. If she is running away, I'll not make it easy for her to take one of my horses with her."

Prospero left quickly, Andrew following in his footsteps.

"Well done, Gabe," Ellie said. *"That should get them going nicely."*

Chapter 28

Prospero

Andrew and Prospero rode mainly in companionable silence, clearly neither in the mood for their usual discussions.

"What are you so worried about?" Andrew ventured after a while. "She's not hurt, is she?"

"I don't think so." Prospero wasn't sure what was wrong. "She seems sort of withdrawn. Her image is fainter than normal. I think she's anxious, or worried, or frightened. I can't tell."

They rode faster after that. Eventually Prospero brought them to a halt and gestured through the trees to one side.

"There's a small clearing just through there – she's on the far side of that."

"You go," instructed Andrew. "I'll tether the horses and bring the bags."

Although he knew where she was, it still took Prospero a few moments to spot Leonie as he entered the clearing. She was sitting against a tree on the far side, curled up into a tight ball, and didn't look up as he raced across to her. Even before he knelt down beside her he was straining every sense to see if she was hurt.

He spoke urgently, but gently, "Leonie, what's wrong? Are you hurt?"

He almost hoped she was; at least he would be able to do something about that. At the sound of his voice she turned her face towards him with a look of such apprehension and sadness that he wanted to scoop her straight into his arms and reassure her. Resisting the temptation, instead he placed his hand on her cheek.

"Not hurt," she whispered.

"Then what is it?" he queried, urgency and concern still in his voice.

She looked at him for a moment. "Why?" she asked. "Why do you come and find me?"

Thrown by the unexpected question, Prospero prevaricated for a moment, "Why us, or why me?"

Leonie shrugged. "Either. Both."

Prospero took the easier option, "Because we care about you and we worry about you. You matter, you're important to us. We want you to be happy and cared for, and you're not safe out here alone in the cold and dark. There's any number of people in the house who care about you; you matter to them, to Lord Gabriel, to your friends." He paused for breath and stood up, reaching to draw Leonie to her feet with him, and sighed, "Heaven help me, Leonie, you matter to me."

He looked at her then, his hand still on her cheek, and saw the tears running down her face. "Oh, Leonie," he said, "I didn't mean to make you cry."

Too much for him to resist any longer, he pulled her into his arms and cradled her head against his chest. She came willingly.

"I'm not a child," she said.

"I know," he confessed, as much to himself as to her.

They both looked up at the sound of Andrew entering the clearing, but Prospero kept his arms around Leonie.

"Come on," he said, "Andrew has food, and I'm guessing you're hungry."

As they crossed the short distance to Andrew, Leonie had one more question. "Why you?"

Prospero smiled at her. "Because I can always find you," he replied. "Now sit down."

Leonie complied, but she hadn't finished. "Will you always find me?"

Prospero looked at her thoughtfully. "Do you want to stay? Do you want me to find you, always?"

She nodded, slowly.

"Then I will," he told her.

"Promise?" she asked, her voice pleading.

She seemed desperate for reassurance. There was no way he wouldn't give it, but he smiled at her, unable to resist teasing her a little. "What's with this need for promises? I said I would."

She just looked up at him silently, eyes full of loss and sorrow, and he was instantly repentant.

"Yes, I promise," he confirmed. He turned his attention to other matters. "Are you warm enough?"

He had kept his arm around Leonie as they'd sat down and wrapped his cloak around both of them so she was benefiting from the warmth both of his body and the cloak. She nodded again.

Andrew held a mug out to her. "Here, drink this." Then he passed her a savoury roll. He communicated telepathically with Prospero. *"Is she okay? Not hurt? What was the matter?"*

"Just overwhelmed that we care enough to come and find her."

"We or you?"

"Either. Both."

Out loud Andrew offered Prospero a choice of hot drinks and then passed him the requested mug of coffee.

"There's some chocolate pastries here, too," he added, which got Leonie's attention.

Prospero indicated her savoury roll. "Eat that first," he instructed, "and make sure you eat it all, no putting half of it in your pocket to share with whoever it is you think needs it more than you do. Who is that, by the way?"

Leonie just stared at him.

"Don't you trust me enough to tell me?" Prospero continued.

Andrew interrupted, "Don't be so unreasonable, Perry. Someone else's identity isn't her secret to share. It doesn't mean she doesn't trust you."

Prospero turned towards Leonie, "Is that right? You can't tell me who but you would if you could? You know I would only want to help whoever it is?"

Leonie, with her mouth full having just taken a bite, shrugged in confusion.

Andrew interjected sharply again before Prospero could speak, "And that means you're asking a complicated question that doesn't have a yes or no answer when she can't talk because she's eating like you told her to."

Prospero looked at Leonie. "And is that right? Just nod or shake."

Leonie nodded vigorously, nearly choked trying not to laugh at Andrew telling Prospero off, and then shrank back against Prospero's side in embarrassment and confusion. Prospero tightened his arm around her.

"I'm sorry," he said, "it's been a long day. Concentrate on eating, the rest can wait."

Leonie swallowed. "Perry?" she said. "He called you Perry?"

"Prospero's quite a mouthful for a small child," he explained. "Everyone called me Perry as I grew up until, well, until I joined the Order. Now there's only Andrew that uses it, and not much at that. I suppose my parents and brothers would still use it, but they don't really get the opportunity."

"Perry," repeated Leonie thoughtfully. "I like it. It suits you."

"Well, I'm so glad my childhood nickname meets with your approval," responded Prospero and then realised that the comment he intended to be sarcastic was actually true.

Leonie just smiled at him. While she continued eating, he and Andrew fell into discussing one of the day's cases where they had a disagreement of diagnosis. Prospero was very aware of Leonie's body next to him, warm and soft, growing closer and heavier as she relaxed against his side. Despite enjoying it, he tried to ignore the sensation, afraid that he would distract her from eating. As a result it was Andrew who noticed that Leonie had fallen asleep, curled up against Prospero.

"I don't think she has any issues with trusting you," he commented.

Prospero twisted to look at Leonie.

"Is she asleep? Now what do we do?"

Andrew nodded in reply. "For a start why don't you see if

you can lift her up onto your lap. I think you'll both be more comfortable. I'll fetch another blanket to keep her warm and then we'll work out how to get her home."

One arm still round her shoulders, Prospero was already sliding his other arm under her knees to lift her as Andrew went to fetch the blanket. Leonie stirred as she was moved but just settled her head against Prospero's chest and moulded her body to his without waking. He rested his cheek gently on the top of her head but looked up as Andrew returned and together they tucked the blanket round her.

"I'd rather not wake her if we don't have to," Prospero said, "I'm sure she sleeps badly because she's afraid the nightmares will happen."

Andrew agreed, "Right now she's able to sleep because she's convinced you'd stop any nightmares."

"I can hardly spend one night, let alone every night, being close enough for her to sleep," Prospero responded with a hint of bitterness in his voice. "Even if it's what I want to do. And anyway, you're just as good at stopping nightmares. You could always stop mine."

"Bet I still could," said Andrew smugly, "but the point is, she believes in you."

They were silent for a moment, and then Prospero spoke again, "She's tearing me apart, and I don't know what to do."

"You don't look very torn," Andrew replied. "In fact, right now you look remarkably content! And anyway," he added, "it's not her doing the tearing, it's you not being able to decide which is the right path to take."

"Oh, stop sounding like Lord Gabriel!" Prospero retorted.

"I'll take that as a compliment," Andrew said with a smile.

Prospero had to smile, too. "Seriously, though," he said, "how do I know what I am supposed to do? Is she a temptation sent to test me or a signpost to what comes next? When we took our vows I thought they were for life, that's how I meant them. Can God possibly be telling me it is time to move on? How do I know the difference between what I want and what I fear and what God is telling me?"

"What does Lord Gabriel say?"

"He says that the vows are for a time and that may not be for life always, that I've got to determine for myself what God is telling me."

"What do you want to do?" asked Andrew curiously.

"That's just it, I don't know. I like belonging to the Order, I enjoy our life here, it has purpose, I feel fulfilled. I don't want to leave. Then I think about it without Leonie here, however much she drives me crazy..." His voice drifted off for a moment before he picked up again. "I didn't expect to feel like this ever again. And it's more than I ever felt before. But if I left the Order, what do I have? What could I offer her? How can I make promises to her when the ones I thought I was making for life turn out not to be?"

"Just a few minutes ago you made a promise to her without thinking twice. Didn't you mean it?"

Prospero stared at Andrew for a few moments as comprehension dawned. "I did, didn't I? And yes, I did mean it." Unconsciously, his arms tightened around Leonie.

Andrew carried on, "And you do have something to offer, don't you? At the very least you could find work as a doctor, but there's that other stuff isn't there? You leave the Order and he'll know. He'll have a role and a home for you."

"Yes, and that terrifies me. It did then and it does now."

"Would you do it for Leonie? If it was the best way to provide for her, to take care of her?"

Prospero was sure of the answer, but reluctant to admit it. "Yes," he said eventually, "yes, I would. But I wouldn't want her to get swept up into it if it would make her unhappy, and I think that's more likely."

"Have you talked about this with Leonie at all?"

"No," Prospero responded shortly.

"Don't you think you should? It affects her as much as you." Andrew's voice was gentle.

"Of course I should!" Prospero retorted in exasperation. "But how can I talk to her? What do I say? She's too young, our backgrounds are wildly different. Or do I tell her she's an evil temptation leading me astray?" Again, his voice held more than a hint of bitterness.

Andrew sighed. "You tell her how you feel, idiot. Then you find out how she feels, and you discuss the options for both of you. It might make one path or other clearer." He indicated the sleeping girl and added, "Not that what she feels isn't obvious!"

"You think?" Prospero's voice held more than a hint of hope this time.

"Come off it, it's perfectly clear she's in love with you and you with her. The two of you are the only ones who can't see it."

"I hope you're right."

Andrew smiled. "I am. Right now, though, I think we need to work out how we are all going to get home. Do you want to try and wake her?"

"I'd rather not," said Prospero, but he shook her gently anyway. "Leonie, wake up, we need to go home, come on, wake up."

Leonie opened her eyes for a moment, whispered one word, "Perry," then settled down to sleep again. The two men looked at each other, and Andrew burst out laughing.

Prospero laughed too, trying not to disturb Leonie again. "Now look what you've taught her," he said. "She's not going to forget that nickname!"

"She'd have discovered it from someone soon enough," Andrew defended himself, and then continued, "Anyway, I think if we do manage to wake her, she's just going to fall asleep again. If I passed her up to you, do you think you could carry her like that on the front of your saddle?"

Prospero was sure he could; he'd been planning to have her ride in front of him anyway. No way was he going to let go of her before he absolutely had to. He needed her where he could see her, touch her, smell the delicious, herbal scent of her skin, and satisfy himself that she was safe.

Once mounted, Prospero found he was able to hold Leonie in front of him without disturbing her. He kept his left arm round her and wrapped his cloak under and around her. That acted almost as a sling and helped transfer the weight to his shoulders. When necessary he used his Gifts to ensure she was secure. He was a very capable horseman, happy to ride with just one hand on loose reins, guiding his horse with his legs. The ride back was slower than the one out but it didn't take long to reach the campus. Instead of requiring them to dismount, the Gatekeeper waved them through to the inner courtyard. There was a small group waiting for them including Lord Gabriel, Benjamin – he must be the duty doctor tonight, Prospero thought – and Lady Eleanor.

Andrew dismounted first. "I'll deal with the horses," he volunteered, taking the reins of Prospero's mount.

Still holding the sleeping Leonie, Prospero swung one leg over his horse's neck and slid to the ground. The welcome party surrounded him while Andrew slipped off with the horses, no doubt glad to escape.

"Is she okay?" Gabriel spoke first, sounding surprisingly concerned for someone who had seemed reluctant to let the search party go out.

"Is she injured?" Benjamin, reached forward to check Leonie's pulse.

Prospero held her closer. "She's fine, not injured, just sleeping, don't wake her."

He spoke urgently but quietly, and Benjamin dropped back a little, giving Lady Eleanor an opportunity to take charge.

"In that case, bring her up to her bed."

She led the way indoors and towards Leonie's rooms. Prospero followed obediently, aware that Gabriel would still require an explanation.

He rested Leonie's weight on her bed, squatting beside it, her head against his shoulder, whilst he and Eleanor removed her footwear and outer clothing. Prospero laid her head down on her pillow, and Lady Eleanor lifted the covers over her. As he slid his arm from underneath Leonie's shoulders, she turned towards him, still fast asleep as far as he could tell, and clung to him.

"Don't leave me!" she pleaded.

He stroked her head gently with his free hand.

"I cannot stay. Lie down now, sleep."

Still she clung to him. Desperate for something to calm her, he reached into his pocket for his little wooden holding cross, which he placed into her hand. "I cannot stay, but you are not alone, you're safe, sleep now."

It seemed to work; this time she allowed him to settle her back into the bed, and he stood up, staring down at her.

Lady Eleanor broke into his reverie by touching his arm. "She'll be fine now; I'll keep an eye on her."

"Yes," he agreed absently, "Of course she will, thank you."

He turned to leave the room. Eleanor followed him and spoke as he was starting down the stairs. "Don't play with her feelings, Prospero, she's far too vulnerable."

He turned back, spreading his hands towards her. "And I am not?" he pleaded.

Lady Eleanor smiled and reached to touch his cheek. "You are too. But this is your decision to make. You're a good lad, Prospero, you'll make the right one."

"How do I know what that is?"

"It'll come. You're trying too hard, just relax. Right now, go to bed—you look like you could do with a good night's sleep."

Prospero shrugged. "I need to see Lord Gabriel first."

"Gabriel will wait, you need sleep. Go to bed."

She turned back down the corridor and Prospero headed down and out into the courtyard. Gabriel was seated on a bench looking up at the stars.

"Father, I—"

"Sit, be still, look at the stars and think about God's

creation, just for a moment."

Prospero sat down beside Gabriel, tipped his head back and looked up at the stars. His mind was in turmoil, racing, but as he sat there staring at the night sky he found it was becoming quieter, more peaceful. Eventually, he looked towards Gabriel, who was watching him.

"Does that help?" Gabriel asked.

Prospero nodded. "But I still don't know what to do. She is so young."

"Only about the same age that you and Lesley were."

"We were too young – look what happened."

"Well, you are older now, and Leonie may be young, but she's got more sense than Lesley. I doubt she'd make the same decisions."

"That situation will not arise, but no, things would be different. It wouldn't happen again."

"I'm pleased to hear that."

There was a glint of mischief in Prospero's eyes. "It never did happen again!"

"That's not such a good answer. I suppose at least you learnt to be careful. Do you ever think about the child?"

"Yes, but I knew so little about it. Lesley told me around this time of year, so always in the spring I think of it, and her. And whenever I see a child about the right age – it would have been ten or eleven by now."

"A girl I think, it would have been a girl."

"What makes you say that? Do you know?"

"No, I don't know. But there's a woman involved in all the major turning points of your life. Haven't you noticed? Jenny, Clare, Lesley and the child, Melanie, Marie."

Prospero shook his head. "I hadn't noticed. There was the other one too, when I left Marie. The vision, the nestling who made me realise what I'd become."

"How does what you feel for Leonie compare with what you felt for Lesley, for Marie?"

"I never felt anything for Marie, that was just wrong. I was hurting and trying to spread the pain. For Lesley, I would have married her, been faithful, supported her and the child, tried to make her happy. I would have done all that. I thought I loved her, at the time."

"I know."

"I would have married her for duty though, not love, I know that now, I knew it a long while ago. It might have grown into love, I guess it never had the chance. What I feel for Leonie is different, so much more, a different quality. I never felt like this before, not for any of them. I want what is best for her, no matter what. What would happen to Leonie if I decided..."

"If you feel that she is a temptation to be resisted, then what happens to her will be none of your business, I'm afraid," replied Gabriel.

"I might make the wrong choice, just to ensure her wellbeing – if she was somewhere else, I'd need to know, wherever she was, that she would be safe, taken care of, content."

"If that is your overriding concern, would it be the wrong decision?" asked Gabriel with a wry smile. He continued more seriously, "What makes you think it is Leonie who would be sent elsewhere?"

He smiled again at Prospero's astounded face. "That's arrogance, Prospero. Consider that I might choose to keep Leonie here, at least for now. Look, whatever happens, your life here will not continue as it was. You have changed and you cannot go back. There is a new path ahead of you, and your only choice is which way forward."

Prospero sat quietly for a moment or two, lost in thought before nodding. "What do I do next?"

"You carry on praying and reflecting – you will work out what to do. But immediately next, you go to bed."

They rose and headed together across the courtyard to the main building.

Chapter 29

The next morning

Leonie

I woke myself up by rolling over and feeling the smoothness of the sheets beneath my hands and face. Something jarred; I had expected to feel the roughness of grass or the grittiness of dirt. I lay for a moment, eyes still closed, trying to work out what else I could feel. The back of my head was warm with the sunshine; that meant day time when I had thought it was night. I could smell rosemary, and thyme. I stretched out my mind; I was in my own room and there was no one else around. Feeling a little reassured by that, I sat up and noticed that I had something clutched tightly in my hand. Uncurling my fingers revealed it to be one of the palm-sized wooden crosses that many of the monks and nuns had. I had no idea how I had come by it. Bewildered, I thought back through the events of the previous evening to try to make sense of everything.

My conversation with Lord Gabriel had disturbed me more than I'd thought at first, and I'd felt the need to run. Not to, or from, or away, just to run so that the rhythm and action could help me sort out my thoughts and feelings. For once, running hadn't helped – perhaps because I couldn't see any good answer or solution to what troubled me – and eventually I had stopped in a small clearing and curled up beside a tree to wallow in my misery. Whatever Lord Gabriel might have hinted, there was no future for me in having feelings for Prospero. He was a monk, so there was no possibility there. Even if, by some strange chance he ceased to be one, I wasn't the sort of person he could have serious feelings for, however much I wanted that. The things I'd been and done made me totally unsuitable for someone like him. And I didn't dare to have feelings for him – too many of the people I'd cared about had... No, I wasn't going there again, I'd descended into that particular misery last night.

I hadn't been aware of the passage of time, nor taken any particular notice of my surroundings until Prospero had appeared beside me. I hadn't been expecting him, but nor had I been surprised at his presence. It seemed to me that we were drawn together, however much either of us might want to avoid it. He'd been concerned that I might be hurt; from the deep, dark place I was in I'd struggled both to understand him and to find the words to reassure him. His touch as he'd placed his hand on my cheek seemed to make it easier despite, or perhaps because of, the electric effect he had on me. It had provided a light in the darkness, a lifeline, a route out of the pit. I'd needed something more but the question had come without conscious thought. I still couldn't comprehend his answer; obviously I was of some value to the House or they wouldn't have done all they had for me but I had no clear idea of what they wanted in return. It was beyond belief that they would do all this just because I existed, which seemed to be what Prospero had said last night and was what he had always said.

He had paused for breath and pulled me to my feet.

"Heaven help me, Leonie, you matter to me."

I wanted so much to believe that was true, even if nothing could ever come of it. Hope, fear and loss had combined, and I hadn't been able to stop the tears that trickled down my cheeks. He must have felt them against his hand, which had been resting on my cheek.

"Oh, Leonie," he'd said, "I didn't mean to make you cry."

Then he had wrapped his arms around me.

I relived the moment in my head as I thought back over the evening. I'd realised last night that I'd found the place I fitted into the world, where I belonged. I had felt safe – such a strange feeling – protected, and yes, both loved and wanted. It had felt like coming home and it had been so many years since there had been anywhere I could truly call home. My response to his words had been automatic; I so wanted him to think of me as a woman.

I smiled now at the memory. He'd kept his arms around me as Andrew arrived. That was just as well because if I'd let go or he had, I couldn't have remained standing with all these feelings overwhelming me. I had needed more reassurance. I had needed to know that he felt this personally, that I wasn't just a duty.

"Why you?" I'd asked.

His smile and the look in his eyes should have told me all I needed. "Because I can always find you."

Still I had pushed for more, "Will you always find me?"

He had looked at me so seriously as he responded that I had realised he was asking me to trust him with everything, even those things I have always kept hidden. It had taken me a moment but I had summoned up all the courage I could find, and nodded. I had asked him to promise; I'd known it was childish but I hadn't been able to help it.

When he'd answered me with "What's with this need for promises?" I had panicked. Had I misunderstood? Had I pushed too far? Did he not mean what I'd thought he did? Even now, hours later, just thinking about it, I felt the panic rise again from my stomach. He had promised, though. I reminded myself of that. He had definitely promised.

I found I didn't have a very clear recollection of the rest of the evening. I was sure there had been food and drink, along with some mention of a chocolate pastry that I didn't remember eating. I did remember being warm and comfortable, and feeling very tired. Prospero had asked me something that I couldn't answer, but Andrew had leapt to my defence and told him off. I guessed it must have been soon after that when I'd fallen asleep.

I couldn't work out how I'd slept so deeply that the journey home hadn't woken me because usually I woke at the slightest thing. It didn't seem likely that they'd put something in my food or drink because it would surely have been easier for them if I'd been awake and cooperative. Had they thought I'd be uncooperative? That didn't seem likely either as both Prospero and Andrew knew that when I ran it was to get my thoughts straight, not to run away. Could it just be that, subconsciously, I'd known I was safe to sleep deeply close to Prospero and in no danger from the nightmares? Was he the person who could do that for me, as he'd once said someone had done for him? Much as I might want that, it seemed totally unfair, under the circumstances but I couldn't think of another explanation.

Another memory was nagging at me, determined to be recalled. Andrew had called Prospero by a nickname – Perry, that was it. I turned the name over in my head, deciding again that I liked it, and stored it away for future reference.

At that point there was a gentle knock and Lady Eleanor put her head round the door. "Oh good, you're awake. I've got some breakfast for you."

She disappeared again then reappeared with a tray of food, which she put down on the table. She turned to look at me, noticing that I was still turning the little wooden cross over in my hands.

"That belongs to Brother Prospero," she stated. "It was the only way he could get you to let go last night."

I looked up at her, eager for more explanation.

"You fell asleep on them," she continued. "They didn't want to wake you, so Brother Prospero carried you back. He and I brought you up here and put you to bed, but you didn't want him to go. He left that with you so you would know that you are never alone. It seemed to do the trick at the time."

I looked at the cross in a new light and then very carefully put it down on the table beside the tray. Lady Eleanor turned towards the tray, too.

"Now, the chocolate pastry is courtesy of Brother Andrew, who said you missed out last night. Brother Prospero sent a message too; he said to eat the healthy stuff first."

As a matter of course, I reached straight for the pastry.

Lady Eleanor laughed. "Brother Prospero also said that he didn't for a moment suppose that you would."

My hand hovered over the pastry, undecided as to what would now be the most rebellious item to eat first, and then I had to laugh too.

"Go on," said Lady Eleanor, still smiling. "Eat what you choose, I won't tell on you."

As I ate, Lady Eleanor continued, "I've got one more message for you then I'll leave you to eat in peace. Gabriel says not to worry about this morning's classes, you've been excused from them, but he would appreciate it if you would join him at his table for the evening meal."

I looked at her rather surprised. I'd assumed I'd be in some sort of trouble after last night, but clearly not.

She hesitated as she made for the door and then turned back into the room. "Leonie, I don't mean to pry into your affairs, but if you ever need to talk to anyone about what's going on, I'd be happy to listen."

Another surprise; the world didn't seem to be working as I'd expected today but I managed to stammer out my thanks before she left. As the day progressed, no one expressed any negative feelings towards my disappearance yesterday. I hadn't meant to run away or stay out that late or require anyone to come and find me. It was just that I'd been so lost in my thoughts I hadn't noticed the passage of time. Pedro was pleased to see me when I turned up for my shift and even had a batch of my favourite cookies tucked away. Lord Gabriel spoke to me pleasantly at the evening meal as did the others at his table, as though nothing had happened. I didn't see Prospero but I did bump into Andrew who mentioned that Prospero was over at the hospital, working, which was nothing out of the ordinary either.

I tracked down Prospero the next day to give him his cross back. I held it out to him but he folded my hand back over it.

"Keep it," he said. "I can get another and it'll remind you that you are never alone."

"I'm not?" I asked, a little puzzled. I'd felt alone most of my life.

"No, you're not. God is always with you. And if you ever need me, you just have to call me. I promised I'd come and find you whenever you need me to and I will."

With that he smiled at me, turned and headed off wherever he'd been going when I'd found him. I didn't see him for several days after that. I almost felt he was avoiding me, but Andrew said it was just his shift pattern and that it was often more convenient to eat over at the hospital. I didn't have too much time to think about it.

Chapter 30

Late March

Leonie

Easter was coming and the preparations were making Pedro – and Lady Eleanor, Edward and Chloe for that matter – exceptionally busy.

I asked Pedro about Easter one evening when we were alone in the kitchen. We were kneading the bread for the next day, up to our elbows in flour, the rhythmic movement relaxing and conducive to confidences. Pedro smiled happily.

"It's my favourite time of the year," he said. "No matter the extra work, or so many extra people here, I look forward to it all year round, and then it's over too quickly."

"But why? And how? And what's going to happen?" I asked.

"All questions, you, aren't you?" he responded. "Next Sunday's called Palm Sunday," he explained. "From Saturday onwards, our family will start to turn up. There'll be people arriving all week, so we're together for Easter Sunday."

I got stuck on one word. "Family?"

Pedro grinned at me, almost as if he'd been expecting that. Sometimes I thought he had to know what I was but he never said anything about it, or acted any differently.

"Anyone who's got some connection here and wants to come. Brothers and Sisters who work somewhere else now, or who've left the Order, or people who grew up in this House and now live elsewhere. Anyone. They're all family still. Lady Eleanor'll find a room for them, somewhere."

"But what are they all going to do, once they are here?" I thumped my dough in frustration at my lack of understanding.

"We" – and he definitely emphasised that word – "We are going to worship, and celebrate and enjoy each other's company and remember what Jesus did for us."

Now, I was no expert, but I'd read and heard the Bible stories about what had happened. It was thousands of years ago, but they still remembered it. I thought of Jesus as being like the heir to a Great House that was ruled by some other Lord, and everyone thought he was riding into town to reclaim it. They had a big celebration when he arrived. Now that sounded daft to me; I mean either you came with a big army and a battle or you sneaked in to overthrow things from inside on the quiet, surely? Didn't a big party warn the other side that you were coming? Not that it mattered, because one of his friends betrayed him to the authorities who arrested him and then executed him.

I looked at Pedro in surprise. "They killed him," I said incredulously. "You're celebrating someone being killed?"

"No," he said. "Although we will commemorate his final meal with his friends and his death at services on Thursday and Friday. What we're celebrating is that he rose from the dead."

I'd read that bit too, but I didn't believe it. I'd seen dead bodies. They didn't recover.

"How?" I asked. I might have thumped the dough again.

Pedro moved it from under my hands and gave me a fresh batch to knead. "Weren't you paying attention at Christmas?" he asked.

Frankly, no, I'd had other things on my mind. But I did remember we'd been celebrating the birth of Jesus, who was – allegedly anyway – fathered by God.

Pedro didn't expect a response and went on, "Jesus is the Son of God, wholly human and wholly God. God sent him to take our punishment for all we've done wrong, that's why he died, so that we can be forgiven and able to be with God. God raised him from the dead to show that death isn't the end, that evil hasn't won. Because Jesus died in our place, for our wrongdoing, we can have life with God after our death as well as working towards a God filled life here and now."

It made a lot more sense when Pedro put it like that. It was clearly very personal for him, and for Prospero and Andrew and many of the others that I knew.

"It can be personal for you, too," he said.

I didn't think so. I mean, these were all good people, of course God wanted them. I couldn't see why he would want me, not with everything that I'd been and done.

Pedro was gently insistent, "It doesn't matter what you've done, it can all be forgiven, it was for me."

But I just looked at him in disbelief and shook my head, and he didn't pursue it further.

Anyway, given all the busyness and the extra hours and effort we were all putting in as preparation, I was pleased to find I had a free afternoon. The weather was sunny, but still cold, so I wrapped up well – it was so good to be able to – collected some food and things from the kitchen and set off to take it to those I knew needed it. They were pleased to see me and even more pleased to see what I'd brought. They were feeling the cold, though, so I left my coat and gloves and scarf and even my jumper – there were other ways to keep warm, at least if you were gifted, and I'd be fine heading back to campus.

It was such a nice day that I dawdled on the way back and

went the long way round by the lake. In the sunshine, the water was blue and clear and inviting and I loved to swim. And there were ways to keep the water around you warm, if you were gifted, too, tricks I knew that Prospero and Andrew hadn't even thought to test. There was absolutely no one around, so I stripped off and dived in, enjoying the feel of the water flowing over my body.

Gabriel

Gabriel and Prospero strolled towards the lake, one side of which formed a boundary with the campus, taking advantage of the pleasant weather. Gabriel was once more acting under Eleanor's direction.

"Things have gone too quiet," she'd told him. "You need to push Prospero into taking another step. At least get him to spend some time with her."

"And how am I supposed to do that?" he'd asked.

She hadn't given him much idea. "You'll think of something," she'd said.

Gabriel agreed with Eleanor that Prospero had made little progress either with Leonie, or in coming to a decision on his future. Now, walking and talking with Prospero, he found himself reiterating what Andrew had said earlier in the month.

"You need to spend some time talking to Leonie about this. It affects her too. And how she feels could affect your decisions."

"Father Stephen said that how I feel about Leonie is incidental to God's path for me," Prospero countered.

Gabriel just looked at him. That was a weak argument and he was sure Prospero knew it.

"Okay," Prospero sighed. "The real problem is that I can't

tell the difference between my feelings and what God wants for me. Is God telling me to leave the Order to be with Leonie or is that just what I want? Do I want to stay in the Order because I'm afraid of what's out there if I leave, or is it God telling me to stay?"

Gabriel had his own views on this but privately he felt equally conflicted between what might be right for Prospero and what he was trying to achieve with Ellie's help. "I still think you need to talk to Leonie," he said, then lapsed into silent prayer both for Prospero and for help in dealing with this situation.

They reached the lake and, as they walked along the small pebbled beach, a movement in the water caught Gabriel's eye. From a distance it looked like a large fish leaping and diving across the water surface but there were no fish that size in this lake. He stopped and pointed it out to Prospero. Almost at the same moment they realised it was no fish, but Leonie, swimming, leaping and diving in the lake with abandoned enjoyment, unaware that she was being watched. Gabriel sent up a quick prayer of thanks and seized the moment.

"Now's an ideal opportunity to talk to her. You wait here," he said. "If she realises that you are alone, I think she'll come to you. If I stay she'll keep her distance. But she's bound to be cold so I'll send Andrew back with blankets and warm drinks in a bit."

"Gabriel, no," Prospero protested. "I can't, I'm not ready, I don't know…"

"You're going to have to sort this out some time soon, you might as well start now!" responded Gabriel, and set off.

Prospero

Abandoned by Gabriel and with little real choice, Prospero made himself comfortable sitting on the bank and waited for

Leonie to approach. He didn't have to wait long before a tightly rolled bundle of her clothes landed on the bank not far from where he was sitting. Well, that was a use for telekinesis he'd never thought of – make your clothes arrive where you wanted to get out instead of having to leave them where you'd got into the water. On the other hand it probably meant that Leonie was swimming entirely naked.

He groaned at the thought, eager desire and his fear of temptation battling inside him. He watched a ripple move across the lake, resolving itself as Leonie's head broke the surface further along the bank. Leonie turned her back on him as she climbed out and the foliage, thin though it was at this time of year, meant that he couldn't see her clearly. Prospero didn't know whether to be relieved or disappointed. He could see well enough to tell that she didn't bother with a towel, just shaking herself like a dog and pulling her clothes on. His irritation with her behaviour started to rise and she was barely dressed before he stormed along the bank taking his own coat off as he went. Swinging her round to face him, he placed his coat around her shoulders and reached to rub her arms to dry her and warm her.

"What do you think you are playing at swimming at this time of year? And not getting dry properly, putting your clothes on wet, you'll catch your death of cold. And you've got no coat, yet again."

Leonie looked at him in astonishment. "But I'm not wet or cold!" she protested. "Feel!"

It was Prospero's turn to be astonished. Her hair, which he knew had been under water only moments ago, was dry and her skin was warm to the touch. Leonie didn't give him time to absorb this before she rounded on him.

"And I haven't missed any classes or any meals and I'm not late for anything and Lady Eleanor knew when I was expected back and it isn't yet, so why are you following me?"

Taken aback by the attack he spluttered, "I wasn't following you, we just happened to notice you and I was worried about you. And I bet Eleanor doesn't know you haven't got a coat, or that you were planning to swim at this time of year!"

"I wasn't planning to swim so how could I tell her? It just looked so inviting so I did. And I was wearing a coat."

"Inviting? In these temperatures? And what about the coat? Where's that now?"

"Someone else needed it more."

"Yeah? Who? Are you going to tell me?"

"No."

"I could make you." He pressed on her mind with his, to indicate how he could find out what he wanted to know.

"Maybe," she acknowledged. "But you won't, not that way."

His anger seeped away as he realised how close he had come to using his abilities wrongly. "No," he admitted, "I won't."

Without further conscious thought, he dipped his head and touched her lips with his. He wasn't prepared for the electric jolt of desire that coursed through him. Prospero drew back slightly, and ran his hands lightly down her arms, nudging her hands together behind her back where he captured them both in one of his. With his other hand he slid his fingers into her hair and brought her head close to his. Their lips met again but he was still not prepared for the pleasure that flooded his body as she responded, her lips and tongue seeking his. Releasing her hands, he slipped his arm round her waist under the coat, pulling her close along the length of his body. Somewhere in the back of his mind he registered that she was most definitely not cold. Freed, Leonie's hands wound round him, one on his cheek, the other round his neck until she was touching bare skin and sliding her hand inside his collar. The contact brought him back to his senses and he pulled away, running his hands through his hair as he realised what he'd done.

"Leonie, I'm sorry, I shouldn't have done that, I don't know what I was thinking, I didn't mean to..."

"Didn't you?" she asked softly, looking at him, although her eyes were still far away.

"Well, maybe I did," he acknowledged, feeling a need to be honest with her even if not with himself. "But what I did, my actions and my vocation are incompatible."

"How can something that feels right be wrong?"

"It did feel good," he agreed with a smile. Feel right! His senses were still swimming, singing with how it had felt. She nodded, and he went on, fighting to regain some grip on sanity. "Sometimes our desires overcome our consciences and we can't tell what's right anymore."

"Do you regret it?"

"No," he answered. "No, I don't, not for myself. I'd only regret it if it, or the consequences of it, hurt you in some way."

Leonie shrugged, but with a smile on her face. "I'm fine."

"Nevertheless, I shouldn't have done that. Look, I need to think things through, work out what is right and wrong, what I should do. Can you be patient while I do?"

She nodded. "Yes, but right now Andrew is looking for us, and he's not far away."

They moved away from the bank onto the main path, and Leonie slipped her hand in his. He looked at their joined hands for a moment, but didn't move his away. He didn't want to let go, in fact he'd much rather put his arm around her, but if he did that he'd be kissing her again. Holding her hand was just about manageable and it wouldn't matter that Andrew saw it; he knew how Prospero felt anyway. Within moments he spotted Andrew making his way towards them.

Andrew raised his eyebrows at the joined hands but made no comment. He had brought blankets, a spare coat and hot drinks just as Gabriel had promised. Leonie accepted the coat, returning Prospero's to him. He put it back on, feeling its warmth from her body and aware of her scent lingering on it. They spread the blanket out on the bank and sat there to enjoy the hot chocolate that Andrew had brought.

Leonie

Sitting on the blanket, sipping hot chocolate, gave me a chance to gather my thoughts and pull myself together. When Prospero had kissed me, it had taken my breath away. Now, not just my skin tingled at his touch, the feeling coursed through my whole body. When he pulled away I had felt both dizzy and exhilarated and unable to focus. Holding his hand and wearing his coat had made me feel safe and able to function, after a fashion. His coat had been warm from his body and I hadn't wanted to take it off.

Andrew had been quite firm about it. *"Sorry,"* he'd said telepathically, *"but you have to give it back."*

I'd known he was right, really. Now Prospero was talking to me and I struggled to pay attention.

"How did you get dry and warm so quickly when you got

out of the water?" he asked.

I looked at him a bit blankly. I'd never been cold. "I just told the water to go away," I said lamely.

"You just told the water to go away?" he repeated sounding incredulous. "Show me."

Andrew butted in, "I don't think this is a very good idea."

But l leaned over the edge of the bank and dipped my hand in the lake. I held it out to show them it was wet and then told the water to go just like I had earlier. Prospero took my hand, turning it over in his to assure himself that it was dry.

"Do it again," he demanded. "Only this time let me watch your mind to see how you do it."

I felt his mind start to reach towards mine.

Andrew spoke urgently, "Really not a good idea."

Prospero stopped. "No," he said. "There's a better way. Leonie, you touch my mind with yours."

"Prospero!" Andrew said, with considerable feeling.

But I reached towards Prospero's mind anyway. As I touched it I felt his shield recede before me and my mind infiltrated the top layers – and more – of his.

"Excellent," he said, smiling at me.

I twisted the threads of my mind into his where they fitted easily. I could have gone much deeper; he wasn't stopping me but I chose not to. His mind was watching mine settle and I could feel his amusement.

"Comfortable?" he asked.

I nodded and he carried on, "Now, I'm going to follow that

link back towards you. It'll be very light and I'll do it very slowly. You're in charge of the link and you can break it at any time, okay?"

I nodded again and felt his mind moving towards mine. The thread was not weak but delicate, gossamer thin and I knew I could break it without trouble. I almost held my breath as he touched my mind and settled there at the top, not trying to go any further.

"That's as far as I need," he said.

But I *needed* to protect this connection and I wrapped my mind around it, weaving my threads around this delicate one to protect it, give it strength and hold it in place. Prospero blinked at me a couple of times like a surprised owl.

"That was unexpected," he said.

Andrew was getting more and more agitated because he couldn't tell what was happening. "I said this was a bad idea," he repeated.

Prospero waved him away. "Not bad," he said. "Very impressive, just unexpected. I like it. Now, Leonie, show me again."

Once more, I dipped my hand in the water and then told the droplets to go away.

"Ahh," said Prospero, understanding immediately. "So that's how you do it. It's based on telekinesis; you move the water somewhere else. Now again, while I shadow you. My hand this time."

He dipped his hand in the lake and held it up in front of me. I made the water go away but this time I felt his mind following every action of mine.

"Okay," he said. "My turn now, with you watching me."

He reached to dip his hand in the lake again but this time Andrew said "No!" so forcefully that we both turned to look at him.

"At least use something inanimate the first time," he said, weakly. "If it goes wrong you don't know what might happen to your hand."

Prospero dipped one of the cups in the lake and put it down in front of us. I followed his mind while he made the water go. That first time he all but splashed Andrew; I was pretty certain that was deliberate. He had a couple more goes using the cup before trying with his hand but he didn't have any problems.

"Thank you," he said to me and then he tried to retreat from my mind. Only the weave I'd made meant he couldn't, and he looked at me in surprise – and amusement – again.

"You're in charge of the link," he said. "You'll have to break it."

I didn't want to. I found the link comforting and pleasurable, but I could see Andrew's 'this is a bad idea' and 'I told you so' face which convinced me I needed to.

"If you can't," Prospero said telepathically just to me, *"it'll break automatically the moment one of us goes into the Abbey or under any dampening shield."*

But I could, so I unwove the threads, all but one which I kept twisted about his. He could have pulled his thread back at any point now but he didn't. He left the connection whilst we collected up our things and walked back towards the centre of the campus. I liked it, it was even better than holding his hand, it made me feel safe.

I'd linked like this before, with Katya when she'd taught me how, and a few times with people or patients who couldn't tell us what their problem was. It wasn't based on telepathy; I couldn't read his thoughts linked like this and I assumed he couldn't read mine. It seemed to be based on empathy, sensing what someone else was feeling emotionally. There was a way to link slightly differently, slightly deeper, where you could feel any pain or sensations a patient felt – which was what made it useful in treating someone who couldn't speak. There was another variant too, but I'd never had cause to use it. I hoped to, one day.

They said goodbye to me as we crossed one of the courtyards. I didn't break the link even then, and nor did he. They were heading for the Abbey and it would break as soon as they entered – which it did, just a moment or two later. Back in my room, I spent a few minutes thinking about the feelings I'd sensed in Prospero. However confused we both might have felt earlier, by the time we mindlinked, his overriding feeling was one of curiosity. It had been tinged with amusement, except that wasn't quite the right word. He wasn't amused at me, it was more that he was entertained and surprised by the way I'd done things, a way in which he hadn't expected or hadn't thought of. Then he'd been concentrating hard, very focused on what we were doing. He hadn't bothered to shield the deeper levels of his mind; at that point I could have looked anywhere in his head if I'd chosen to and he wouldn't have noticed until too late. That was interesting in itself – was he being careless, or was he deliberately showing me he trusted me?

On the walk back, he'd been mostly the cocky, confident Prospero, pleased with himself at learning this new skill. But under that somewhere he'd been happy, pleased that I hadn't broken the link and I'd also found a sense of reassurance which had helped me. I tried, very hard, not to think about that kiss, but that proved impossible.

By the time the evening meal came round I was feeling pretty tired. I'd used my gifts a lot today for one reason or another and it tended to have that effect. There wasn't much you could do with gifts that you couldn't do some other way without them, and using them usually took more effort or energy than not doing so. It was just sometimes they were far more convenient. Although I tried to hide it, I yawned my way through the meal.

Lady Eleanor and I left the table together, heading towards our rooms which were close to one another.

"I saw you yawning," she said, with a smile. "Have you got much school work that needs to be done tonight?"

I shook my head. "Nothing due for a couple of days."

"Then why don't we go and sit in the library and read for a while," she suggested. "And then you can go to bed early."

"I'd like that," I said and then turned at the sound of hurried footsteps behind us. It was Prospero.

"Leonie," he called, "wait a moment."

I stopped and waited. When he reached us he took my chin in his hand and stared in my eyes, then reached for my wrist to check my pulse and also checked my temperature with his hand.

"I saw you yawning," he said. "Have you been using your Gifts a lot today? More than I already know about?"

I nodded, not sure I could trust my voice. My feelings were swinging between pleasure at his concern and annoyance at his fussing.

"You need to get a good night's sleep," he said. "Make sure you go to bed early. And have you got anything to eat in your room, in case you wake up hungry?"

I nodded again, annoyed with him trying to tell me what to do. Pedro always tried to make sure I had something in case I felt peckish.

"I'll make sure she's fine," Lady Eleanor said, dismissing him.

I felt Prospero's mind stroke mine before he left. The care and concern I felt there dissipated my annoyance but brought back more thoughts of that kiss. I did go to bed early, I couldn't stay awake.

Chapter 31

Easter Week – April

Leonie

Kitchens are dangerous places, full of heat and flames, weights and stress, pressure and speed, and…accidents. I always tried to watch for the accidents that were about to happen, and stop them or minimise them, but sometimes something had to happen, and sometimes people were going to get hurt. All I could do then was make the injury as light as possible, and try to take it myself, of course.

This time, something fell or was dropped and it caught my foot. I made as little of it as I could and held the pain at bay until I could get away. In the end though, I couldn't avoid the pain, merely delay it. Eventually, I was going to have to feel it. So, as soon as I could I made for the ice cold waters of the river. There was a place where a series of large rocks, boulders with flat tops, formed a sort of jetty out into the river. I sat on the end one, lowered my foot into the water and allowed the pain to come. The cold helped and once my foot was numb I curled up on the flat surface of the rock to decide what to do next. The stone was warmed by the weak spring sun and I was tired from using my gifts first to reduce the accident and then to delay the pain. Besides, I was unlikely to be disturbed here and, as I told myself, sleep helped healing, so a short doze would be all to the good.

I slept both deeper and longer than I'd intended and when I woke it was close to lunchtime. Given the choice between hobbling back in time for lunch or numbing my foot in the river again, I chose the river. If anyone noticed I hadn't turned up for lunch they would assume I was eating somewhere else as I sometimes did. I wouldn't go hungry either – later it would be easy enough to find something in the kitchen. Once my foot was sufficiently numb, I moved back towards the bank and sat there for a few moments lost in thought.

My thoughts were dominated by Prospero as they had been ever since he kissed me. In my head I called him Perry, I liked the name, I thought it suited him better. Prospero was calm, confident, self-assured, always in control, always did the right thing, always knew what the right thing was. Perry seemed more human, with feelings and uncertainty. I felt it had been Perry who kissed me the other day, down by the lake, Perry who needed to think things through and work out what was right. Or perhaps I had this all wrong – it had been several days since the lake and there had been nothing more from him. Our paths hadn't crossed naturally but could he have made the opportunity? Perhaps there was only Prospero, perhaps I was imagining the rest, and perhaps he really did regret that kiss and was now keeping clear of me.

Prospero

For Prospero the days up to Easter passed too fast, with little spare time to contemplate his problems. The nights dragged as his thoughts teetered from one option to the other. Unable to sleep, he would retreat to the Abbey chapel to pray. He felt the answer hovered at the edge of his reasoning but however hard he tried he couldn't capture it.

From the day before Palm Sunday, previous residents, monks and nuns started to arrive and the campus, briefly quiet from the end of quarter student exodus, rapidly filled up again. Sitting at lunch in the middle of week, Prospero spotted a past colleague, Aidan, entering the dining hall and waved for him to come over to the same table. Aidan had left some four years earlier, but he and Prospero had often sung together and were good friends. Deeply involved in their conversation – after the usual small talk it had moved onto Aidan's experience of leaving the Order – Prospero ignored the hurried footsteps as someone passed behind him.

Then he heard Pedro's voice, "Lord Gabriel, I'm concerned about Leonie, she hasn't appeared for lunch."

Prospero looked up sharply at the mention of Leonie's name.

"It's hardly compulsory. She's probably eating somewhere else, or gone into town." Gabriel didn't seem worried.

"Well, normally, yes," Pedro agreed. "But there was an accident this morning. Nothing serious, but Leonie ended up with a bruised foot while trying to protect someone else. She's not likely to have wanted to walk far on that. I'm concerned it's worse than we thought and I can't find her."

Gabriel glanced over at Prospero. "Do you think you can find her?"

"Seriously?" Prospero asked. "Does she think she can solve everyone's problems by taking them on herself?" He closed his eyes as he started to search for her. It didn't take long.

"She's not far, just down by the river."

"Is she hurt? Some Trader women can delay the pain."

"She's hurting now, and hungry," Prospero was certain of that. "I'll get my medical bag and go get her."

As Prospero stood up, Pedro passed him a lunch bag. "Here, this is for her, she's always hungry."

Gabriel put out a hand to stop him, too. "I have no one to send with you, this time."

"It's okay," Prospero assured him. "She's close enough that I could call for help if she can't walk."

Aidan

Aidan watched the conversation between Gabriel and Prospero with interest.

"A Trader girl? Here? Isn't that a little disruptive?" he asked as Prospero left.

"To say the least," agreed Gabriel dryly. "My latest ward is highly independent, highly Gifted and highly disruptive. Prospero is about the only one who comes close to being able to manage her and her abilities so he tends to bear the brunt of the disruption. She's an orphan, not really a Trader, she just spent a few years with them on her way to us."

"She's not really disruptive, either," Pedro stated, defending Leonie. "And she's the best worker I've had in the kitchens for a very long time."

Gabriel stood up to leave. "As you can see," he said to Aidan, "she has her champions."

Pedro watched him go. "He's pretty worried about something," he said. "He's as fond of her as any of the rest of us."

"So, will I get to meet this bad influence?" Aidan asked. "And would there be any connection between her and the fact that Prospero is asking about what it's like to leave the Order?"

Pedro sat down next to him. "Is he? I didn't know that. Leonie'll be sitting at Lord Gabriel's table tonight. You'll have no problem spotting her."

"So, as Prospero's smitten with her..."

"I didn't say that!"

"No, no, you didn't, did you? I take it Andrew is not one of her champions?"

"On the contrary, she and Andrew are good friends. I think at least part of the disruption comes from them ganging up on Prospero."

Aidan raised his eyebrows. "Is that so? Interesting. Perhaps it's Andrew that's smitten?"

Pedro didn't deign to answer that. "Seriously, though," he said. "What did you tell Prospero?"

"About leaving the Order? I told him it was hard, incredibly hard, even when you are specifically called out to something, and have the full support of your family and friends outside." He looked Pedro straight in the eyes. "And Prospero doesn't have that, does he?"

Pedro shook his head in agreement, but refused to be drawn further on the matter.

Prospero

Prospero saw Leonie as soon as he approached the river bank and thought she had probably been easing any pain in her foot by soaking it in the cold waters. She was sitting on a large boulder, knees drawn up to her chin and her arms wrapped around them. Even if she looked lost in thought, Prospero was pretty certain she was well aware of her surroundings and that she would try to run if he took her by surprise. He tried to make some sound as he got closer, calling out her name from a short distance away. By the time he reached her she was sitting upright on the boulder looking towards him.

"Perry," she said, by way of greeting.

"Just because you know that nickname doesn't mean I've given you permission to use it," he said with a smile, aiming to bring some humour to the situation.

"I rather think you have," Leonie responded.

He ignored the challenge in her voice as he got to the point, "I hear you hurt your foot. May I have a look?"

"It's nothing," she said, shrugging, but she didn't object when he bent down and took her foot in his hands. She winced once or twice as he examined it, which caused him to look back up at her and apologise. She shrugged again. "You have gentle hands."

He smiled. "Thank you." Carefully he placed her foot back on the boulder. "I'm sure you haven't broken anything," he said, "but it's going to be bruised and painful for a while. Would you let me strap it to make it more comfortable for you?"

For a third time she shrugged, clearly finding gestures easier than searching for the words to express what she felt.

He went on persuasively, "I'd feel better too, knowing it was properly treated."

She nodded acquiescence and watched as he reached for his bag and bandaged her foot, slipping her shoe back over it. He straightened up, standing in front of where she was sitting, her eyes now barely lower than his.

Leonie started to speak. "I... No one... Never..." She came to a stumbling halt.

Prospero half smiled at her. "Let me try," he said. "No one's ever cared enough before to come find you and make sure your injuries are treated, and you can't get your head around it."

"Something like that." She nodded in relief.

Prospero continued, "I'm falling in love with you. Can you get your head round that?"

She looked at him in some puzzlement, and tentatively shook her head.

"No," he agreed, "me neither."

He slid his arms around her and bent his head to touch her lips with his. Without hesitation, Leonie responded, moulding her body and her mouth to his, and the same passion that he had felt before flared between them once more. Prospero was the one to break the kiss, moving back only slightly, unwilling to let go of Leonie. He looked down into her eyes, reaching to stroke her hair and tuck a stray curl back.

"I probably shouldn't have done that," he said shakily but his voice held no regrets.

"Do it again!" Leonie whispered.

"No," he said and this time his voice was full of regret, "Leonie, you are awakening in me feelings I never expected to experience again. I thought I had them under control but now..." He paused and ran his hand through his hair, "Now, I don't think I do have. I don't want to risk anything more that either of us would come to regret."

Leonie studied his face for a few moments then nodded and moved a little away from him. Her stomach rumbled, and Prospero laughed at the surprised look on her face, breaking the tension between them.

"You did miss lunch this time," he said. "Pedro was worried about you. I think he's sent enough food for an army."

He reached for his bag and pulled out the provisions, handing them to Leonie, who smiled silently at him and took them. Prospero sat down beside her, taking pleasure in watching her eat.

Eventually, he spoke again, "Leonie, how do you feel about me?"

She looked at him as if almost surprised that he had to ask and then said, "I belong to you?" with a rising inflection suggesting it was a question.

"You mean belong with me," he corrected her. "Belong to suggests ownership and people don't own other people, that would be slavery."

Leonie shrank away from him and the blank look on her face made it clear to him he had said something very wrong.

"I'm sorry," he said. "That was thoughtless of me. Just because slavery is outlawed doesn't mean it doesn't exist." He hesitated, thinking fast and then worded his next question very carefully. "Leonie, are there people out there somewhere who might think that they own you?"

She nodded.

"And you've run away from them and are afraid that they might still be coming after you?"

Another nod.

"You know that you are quite safe here? We wouldn't let anything happen to you or let anyone take you."

Slightly more hesitant this time, but it was still a nod.

"But it still makes you feel safer, if you can say you belong to me?"

She didn't hesitate this time but nodded energetically and he was pleased to realise that he had understood the issue.

"Okay then, you can belong to me if it helps." He smiled at her. "Do you belong with me as well though?" he asked lightheartedly in relief.

She grinned back at him and nodded yet again. "This is where I'm supposed to be, the place I fit in the world," she explained.

He had one more question for her. "Do you think, in time, you might come to love me?"

Leonie's reaction was instant but unexpected. She launched herself away from him, trying to gain her feet and run, tripping and stumbling when her bandaged foot didn't responded as she anticipated. She looked at it blankly, not understanding. That moment of confusion gave Prospero time to gather his own wits and leap to his feet after her. She looked at him in terror and continued to try to move away. He didn't understand what had scared her or what he might have said, but the more immediate problem was to get her to stop before she injured herself further. He stood still and held his hands out, palms forward.

"I'm sorry, I didn't mean to scare you. It's okay, I'm not going to chase you, you're safe, you're free to go if you want, I won't stop you."

It had some effect; she stopped trying to back away, but she was still looking at him with what he could only interpret as fear. His mind raced as he tried to work out what was going on, how to reassure her, how to get her to trust him again, when what he wanted to do was wrap his arms around her and hold her until the fear went away.

He tried again, "Leonie, if I'm scaring you with all this, you don't have to run. I can go, Gabriel will send me away, you'll be..."

He didn't get to finish his sentence because Leonie had closed the distance between them and was clinging to his coat.

"Don't go, don't go, don't go," she kept repeating.

He wrapped both arms around her, holding her close as he had so wanted to. "It's okay, I won't go anywhere, shush now, you're safe. I'll stay as long as you want me."

Much later Prospero would acknowledge this as the moment he made his choice, the moment he realised that he and Leonie were inextricably linked and that the way forward was together not apart. For now he just held her, soothing her and trying not to drown in the pleasurable sensation of her body against his.

Chapter 32

Leonie

I couldn't handle losing the place where I belonged just as I'd found it. Without thinking, I flung myself at Prospero and he wrapped his arms around me, holding me close and carrying on being calm and soothing and reassuring. I felt his mind wrap around mine, too, protective not invasive, so I reached out for his, entwining myself in it as I had the other day. We stood there for a while, entangled in mind and body, as my heart rate and breathing slowly returned to normal, and so did his. Then he sat us down back where we had been but without letting go so we were still wrapped up in each other. Once more, I'd got myself in a mess, a place I wanted to be but couldn't risk. *How had I let it happen?*

Earlier, I'd been deep in thought and hadn't noticed someone approaching as soon as I should have done. I'd known it was Prospero before he called my name.

My head was so full of thoughts of him I was hardly surprised to see him. I whispered "Perry," to myself, but it must have been out loud because he responded.

"Just because you know that nickname doesn't mean I've given you permission to use it."

I was afraid he did regret kissing me, that he was going to deny what had been between us. Miserable, rejected and confused, I didn't trust my voice and just shrugged and let him examine my foot. The feel of his hands on my skin confused me further; his touch still felt electric, making all my senses dance. It hurt some as he examined it and I know I winced or exclaimed because he apologised.

I said the first thing that came into my head, "You have

gentle hands."

I regretted it instantly because it sounded so silly and I meant so much more. He just smiled and thanked me and then proceeded to bandage my foot which made it feel a lot more comfortable. He stood up in front of me and I feared he was going to leave; I didn't want him to go. I wanted as much time with him as I could get. I tried to speak but couldn't find the words.

"I . . . No one . . . Never. . . "

He smiled gently and said, "Let me try."

How could he possibly know what I wanted to say when I didn't?

But he went on, "No one's ever cared enough before to come find you and make sure your injuries are treated and you can't get your head around it."

It wasn't what I'd been meaning to say – I didn't know what I'd been trying to say – but it was certainly true, and I did feel like that.

"Something like that," I agreed weakly.

He carried on, "I'm falling in love with you. Can you get your head round that?"

He took my breath away. I thought he'd come to regret kissing me the other day and was acting as though it had never happened. I struggled to believe that he felt like this about me and I just stared at him and shook my head in disbelief, trying to clear my thoughts. He took that as an answer to his question.

"No," he said, "I can't either."

He was as thrown, as disorientated as I was by this. Once, I had wanted to disorientate him, knock him out of his self-confident assurance, but now . . . now I needed him to be certain how he felt so that I could be certain of it. Even as all this was going through my mind, he slipped his arms around me and touched his lips to mine. My body responded and I gave myself up to the passionate sensation of his body against mine, feeling his warmth even through my coat. Underneath the excitement there was a different feeling and I, who had always been an outsider, realised that I had found where I belonged and it was not a place, he was a person.

When he moved back it felt as though part of me was tearing away. I didn't want him to stop holding me and I held on to him. He looked so vulnerable as he tried to explain to me why we had to stop. There was nothing he, or we, could have done that I would regret but he was asking this of me and I couldn't refuse this either. As I studied him I understood that his life choices gave him different constraints from mine and that he was trying to do what he considered the right thing even if he didn't know what that was.

I moved away a little to make it easier and then my stomach rumbled, complaining about that missed lunch. He laughed and handed me some food that Pedro had sent, knowing I was always hungry. I ate gratefully, happy just to sit next to Perry.

Eventually he spoke, "Leonie, how do you feel about me?"

He had to ask? Couldn't he tell? Or did he just need reassurance? I tried to explain how I'd felt when he'd kissed me but I struggled for the words.

"I belong to you," I said.

That brought the always-right Prospero back, correcting my language and talking about slavery. I hate that word, it brings back so many bad memories and for a moment I retreated into myself as I tried to squash them. He didn't help.

"Leonie, are there people out there somewhere who might think that they own you?"

Well yes, that was where the memories came from.

"And you've run away from them and are afraid that they might still be coming after you?"

Near enough. I was still a child when I ran. They didn't recapture us orphan brats, we weren't worth it, they just left us to live wild and used us as prey for their hunts. But I was still afraid they'd come after me if they thought there was anything to gain from it.

"You know that you are quite safe here? We wouldn't let anything happen to you or let anyone take you."

Actually, that kind of did help. I knew I was safe here and that Perry would protect me. But if Lord Gabriel thought it was right to hand me over to someone, I suspected that he would and I didn't know what he might think was right.

"But it still makes you feel safer, if you can say you belong to me?"

I agreed with that even if it wasn't safer exactly; I knew he was on my side no matter what. I was just trying to explain how I felt and I didn't really understand the difference between to and with. It mattered to him.

"Do you belong with me as well though?" he asked.

I tried to explain it better, "This is where I'm supposed to be, the place I fit in the world."

I wasn't doing a very good job because he had another question.

"Do you think, in time, you might come to love me?"

I had to get away. He didn't understand the danger he was putting himself in. Every time I'd admitted out loud that I loved someone, something bad happened to them. Really bad. Like, dead. I had to get away before I risked that. For some reason my foot didn't seem to work. I didn't understand why. I stumbled and tripped and I could feel Perry trying to radiate calm and reassurance. He stopped coming after me and I turned to look at him.

"It's okay," he said, "Don't be scared. Don't run. I won't chase you. I'll go away."

I couldn't handle that.

Perry's gentle voice brought me back to the present. "I don't know what I said to scare you. But I'm sorry. I think you feel the same about me as I do about you but I'm not going to ask you to say it if that's a problem for you somehow, okay?"

I nodded, grateful to him for understanding.

He went on, his voice still soft and gentle, "I don't know what to do about all this. And Easter, with all that's going on, it's no time to be causing upsets and disruption. Can you wait until after Easter, once things calm down, and then I will talk to Lord Gabriel and we will work it out?"

I agreed. I could wait forever if it was what he wanted, as long as he didn't go away.

"Okay," he said, smiling at me. "Now, Pedro had everyone getting worried about you, so I think we'd better get you back and relieve their minds. Can you walk on that foot?"

Of course, my foot was bandaged, that was why it hadn't seemed to work earlier. Now I realised that, I was sure I could walk.

"Yes, I think so," I told him.

"That's a shame," he said, which surprised me. Then he grinned at me and I saw the mischief in his eyes and felt it in his mind. "If you hadn't been able to, I'd have had an excuse to carry you."

As it was, he put his arm round me and suggested that I put mine round his waist. That did make walking easier and more comfortable as well as being an excuse to keep holding on to him. He escorted me right back to my room carrying off the fact that our arms were around each other with bare-faced confidence, even when Lady Eleanor met us outside my room.

"Nothing broken, fortunately," he said to her. "Just some bad bruising that could be quite painful."

He sat me down in a chair and turned so that his back was to her and he was looking at me.

"Now," he said, his voice sounding serious and strict but his eyes dancing with mischief, "you're to keep off your feet as much as possible for the rest of the day. Keep your foot up and rest. Understood?"

I nodded, well aware that if I said anything it would turn into a giggle and that I wouldn't be able to keep a straight face. He turned back to Lady Eleanor before he left.

"I'm sure she'll be fine with a bit of rest," he told her.

He didn't break the link between our minds when he went and I wasn't going to either. We stayed linked until he went into the Abbey before the evening meal and although I couldn't tell what he was doing I found it comforting to know he was there, within reach.

Lady Eleanor fussed around me for a bit, making sure my

foot was comfortable and that I had anything I might need readily to hand.

"Did Prospero come and find you?" she asked.

"Yes," I told her, "I'd only gone down to the river. I didn't realise how bruised my foot was, or that anyone might be worried. I didn't mean to worry anyone."

"That's alright," she said. "It's just because we care about you. Now, I'd better go and tell Lord Gabriel you're going to be fine."

I was left alone with my thoughts until it was time to prepare for the evening meal. It would be a formal meal, in honour of all the visitors, so it was an opportunity to dress up – and Edward had made me a new outfit. I found I was eager to see Perry's reaction to me wearing it.

Aidan

As predicted, Aidan had no problem working out who Leonie was at the evening meal. Even if her red hair hadn't drawn his eye immediately, she was the only female at Lord Gabriel's table of a suitable age to be his ward and certainly the only one dressed as befitted the ward or daughter of a High Lord. The more sombre outfits of the monks, nuns and visitors made an excellent background against which she shone like a jewel in a setting designed to show it off. He was curious as to whether that was deliberate or sub conscious. He rather thought Leonie was unaware of the impression she made; Edward was probably responsible for her clothing and he would be very well aware of it.

Prospero was sitting some distance from her; both were conversing with their neighbours with every evidence of concentration but a close observer – which Aidan had chosen to be

– would see that their eyes kept being drawn to each other. *Not smitten, indeed!* Prospero was clearly in love with the girl and she with him.

Aidan wondered what Lord Gabriel planned to do about it. That particular shade of red hair would suggest to anyone that she was some Chisholm by-blow but it was unusual to find them as orphans or wards in other Houses. Lord William of House Chisholm would pick his heir from any of his descendants, whether born inside or outside a legitimate marriage and equally any of his descendants could challenge for the House. With a family of lusty sons he worked on the principle of keeping your friends close and your enemies closer, and provided generously for all those offspring he could trace.

Safe inside the Order, Prospero was insulated from the politics of the Great Houses; should he choose to leave and marry this girl then the link between his family and a Chisholm challenger – if that's what she was – could be considered quite threatening by a number of parties – and very attractive to his High Lord.

Leonie's eyes reminded him of someone and although he thought it was important he couldn't remember who. When he did discover who, some months later, it was far too late to matter.

Chapter 33

Leonie

With all that was going through my mind, on Thursday evening I took the opportunity to retreat to one of my hiding places to think things through, climbing up to the space in the gallery where the arms of the Abbey intersected. Enjoying the peace of the Abbey and lost in my thoughts, I felt the dampener shield disappear. I sat up sharply, stretching my mind out to investigate. The shields in the Abbey, the full set, were supposed to be on permanently. *Is something wrong?* Before I could react further I heard Lord Gabriel's voice in my head.

"Shield your presence, child, and you may stay."

His mind showed me how to shield, but of course I knew anyway and did so promptly, very curious as to what might be happening. I peered down into the Abbey, making sure I couldn't be seen either physically or mentally. For the moment, only Lord Gabriel was present but then other monks and nuns and all the visitors who were or who had been monks and nuns started to pour in. I spotted Pedro, Andrew, Edward, Perry, Chloe and many others. I hadn't realised there was to be another service.

This was a family, coming together to enjoy each other's company and to worship together. For once, those with gifts used their abilities to enhance the worship. I supposed there was no one there – except me – who was in any danger of being influenced as they were all already committed. There were readings, speaking, music – more than enough instruments for a full orchestra – poems, dancing and singing. Perry sang, not a solo this time but a duet with one of the visitors, a dark-haired man I'd seen around. I got so lost in that I nearly let my shield slip. I realised then that Lord Gabriel was also protecting me with a small part of his mind. I tended to think of Perry as the most gifted person around but I was beginning to suspect that Lord Gabriel was at least as powerful but far more subtle. Subtlety didn't seem to be one of Perry's characteristics.

It was different from anything I'd seen before. I found it a very powerful and moving experience and I was overwhelmed by the feeling of belonging, a little like the tight bond that existed in a Trader caravan. I'd come to know many of these people over the last few months and I'd seen them care for each other, but also bicker and squabble and irritate each other. Now they were expressing such joy and love and togetherness in their worship all that seemed minor. Everyone had their faults, their problems, their bad days and yet they were forgiven and loved and accepted and belonged despite that, and nothing could break their bond.

However long it went on, it ended too soon for me. I watched them filter out with regret. Lord Gabriel was the last to leave. He spoke in my head again just before he switched the shields back on.

"You belong too, child, to God and to us," and then he left.

The silence with the shields on was deafening. For once, it was too quiet for me there and I scarpered back to my room as fast as I could, listening to and enjoying the background noise of everyone around me. Even that seemed subdued, much quieter than normal, despite all the visitors. Eventually I realised that all the monks and nuns were missing, along with a large proportion of the guests, and deduced they had to be within the restricted area, behind the shields. My mind was occupied with what Lord Gabriel had said to me. *Do I belong?* I wanted to, but I didn't know what it involved, what it meant, what I had to do – or whether they would want me, if they knew all about me. I thought about that all through Friday but there wasn't anyone around to ask – and those people that were around, like Lady Eleanor, were very busy. I didn't want to pester them. I stayed away from the Abbey, confused both by what I had felt on Thursday evening and by my feelings for Perry. I didn't want to be able to see him across the building and yet not be able to sense him, or touch him, or talk to him.

***

The Them came after me, hovering around me, looming over me. I ran; they followed. I stopped; they surrounded me. I stared at them for a moment. No, I thought, you're not getting me. Someone will come and help me. It won't be Perry but someone will come. I didn't waste time with weapons but gathered up the power and threw it at them in a great arc as I spun round on my heel. They backed off for a moment, and then surrounded me again. I kept pushing at them; they kept retreating and returning. We were at a stalemate and I didn't know how long I could last. I'd used fire before, but I wasn't doing that again; it had caused too much damage. A Trader caravan appeared beside me. That didn't make sense, but it reminded me of the advantage of the high ground. Quickly I climbed onto the roof. Gleefully I realised, the Them couldn't climb. They stood in a ring below me and every time one got too close I whacked them with a bolt of power.

Prospero

Prospero had already retired to his room on Friday night when he was summoned by Lord Gabriel. Sleep had been eluding him anyway, as had become common. He had shrugged his tunic back on and gone to see what was happening.

"Leonie's having a nightmare," Lord Gabriel told Prospero. "The watch team can't cope and have sent for our help. They're in the central courtyard. Go sort it out. Do whatever seems appropriate."

The Order always took the period from Thursday evening to Easter Sunday morning as a retreat, starting with the service on

Thursday evening, and spending the time in prayer, worship and fasting. With the exception of services, they stayed within the restricted area of the campus. This wasn't as disruptive to the rest of the community as might be imagined. Most activities were staffed by lay workers as well as nuns and monks so the impact was minimised by careful adjustment of shifts and rotas. One area that was disproportionately affected was the night-watch team as many of the most Gifted adepts tended to be monks or nuns. Even here the impact was mitigated by circumstances. Those most likely to have nightmares were the student adepts, who had returned home for the holidays, or the younger novices, who were on the retreat and would be cared for by the Brothers and Sisters. The chances of the under-strength watch team having to deal with a severe nightmare in these three nights was small but not non-existent.

Prospero found Leonie perched on a high ledge in one of the courtyards, still deeply asleep, out of physical reach and holding off any attempts by the watch team to restrain, wake or calm her. He was able to walk across the courtyard untroubled by any attack; it almost seemed that Leonie was unaware of his presence. He looked up at where she was perched.

"I've come to find you. It's time to go home," he said.

She blinked, waking, and dropped off the ledge straight into his arms. "You came," she said, wonderingly.

"Of course I came," he responded, "I wouldn't leave you lost and frightened and alone."

"I thought you wouldn't be able to come."

He smiled at her. "Well, I'm here. And it's time you went back to bed. Come on."

He scooped her up into his arms where she settled with her

head on his shoulder and her arms round his neck. She was almost asleep again by the time he got her indoors and sorted out who would monitor her for the next few hours; he had no intention of being left out of this task. In the end the watch team leader agreed she should be taken to her own bed where Prospero and Lady Eleanor could watch her until morning. Assuming she was fine then, Prospero would return to the retreat and she could spend the morning with Eleanor.

By the time they reached her bed Leonie was sleeping peacefully, and Prospero was able to tuck her back in without waking her. It meant he couldn't give her a dose of the inhibitor sedative as normal but he was confident of his ability to soothe her should the nightmare start to return.

He turned to offer Lady Eleanor the bedroom's one chair but she smiled at him.

"Don't worry," she said indicating the outer room, "one of the chairs unfolds into a mattress. I'm going to find a pillow and a blanket and sleep there. You can watch Leonie. I don't suppose you'll need the chair."

He frowned at her. "You trust me with her?"

"Totally," she confirmed. "I trusted you with Mel, and I've never had cause to regret that. I'm quite certain that Leonie will come to no harm whatsoever in your care. If necessary, I'll wake you about seven."

With that she smiled at him and left the room, shutting the door behind her. Alone with Leonie, Prospero stood watching her whilst his mind slowly processed what Eleanor had said. To him it implied that she expected him to share the bed with Leonie and it took him some time to come to terms with this. He wanted to, very much, and he could see there were advantages to it; he was certain Leonie's nightmare would not then come back, and he'd be able to sleep too. He wanted to; he just wasn't sure whether he ought to. He needed to do the right thing, whether or not anyone would ever know.

Lady Eleanor clearly trusted him not to do anything inappropriate, though his behaviour with Melanie certainly hadn't been innocent. Lord Gabriel trusted him to look after Leonie and had from the beginning even though he knew how Prospero felt about her. Most of all, he knew Leonie trusted him, or he wouldn't have been able to calm her nightmare. In the end he supposed the question was whether or not he trusted himself. He kicked his shoes off and sat down on the floor to pray, resting his head on the edge of the bed. When Leonie stirred and he felt the first tendrils of the nightmare return, he reacted instinctively, without thinking.

Leonie

The nightmare didn't come back, but I dreamt again. I dreamt that I woke up and someone's arms were around me keeping me warm and safe and protected. It wasn't that I didn't know who they were; in my dream they were all the people that I've loved and who loved me. A voice spoke.

"You're safe," it said, "I've got you. Go back to sleep."

So I curled more closely into the arms and went back to sleep, even in the dream.

When I woke properly, Lady Eleanor was sitting in the chair by the bed. Perry was sitting on the foot of the bed with his back against the wall.

"How are you feeling?" he asked, smiling at me as he moved towards me. I knew he was doing that to check my pulse and things but I slid as close to him as I could manage.

"I didn't expect you to come," I told him. "But I couldn't

find the watch team."

Lady Eleanor laughed, making me look round and Perry smiled too. "You certainly did find the watch team," Lady Eleanor said. "You were holding us off very easily. No one could get close."

I looked back and forth between them, puzzled, shaking my head. "There was only the Them. I couldn't get away, I could just keep Them off..."

My voice trailed off as I realised what had happened, as it had before, and Perry confirmed it.

"That was the watch team. They got confused in your head. Don't worry, it often happens." He put one arm round me and held me close to him, reassuringly. "I have to go back now, but I'll see you again on Sunday. Lady Eleanor is going to look after you this morning, okay?"

I nodded. It wasn't okay, I didn't want him to go, but I knew he had to. He kissed the top of my head, looked almost defiantly at Lady Eleanor, then touched his lips to mine and he was gone. I sat there staring at where he had been, utterly bewildered.

"He loves you, you know," Lady Eleanor spoke.

I turned to look at her. "But he can't! He mustn't, it isn't safe. And it's not allowed."

She looked thoughtful for a moment before speaking again. "When I first knew Prospero he was a very messed up young man. There'd been some relationship with a young lady that had gone wrong and then he met up with my daughter. She wasn't a good thing for anyone right then, but he turned out to be very good for her. He helped her get her life sorted out for which I shall always be grateful, but in the process he got even more messed up. His call to the Order was absolutely genuine but in some ways I think it was also a refuge, his only way out of a situation he couldn't cope with. Since then, with God's help, he's sorted himself out and matured. In my opinion, he and the Order have done all they can for each other and it's time he moved on."

"You mean stop being a monk?" I asked her.

"Yes," she replied. "But the important thing here is, he loves you, but how do you feel about him?"

I couldn't answer that. If I said it out loud something bad would happen and I had to protect him. But I couldn't deny it either, so I just sat there, silent and miserable.

She was very gentle. "You don't have to tell me, but if you don't feel the same way about him, you do have to tell him."

I knew that, but I couldn't do that either, for the same reasons; I couldn't lie to him, but I couldn't risk putting him in harm's way.

"This is all a bit heavy so early, isn't it?" Lady Eleanor asked. "Come on, let's go and find some breakfast. Things are always better when you've eaten."

***

The day was as quiet as Friday in mood, although rather busier in preparation for Easter Sunday. I stayed with Lady Eleanor during the morning; she didn't say anything but I thought watching me must be rather a hindrance for her at such a busy time. I tried to make myself useful but she wouldn't let me do any of the more energetic chores. I kept away from the Abbey again, more confused than ever about my feelings for Perry and what I could do about them.

Once Lady Eleanor released me, after lunch, I threw myself into chores in the kitchen. Even there I ran out of things to do eventually. I knew I needed to find somewhere I could think about what I was feeling and decide what to do about it—I was just afraid of what I might decide. Would I be strong enough to do the right thing, whatever that was?

Right now I couldn't even decide where to go to think. The Abbey was definitely out; I didn't want to risk being there if another unexpected service started – or even one of the regular ones. My room and the library offered too many distractions, the Old Chapel felt too quiet. In the end I walked down by the river to the place I'd taken Perry once after a nightmare. I climbed out over the boulders and sat where we'd stood, on a boulder in the middle of the water with the river rushing past me. I tried to put my thoughts in order.

Did I want to belong here with these people? To have that sense of belonging I'd felt on Thursday? Yes, I did, without doubt, and I realised that applied with or without Perry. I was pretty sure I didn't have to be a nun to belong. I knew many people I'd class as belonging who weren't nuns or monks.

Did I know what I had to do to belong? Or even if they'd have me? No, not really, although Lord Gabriel had inferred that they would welcome me when he'd spoken to me on Thursday night. But over the last few months I'd been reading and studying, asking and listening and now I had a fair idea of what they believed. They believed in one God; so did I. The things I'd seen, travelling, the beautiful parts of this world, where it had either recovered or hadn't been destroyed in the first place – well, they'd convinced me of a creator God.

And they believed everyone had done wrong, no one was, or could be, good enough for that God through their own actions. Again, I could sign up to that; I knew I wasn't good enough for anyone, that's why I was worried about them rejecting me. But they said that this God had chosen to be born as a man, Jesus – his birth was what we'd celebrated at Christmas. Then that man, the only one who was good enough, had chosen to be punished, killed, in our place, so that having atoned for what we'd done wrong, we were good enough for God. That was what we'd commemorated on Friday. Each of us just had to accept this gift from this God/man – that was the personal bit. But the best bit, the bit that we would celebrate tomorrow, on Easter Day, was that he didn't stay dead. He came to life again. And that meant that even when our bodies died, we wouldn't, the essential part of us would be with God and with everyone else who had chosen to accept this.

Could I accept this? I decided that I wanted to.

Would they accept me? I figured my only option there was to tell Lord Gabriel everything I had done and been and risk it. That would have to wait until after Easter. If he threw me out after that, I supposed that would be better than living a lie here even if I had nowhere to go.

That left me Perry to think about. I knew how I felt about him and I knew that, for his protection, I couldn't acknowledge it. From what he'd said a couple of days ago I knew how he felt, and I figured he knew I couldn't tell him my feelings. But he was a monk so it was irrelevant anyway; I couldn't expect anything more than friendship at the most, however much I wanted more. Whatever anyone said about him leaving the monastery, and whatever he'd meant about talking to Lord Gabriel, I couldn't let him make that decision for my benefit. I wasn't worth it; there was nothing I could offer him in its place. If I truly loved him perhaps I should leave, but I didn't think I could bring myself to do that. I laughed ruefully to myself; if I didn't love him enough to leave for his benefit, perhaps I didn't love him enough for him to be in danger.

It had grown dark while I'd contemplated all this and was

now full night. I needed to get back or Lady Eleanor would be concerned about me. Unable to resolve my issues with Perry in my head, they continued to nag at me as I returned to my rooms and got ready for sleep. I was afraid that I wouldn't be able to sleep or that I'd be tormented by another nightmare but I was tired and tomorrow would be an early start.

Chapter 34

Easter Saturday

Prospero

Prospero walked back to the monastery early on Saturday morning, having left Leonie with Lady Eleanor. Over the last few weeks he had been torn between his vocation, his fears and his desires. What he had done last night when left with Leonie should have increased the conflict but to his surprise he felt calm and at peace. He realised that at some point during the night he must have finally recognised that he'd made a decision, a choice about his future and he was feeling the relief that came with the resolution of a major issue.

This morning he had woken early, feeling rested and relaxed. By the time Eleanor had returned to the room he'd been sitting on the foot of the bed watching Leonie sleep, curled up like a cat. She'd had one hand outside the covers so he'd held it and hadn't let go as Lady Eleanor had entered and sat down.

"Like that, is it?" she'd asked quietly.

He'd nodded. "Is it that obvious?"

"To me, yes. To others, maybe not so much, though I think there are a number who suspect. Talk to Gabriel, I'm sure you'll find him sympathetic."

He'd nodded again. "I have. I will. I plan to, as soon as Easter is over."

Their conversation had been curtailed by Leonie stirring.

Once Prospero reached the restricted area of the monastery he sought out Lord Gabriel as soon as he could, unable to wait any longer, despite the Easter festivities. Lord Gabriel looked at him and sighed.

"You've made a decision then." It was a statement, not a question.

"I'm sorry, Father. I have to ask to be released from my vows and from the Order."

"And Leonie?"

Prospero hesitated a moment before answering. "I love her, Father, you know that. I want to be with her, I want to ensure her well-being. But my request to leave the Order is not dependent on that. It's time for me to move on, anyway."

"Leonie is my ward. It's up to me to consent to any relationship with her. I will not have her hurt by you, you understand?"

"I understand."

Gabriel nodded in resignation. "Very well then. I will agree both to your request to leave the Order and to your relationship with Leonie. I think you've made the right decisions, if that is any help."

Prospero was both grateful and relieved and said as much.

Gabriel carried on, "We'll sort out the formalities after the Easter festivities. In the meantime, have you given any thought to what you will do once you have left the Order?"

Prospero shook his head. "No, I haven't got that far. I only realised this morning that this was what I had to do."

"I'd like you to consider staying as part of this House. I don't want to lose you and you could continue your current work in the hospital. This option is always open to you, even if it ends up just being short term whilst you decide what comes next."

"Thank you. I don't want to leave, either." Prospero looked

up at Gabriel, the feeling of mischief returning to his mind. "And it would certainly help to stay close to Leonie!"

Gabriel clearly tried not to show his amusement and failed, a slight smile spreading across his face for a moment. "How does Leonie feel about you?" he asked.

Prospero didn't know how to explain what he knew. "I'm certain she feels the same about me as I do about her but she's scared, really scared of something and I'm not sure what exactly."

"Not of you, though?" Gabriel sounded puzzled.

"No, not me, and not of how I feel about her; she may find that difficult to believe but it doesn't scare her."

"Her own feelings then? She's still very young, this could all be very confusing to her."

Prospero shook his head. "No, I don't think that's it. From her reactions it's not about how she feels, more about saying how she feels, and I don't understand why there's a difference but there is."

Gabriel sighed. "Katya sent me a letter about Leonie. It reached me sometime after Christmas. She likens Leonie to a jewel, but she says that when they came across her she was badly damaged. Katya did what she could, but she said she didn't have the time or the skills to treat all the damage and nor could she tell whether it was inherent in her or imposed from her experiences. You are going to need to be very careful."

"It's not inherent." Prospero was very certain.

"And you are sure of this how?" Gabriel asked him. "No, don't answer that. There's no answer you could give that I would possibly want to know."

Prospero grinned, well aware that he was either making an

unjustified claim or that he'd been a lot closer to Leonie, both in body and mind, than should have been appropriate. Not that he'd been that deep into Leonie's mind, still he was certain that whatever damage might be there was entirely rectifiable.

Gabriel dismissed the subject with a wave of his hand. "And what about your own issues with leaving the Order?"

"I'm going to have to face them, aren't I? They haven't gone away while I've been here. I can't change my birth so I shall have to deal with their expectations. But I can't fulfil both and I don't want to fulfil either."

Gabriel nodded. "Fair enough. This is one reason I'd like you to stay here in this House, at least to start with. We'll talk more about it later but I'll do what I can to help. "

With that, he dismissed Prospero who left humming quietly to himself with pleasure as he thought of Leonie.

***

Despite having made a decision on his future, Prospero was still unable to sleep on Saturday night. Instead, he went up to the private roof garden and leaned on the parapet looking out over the campus and towards the Abbey. The garden extended from the restricted area towards the lay House. Standing at the far end, he realised that, due to the intersection of Shields, he could sense Leonie asleep in her room. She was a beacon of colour in his mind and right now she was an edgy orange with flame-like flashes of deeper reds. To him that meant she was restless, unsettled, and possibly even on the verge of another nightmare. He reached towards her with his mind, touching hers, stroking and trying to soothe it. The colours faded back through yellow to the calm green he associated with her being at rest, and he withdrew his touch slowly.

Knowing that he was stepping beyond the boundaries of what was appropriate, even if it was for Leonie's benefit, he walked away from temptation, back along the garden out of range of the House shield and leaned on the parapet once more. After a short while Andrew joined him and they stood silently, shoulder to shoulder.

Eventually, Prospero spoke, "Andy, I'm leaving."

"I know." Andrew's voice was peaceful.

"How? I only knew myself this morning."

"I know you better than you know yourself. Besides, this was never going to be lifelong for you as it is for me. For you, this was a place and time to heal and grow strong enough to face whatever you are meant to do out there."

"Have I? Healed and grown stronger, I mean?"

Andrew smiled. "Yes, you have. But more importantly, you've learnt to rely on God's strength, not your own."

They stood quietly until Andrew spoke again. "And Leonie?"

"What about Leonie? I'm not leaving because of her."

"No, perhaps not. But she'll be part of your future too, won't she?"

"If she'll have me."

"Like that's in any doubt. I've told you before how she feels about you. And she knows you better than you know yourself, too. You need her. She'll keep you grounded."

"I know."

"Be careful with her. She's tough but she's vulnerable.

Don't hurt her."

"Or you'll come after me, right? Gabriel's ahead of you and I expect there are any number of others...Pedro, Chloe, Edward, Eleanor...Besides, why would I hurt her?"

"Well, because you're impulsive, act without thinking things through, always sure you're right especially when you're wrong... Need I go on?" Andrew was smiling and, well used to this litany, Prospero couldn't help but smile back.

"Okay, okay," he said, putting his hands up in mock defence, "I promise to look after her to the best of my ability. Will that do?"

"I guess it's the best I'm going to get."

They both turned back to looking out over the parapet, and Andrew carried on, "What will you do, after here?"

"I don't know. Gabriel says to stay here, for now at least. I want to stay here and I'd like Leonie to have a chance to get the education she needs. I have to sort out everyone's expectations of me because no way am I taking the farm from my brother Matt. He deserves to inherit it, not me. But how do I go back to my birth House and yet deny my duty of service required by that High Lord?"

Andrew shrugged. "Seems to me that your duty is still to serve a higher Lord than him. That doesn't change even if you leave the Order. You'll have to work out what God wants you to do, not any mortal High Lord. While you do, stay here. No point in disrupting your life – or Leonie's – more than you have to."

Now it was Prospero's turn to smile. "You're right, of course. As always. What will I do without your advice and common sense?"

"You'll be fine. You know this for yourself really. And you'll have Leonie. And I'll always be here if you need me. And right now my advice is that we both go to bed."

That drew a quiet laugh from Prospero in agreement and together they returned to the sleeping quarters.

Chapter 35

Easter Sunday

Leonie

I woke early on Sunday morning, surprised to find that I had slept well, with no nightmare. I didn't have time to think about it, but pulled my clothes on and hurried to the kitchen. The first service of the day was always before breakfast, but today it would be as the sun rose, considerably earlier than normal. It was still dark as I ran across the courtyard and slipped through the kitchen door.

Alan – Pedro's deputy – was there already, rushing back and forth, frantic over everything that had to be completed. He'd been in charge while Pedro was on the retreat so I figured he was anxious to show how well he'd done. I grabbed my apron and shot over to my workstation. I didn't want to let Alan down. The time passed too quickly and there seemed to be too much to do. But somehow I was done just as Alan rushed back through, calling out, "Come on, everyone. Service is about to start. Everyone out. Come on, come on."

Despite my reservations over the last couple of days, I got caught up in the rush, swapped my apron for my coat and went along.

The service was outside, in one of the courtyards but with shields over it. I watched as the sun appeared over the Abbey roof, making it glow in shades of pink and gold. The courtyard was probably chosen so we could see just that. It wasn't a long service; all those who had been secluded for the past few days were there, but in a group together, not mixing with everyone else. Most of those from the lay House were there too, along with quite a number from the town. Many of them would stay for breakfast too, another reason for Alan's panic.

I didn't mean too but my eyes kept looking for Perry, unable to settle until I spotted him. My thoughts kept wandering and I kept glancing up to watch him then look away in case he saw me. I tried to stay unnoticed in the crowd and concentrate on the service but it was a struggle. I meant to leave quickly once it was all over because I was needed back in the kitchen but I had to go with the movement of the crowds. For just a moment Perry was beside me and everything else faded away.

"Hey," he said softly, just brushing his fingers lightly down the side of my face. "Later, okay?" and then the crowds moved again and he was gone.

***

Later took a long time coming even though I was busy. As soon as I could get through the crowds I rushed back to the kitchen to finish preparing and start serving breakfast. Pedro was just a few minutes behind me. He ambled through the door in his usual calm, laid-back manner, a smile spreading across his face. I saw him pat Alan on the back and whisper something in his ear. It must have been a compliment because Alan's whole body relaxed. Then Pedro strolled through the kitchen, stopping at every work station, saying something to every worker. When he reached me he put his arm round my shoulders and took a deep breath.

"The bread smells good," he said. "Have you flavoured it with rosemary?"

I nodded.

"Good choice," he said and then moved on.

We had barely finished clearing up after breakfast when it was time for the main morning service, back in the Abbey proper. Again, I hadn't intended to go.

"There's still lots to do," I said to Pedro. "I'll stay here and start getting things ready for lunch."

He just smiled at me and put his hand on my back, pushing me towards the door. "There'll be plenty of time for that later," he said. "The service is far more important. And more fun."

So I went, finding a place beside Lady Eleanor who greeted me as I sat down. Actually, Pedro was right. The service was a lot of fun. There was music and singing and even chocolates passed around, and everyone had beaming faces. I saw Perry amongst the monks also smiling, and admittedly my eyes were drawn to him but this time that didn't distract me from everything else that was going on. It all felt more like a party, or a Trader rest day celebration than a church service.

I hurried back to the kitchen again afterwards to help with lunch. But once that was cleared Pedro put his hand on my shoulder and shepherded me to the door. "This evening you're to play your role as Lord Gabriel's ward," he said. "This afternoon you're to rest and relax so you're ready. Understood?"

I did understand, really. And I didn't want to let Lord Gabriel down any more than I'd wanted to let Alan down this morning. But as I now had free time, there was something else I planned to do. I started looking for Perry with my mind but couldn't spot him. I didn't know where he might be and I decided that my best bet was to go along to the office and see if Chloe was there. If Perry was rostered on to work at the hospital or likely to be somewhere else shielded, she'd tell me. I cut across the courtyard by the side of the Abbey and realised I could hear singing through the slightly open door. Curious, I pushed the door open further and went inside. The monks' and nuns' choir was rehearsing, ready for the evening celebration. Well, that explained where Perry was and it also meant that he wasn't going to be free to spend any time with me.

I sat and listened for a while, taking care to stay in the

shadows where they couldn't see me. And then, reluctantly, I headed back to my room to do exactly what Pedro had told me to – rest and prepare for the evening.

I was beginning to not mind my role as Lord Gabriel's ward at all. Edward had brought me yet another new outfit and again he seemed to have woven some magic into it. This one was a shimmering emerald green silk which made my hair look redder than ever. There was no undershirt, just a short-sleeved tunic which fitted closely to my hips and then flared out, worn with matching leggings and ankle boots. The embroidery at the neck and hem line was in silver, little castellations like a picture book castle, interspersed with the cross keys of House St Peter. I found I was eagerly looking forward to wearing it, to Perry seeing me in it.

My hair was longer now, though still very curly, and Lady Eleanor came and styled it for me. She insisted I wore my necklace and bracelet too, even if the jewels weren't the same colour as the dress. I looked in the mirror when she was done and thought I looked almost as grand, as beautiful as any of the ladies I'd seen at other Houses. The green of my outfit seemed to reflect in the stones of my jewellery and they enhanced one another rather than clashing.

Lady Eleanor and I went along to the dining hall together. Lord Gabriel raised his eyebrows – at her I think – as we reached him, but greeted me with a smile and told me how beautiful I looked as he pulled my chair out for me. Brother Benjamin was doing the same thing for Lady Eleanor on Lord Gabriel's other side. I couldn't believe this. The High Lord of a Great House was assisting me. How far had I come? And how much trouble would I be in if he thought I'd been deceiving him about what I was?

I kept my head down and concentrated on my food as I regained my composure. Brother Richard was on my other side and he spoke quietly to me, apparently not noticing my limited responses until I had recovered. I was too far from Perry to talk with him during the meal. I didn't dare do more than steal quick glances at him, though I could feel his eyes on me almost constantly.

***

The evening celebration service was almost immediately after the meal. Given where I'd been sitting for the meal I had no way of avoiding it. Again it took place outside, this time on the grounds around the town side of the Abbey. Edward had made me a jacket to match my outfit, but I forgot it. It didn't matter. I was plenty warm enough. The place was packed with people from the House, the Order, the town, all mingling together. The choir and those who were leading or participating in some way were close to the Abbey on a low platform with lights strung around. Others had torches and lanterns to see by. But even those who were involved merged into the crowd when it wasn't their turn.

Early on there was a part when they remembered those members of the Order and the House who had died during the past year. Their names were read out and then Perry sang a solo as those who knew them remembered them. It sent a shiver down my spine as I realised that so many of the people I now knew would be named like this one day – and I thought of how many people I once knew that now had only me to remember them. What if I forgot them? And who would remember me? Perhaps Perry, I hoped.

The service moved on; now they were praying for and blessing those who had left the Order during the year for other things. It seemed as though some of those were still part of the Order, just living and working elsewhere, whilst one or two had left altogether. The difference was a little hazy to me. Again Perry sang, this time a duet with the man he'd sung with on Thursday night. I knew his name now; he was called Aidan and had been a monk until a few years ago. Although he and Perry seemed to be friends, I was a bit wary of him. There'd been a couple of times, at and after meals, when I thought he'd been staring at me, watching me. I'd decided that he'd be gone in a day or two and I should just keep out of his way.

Next they welcomed all those who had formally joined the House or the Order since last Easter. I was filled with such a longing to be one of them, to belong to this family. The crowd ebbed and flowed and now Andrew was standing beside me.

"Hi," he said, smiling down at me. "Enjoying the singing?" He inclined his head towards the front, where Perry and Aidan had just finished.

"I'm enjoying it all," I told him.

He had to have heard the longing in my voice because he answered that with, "You know, everyone is welcome here. Anyone can belong. It doesn't matter what they've done in the past, however bad. We all start here with a clean slate. No matter what."

I looked at him. "No matter what, however bad? Whatever you've been?"

"Everything can be forgiven, if you're prepared to accept that forgiveness."

"I want to," I whispered. "But I don't know what to do for the best?"

He smiled at me. "I'm really glad you want to. Tell Prospero that. It won't be long before he comes and finds you. I think what to do next will become clear pretty quickly."

Andrew slipped away, but even as he left I was overwhelmed with such a feeling of...pleasure? Of happiness? No, of joy. I'd never felt like this before. It encompassed me, swirling around me, told me that I belonged, that I was wanted, and I gave myself up to it, letting it soak through me and fill me to overflowing.

Perry appeared in the crowd behind me. "No coat again, I see," he said smiling.

I twisted my neck and looked up at him. His eyes were sparkling, full of life and his mood seemed exuberant as if he too was full of joy. If I didn't know better I'd have thought he was high. Regardless of appearances and who might see, he pulled me back against his chest and wrapped both his arms and his cloak around me so I felt the warmth of his body behind mine.

"Better?" he whispered in my ear.

I nodded although I hadn't been particularly cold. The feeling of joy encompassed me again; I couldn't remember ever having felt this happy.

"Shouldn't you be over there?" I asked him, nodding at the front where many of those taking part in the service were standing.

"I've chosen to be here with you, while I can," he said.

I didn't think it was possible to feel happier.

His lips brushed my ear again. "Marry me," he said.

It was what I wanted most, and the one thing I knew I couldn't have. I tipped my head back against his shoulder to look at him, but he put a finger on my lips.

"Don't answer yet. I have to go but I'll find you again, after this."

With that, he left and a moment or two later I saw him re-join the choir as they took their places in front of the crowd for the next item. I figured I had perhaps half an hour before he would come looking for me so I slipped away through the crowd. Even as I raced back to my room I could hear his voice as he started his solo.

I spent a few minutes panicking about what to do. I had to get away; to marry me, Perry would have to leave the monastery, the place where he belonged and was happy. And if I acknowledged that I loved him – and marrying him would certainly do that – something very bad would happen to him as it had to all the others I'd loved. I couldn't handle that, not again. Yet how could I stand in front of him and say no, when my heart was shouting yes, when marrying him was the very thing I wanted? If this was what he truly wanted, if he loved me, how could I bear to watch while I broke his heart by saying no?

I needed to go where he couldn't find me because he'd certainly come looking but I had no idea where to go. He'd be able to sense me, even if he couldn't see me; I didn't know his range but I suspected it was several miles and I did know that I stood out like a beacon for him when he was looking for me.

I could shield mentally but it took too much energy to do so for long and the shield would drop as soon as I slept. That wasn't more than a very short-term solution. No, I needed to be far enough away from him that he couldn't sense me, preferably in a direction he wouldn't look straight away. Normally, I'd head up into the woods and the hills. They'd be difficult to search physically at night but if I was moving through the woods I'd struggle to shield and I wouldn't get far enough ahead. Besides, that would be what Perry would expect me to do and where he'd search next.

It struck me that the only way I could get far enough away quickly enough was to use the train. I'd never been on a train, so that was a pretty scary thought but I knew where the station was and they certainly went fast. But I also knew they didn't run at this time of night. So I needed to find somewhere shielded to hide overnight, where Perry wouldn't think of looking, then in the morning I could escape on the train which would get me so far away from him that he'd not be able to find me.

If I went in the opposite direction to the woods, that would take me into the town. The riverside shopping area was enclosed and of course it was shielded. No one would look for me there because it would be locked and they'd think I couldn't get in. But I could, and I knew somewhere within it to make myself comfortable for the night. Flooded with relief that I had at least the start of a plan I changed my clothes, grabbed my backpack and started to throw in the things that might be useful.

Most of what I had was provided by the House so it didn't seem right to take any more than essentials. But I took my Bible and the little wooden cross that Perry had given me and a few items of warm clothing. I left the necklace that Lord Gabriel had given me at Christmas with regret. I loved it and what it represented but it was too valuable. I couldn't take it. I hated having to leave all the little plants that Perry put in my room on my birthday but there was no way I could carry them. I made sure they were all watered and hoped someone would find them and look after them. After a moment's thought, I decided to leave a brief note on the off chance it might stop them looking for me. Then I picked up my backpack and slipped out into the dark while everyone was still involved in the service.

I raced across the dark, quiet town, trying to ignore the tears that kept creeping into my eyes. I found it easy to get into the riverside shopping area and into the back room of one of the shops. I knew this bakery well because I'd worked here after the Traders had left me behind and before I joined the Great House. There was an old couch there and a blanket so I curled up in the dark, confident that I wouldn't be disturbed for several hours. I went on shielding although I knew the shopping area had its own shields. It was much easier to do when I wasn't doing anything else and it was just an added layer of protection. Safely hidden, I succumbed to the overwhelming feelings of loss and grief. Only a few hours ago I had felt so happy, so full of joy and now I was alone again.

Maybe not entirely alone. I scrabbled in my backpack for the little wooden cross and held it tight in my hands. When he'd given it to me, Perry had said that it would remind me that I was never alone, God was always there, so I clung onto that thought. With that hope at the forefront of my mind I tried to sleep. Tomorrow I would face the world again, and start to carve out a new life for myself, away from Perry and the danger I had brought to him.

The story continues in

Choices and Consequences Book 2 : Thread of Hope

Choices and Consequences Book 3 : Weave of Love

Choices and Consequences Book 4 : Cloth of Grace

Interested in more? There are sneak peeks, early extracts and sometimes giveaways in my occasional newsletter. And I'll let you know when the next Choices and Consequences book is due out, along with a chance to be an early reader. Sign up at www.racheljbonner.co.uk.

Please consider leaving a review! Reader reviews are crucial to a book's success by helping other readers discover them. Please consider taking a moment to review Strand of Faith at www.amazon.co.uk/dp/B07GKZT8LF. Your review doesn't have to be long or detailed – one sentence about how the book made you feel would be great.

Want to make contact? I'd love to hear from you. Please visit my Facebook page at www.facebook.com/rachelbonnerauthor or connect with me on Twitter at www.twitter.com/racheljbonner1 – or both!

Acknowledgements

They say it takes a village to raise a child. It certainly takes more than an author to produce a book. There are so many people who have helped me on this journey. You have my deepest thanks; I couldn't have done it without all of you.

Firstly, the professionals. The cover was designed by the amazing Oliver Pengilley. Thank you, Ollie. It's exactly right for the book, even though I didn't know what I wanted it to be like. If you'd like to see more examples of Ollie's work, visit his website at www.oliverpengilley.co.uk or his Etsy shop at www.etsy.com/uk/shop/oliverpengilley.

My editor is the equally amazing Sarah Smeaton (and thank you to www.reedsy.com for introducing us). Sarah, you took my manuscript, polished it, nudged me in the right directions with rewrites and gave me back something so much better than I had written originally. Thank you with all my heart.

And to the other Rachel, who can be found at www.rachelsrandomresources.com. You led me through the nightmare of social media marketing, blogs and reviews and made it easy. Again, my heartfelt thanks.

I couldn't even have started this without my family and friends. My husband, David, I have no words to describe how much I love you and how much support you have given me. From being the very first to read the manuscript, and then doing so another four times (at least) to plying me with cups of tea and cricket scores while editing, I am indebted to you. My sons, Adam and the other one, thank you for your love and support (both emotional and technical) while your mother was doing this daft thing. I am so proud of you both. My first readers, my Mum and Kathy – your enjoyment of the early version of this book gave me the strength and courage to continue. And my house group (yes, you know who you are). Thank you for your love, encouragement and enthusiasm, and even your casting suggestions. Who knows, maybe one day?

Finally, thank you to you, the reader. Without you this book would have no purpose. I hope you've enjoyed reading it as much as I enjoyed writing it and will be back again to read the next in the series as soon as it is available.

Deo gratis.

Rachel J Bonner

November 2018

Lightning Source UK Ltd.
Milton Keynes UK
UKHW040355081118
331975UK00001B/61/P